PRAISE FOR STANLEY EVANS

"Evans' combination of [Coast] Salish lore and solid plotting is a winner." —*The Globe and Mail*

"A fast-paced, entertaining story with enough plot twists to keep the reader guessing." —*Times Colonist*

"A mystery novel worth reading and lingering over."
—*Hamilton Spectator*

"A gritty murder-mystery with some violence and suspense thrown in for good measure." —*Oak Bay News*

"Tightly written mystery . . . a pleasure to read." —*Comox Valley Record*

"Evans does not disappoint." —*WordWorks*

"Well worth reading. Evans knows how to set a scene, creates vivid minor characters, and is capable of spitting out the requisite snappy dialogue." —*Monday Magazine*

"An exciting introduction to a Coast Salish cop with a lot more entertaining stories to tell." —*Mystery Readers Journal*

"Sharp, calculating and extremely convincing style of writing."
—*Victoria News*

"Evans is a forceful story teller." —*Parksville Qualicum News*

"[An] evocative series." —*Montreal Gazette*

SEAWEED IN THE SOUP

Stanley Evans

TouchWood
Editions

VICTORIA • VANCOUVER • CALGARY

TouchWood Editions
www.touchwoodeditions.com

LIBRARY AND ARCHIVES CANADA CATALOGUING IN PUBLICATION
Evans, Stan, 1931–   Seaweed in the soup / Stanley Evans.
ISBN 978-1-894898-92-8
I. Title.
PS8559.V36S37 2009   C813'.54   C2009-902906-5

Edited by Lee Shedden
Proofread by Karla Decker
Front cover image by Susanna Pershern, istockphoto.com

BRITISH COLUMBIA
ARTS COUNCIL

Canada Council   Conseil des Arts
for the Arts   du Canada

We gratefully acknowledge the financial support for our publishing activities from the
Government of Canada through the Book Publishing Industry Development Program
(BPIDP), Canada Council for the Arts, and the province of British Columbia through the
British Columbia Arts Council and the Book Publishing Tax Credit.

1 2 3 4 5 12 11 10 09

PRINTED IN CANADA

For my sister Marion, and Douglas Bee

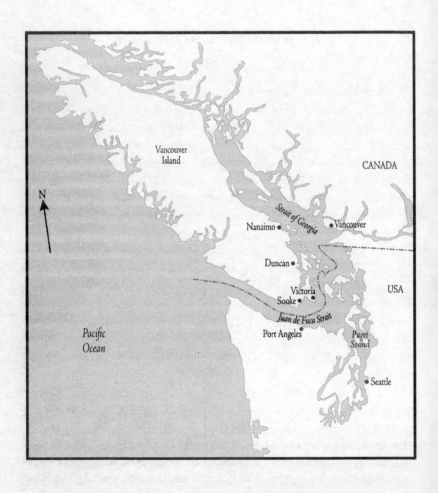

BEFORE

Victoria is surrounded by forest, and when I go out of an early morning, checking up on the homeless people sleeping in parks and doorways and alleys, I often see wild animals as well. Raccoons, skunks and squirrels are common. Coyotes, deer and cougars wander our streets occasionally. Moreover, because we'd had a long cold spring that year, huckleberries, salmonberries and blackberries were scarce, and hungry bears had been coming down from the mountains to forage on garbage.

But ravens seldom nest in the inner city, and when a pair moved into a tree on Pandora Street, I kept a wary eye on them.

Because of its black plumage, croaking call and carrion diet, the raven has since ancient times been regarded as a bird of ill omen. To Canada's West Coast Natives, Raven also symbolizes Creation, prestige and knowledge. In Coast Salish mythology, Raven placed the sun in the sky and put fishes in the sea. In the Coast Salish language, Raven's mystical name may be also be translated as "Trickster," a powerful god with the power to change itself into anything it chooses—a woman, say, or a tree, or a whale.

That morning, though, it was easy to overlook the ravens' Trickster reputations as they soared joyously upwards wing-to-wing, before plummeting recklessly back to earth half out of control, calling raucously. Possessed by love, the ravens spent hours cheek-to-cheek cooing, warbling, and preening each other's purplish-black feathers. Next, a couple of fluffy brownish chicks appeared. The doting parents spent their days airlifting rotten meat and other delicacies to the nestlings. Well-fed raven babies don't croak; they coo and they gurgle.

One warm August morning, the nestlings were flapping their wings on a favourite bough when a couple of young women came by. Both were wearing cut-offs, flip-flops, *Jesus loves you, everybody else thinks you're an asshole* T-shirts, and shades.

The women were on the chunky side and looked like fresh-off-the-reserve folks to me—doe-eyed Indians with long black hair, copper-coloured skin and pretty faces. As they marvelled at the ravens, I took their measure. Statistically, one or both women would be skinny crackheads within two years. Maybe this pair would beat the odds, although, given those four harbingers of mischief watching us from above, I somehow doubted it.

I went over and said, "Good morning. I'm Sergeant Seaweed. Call me Silas. You're both new in town, right? Anything I can do for you? No? Well in case you're wondering, I belong to the Warrior Tribe, that's my office over there. If you run into a problem drop in and see me . . ."

That's as far as I got, because Nimrod Wright shoved himself into the picture. In a soberer incarnation, Nimrod Wright had been a fisher-man. By then, he was an incoherent panhandler who oscillated between the drunk tank, rehab and the funny farm. When Nimrod staggered up to the women with his handout, they turned their backs on us and cleared off around the first corner.

CHAPTER ONE

It was about eight o'clock in the morning. A nice sunny August day. I found Chief Detective Inspector Bernie Tapp in Lou's Cafe. Bernie is a tough-looking guy with hair a quarter of an inch long, an eighteen-inch neck, and eyes the colour of coal. He has the same hard leanness as men who chop down trees for a living. He was wearing a white shirt with the top button undone, a maroon necktie that had been slackened off, and a pair of blue denim pants. His red golf jacket had burn marks on both pockets. He didn't look like a detective, but that was the whole idea.

Bernie was sitting alone in a booth by a window, eating steak and eggs. There was a paperback book propped up on the table in front of him. A trace of runny egg, visible on Bernie's chin, led me to conclude that Bernie was more interested in what he was reading than in what he was eating. Lou was busy serving customers. I helped myself to a cup of coffee and carried it over to Bernie's table. I didn't say hello until I was seated opposite him. Taken by surprise, Bernie grabbed the book and put it down on the seat beside him where I couldn't see it. He was too slow. I grinned, but I didn't say anything. The book's title was *Mood Disorders—How Sudden Impulses Can Ruin Your Life.*

Bernie drank some coffee and stared at me expectantly. He's the best friend I've got. We go fishing occasionally whenever Bernie takes a day off work, which isn't often. Not nowadays. Being a CDI is a big deal, but Bernie used to get more fun out of life when he was a sergeant. He was waiting for me to rib him about the book, but he was saved by the ringing of his cellphone.

One minute later, the pair of us were aboard Bernie's Interceptor, and he was driving too fast on a winding stretch of blacktop through a stand of half-tamed rainforest. An occasional secluded mansion told us that rich people lived around there. After a couple of screeching turns, we ended up on Collins Lane, a winding gravel road suddenly dead-ended by a giant shingled house. Bernie hit the brakes. With gravel spitting and snarling from beneath our wheels, we skidded to a halt alongside a blue and white patrol car. I noticed a shiny new BMW convertible and an '88 Toyota Corolla parked in a detached garage.

There are places in Victoria where you can't get down to the waterfront unless you own it. This was one of those places. "Must be nice," Bernie remarked, as we tramped up a flight of granite steps to the front door. The house had about twenty rooms. It was the kind of residence that people like the Astors and the Vanderbilts would call a summer cottage. Instead of knocking, Bernie and I barged straight into a vestibule with a full-size Chinese rickshaw parked in a corner. An Inuit kayak was propped up in another corner. The remaining space was large enough for a ping-pong tournament. The ceilings were twelve feet high. A single yellow driving glove lay on an oak table. The door leading from the vestibule into the house was held ajar by a hideous but no doubt expensive elephant's-foot umbrella stand. The house—full of museum-grade art and furniture—smelled of beeswax, and the parquet floors gleamed. We tramped through a vast echoing hall and on into a formal dining room with a mahogany table, chairs for sixteen people, and enough heavy silver candlesticks, rosebowls and platters to ballast a ship.

A woman's laughter drew Bernie and me through an archway and along a passage to a kitchen at the back of the house.

Lightning Bradley—Victoria's oldest uniformed constable—was seated at a table drinking coffee, smoking a cigarette, and telling jokes to a woman who was washing dishes at the kitchen sink. The woman wore a lace-trimmed white apron over a black dress. The lines on her face put her at fiftyish; her eyes twinkled with amusement. Bradley was appraising her with a gaze too frank to be innocent.

Bradley turned his big square face towards us. Instead of showing some ordinary polite respect for Bernie's rank, Bradley remarked idly, "This pretty lady is Mrs. Milton, the housekeeper. She's the one who found it." After a moment, Bradley added as an afterthought, "Ricketts is watching it downstairs."

I groaned inwardly, thinking, *here we go again*. Barely controlled rage was fast becoming Bernie's default mode, and it looked as if everybody was in for a bad day. "Say, Mrs. Milton," he snarled. "Why don't you just leave those dishes for now, and wait for us outside? We'll have some questions for you later, so don't wander too far."

Mrs. Milton's smile faded. Startled and upset by Bernie's unnecessarily harsh tone, she hurried out to a back patio, her black skirts swishing around her legs.

Bradley stubbed his cigarette in a saucer and stood up quickly. "Oh yeah, right, Bernie," he said, holding his hands up as if to admit his folly. "You know how it is, we got to talking and I never thought. It's this way, let me show you."

Bernie bottled his anger. We followed Bradley through a doorway off the kitchen, down a flight of wooden stairs to the basement, and along a hallway to an L-shaped bedroom. When we entered, the thick meaty odour of freshly spilled blood enveloped us like a mist. It was a gruesome scene. The rumpled blue duvet covering the room's double bed looked as if somebody had emptied a can of red paint across it.

The room's other occupant was Constable Ricketts, a new recruit. Ricketts was gazing fixedly at a slim Asian male stretched out naked on the floor's blue carpet. Appearances suggested that during his final agonies, the doomed man had rolled off the bed.

Ricketts' face had a sickly pale tone, and he appeared to be deeply shaken. He made a noise in his throat when we joined him, but didn't say anything comprehensible. Bernie took latex gloves from his pockets, blew on them to inflate and stretch the rubber, and went down on his haunches to examine the corpse.

The dead man lay on his back. His neck had been slashed. The wound had severed both of his carotid arteries, as well as the jugular veins. The incision was so deep that the dead man was almost decapitated—his head lay at an unnatural angle to his body. Flies buzzed around, feasting on the dreadful wound and on the splashes of blood that Rorschached the surrounding area. "There's a word for this kind of blood loss," Bernie said. "I just can't think of it now."

"How about messy?" I suggested.

Bernie bared his teeth. When we straightened up after looking at the corpse, Bernie said, "You're Ricketts, right? Do you know who I am?"

Ricketts emerged from his trance and snapped to attention. "You're CDI Tapp, sir?" he answered uncertainly.

The ghost of a smile flitted across Bernie's face. "Twenty years ago I pounded the pavement with your old man, Ricketts," Bernie replied in a consciously gentle tone. "Is this your first murder?"

"Yes, sir," Ricketts answered. Pointing at the corpse, he said with a bewildered face, "Only, it kept twitching."

"What kept twitching?"

"The body. Its arms . . . It's stopped now, but for a while earlier its arms and fingers kept twitching like it was alive. Like it was trying to stretch out and reach for something."

"That happens sometimes. It's something to do with changes in the body's chemistry after death," Bernie said, his arm going around Ricketts' shoulder. "The first time I saw it, it scared the hell out of me too. Are you going to be okay?"

"I don't know, sir."

"Have you or Bradley touched the body or anything else in this room?"

"No, sir."

"Fine, I'm glad to hear that," Bernie said, guiding Ricketts across the room to a window that overlooked the driveway.

"Easy does it," said Bernie, unfastening the window catch and pushing the window wide open. "Take a deep breath and get focussed. When you're ready, tell us what went on. Pretend we don't know anything, which we don't. In your own words?"

Ricketts filled his lungs with clean fresh air. "The housekeeper found the dead man when she came to work this morning. She told us that his name is Ronnie Chew. He's the gardener-cum-handyman."

"That's it? Mrs. Milton comes to work and finds a dead gardener?"

Ricketts moved his weight from foot to foot. Straightening his shoulders, he said with growing assurance, "Chief, a neighbour walking his dog this morning saw two young women on Collins Lane. They were walking, which aroused his suspicions. The neighbour thought that the women were Native Indians. After speaking to them, he called

911. Constable Bradley and I were in a radio car nearby and were the first to respond."

"What time was that?"

"It was about a quarter to eight when the dispatcher's call came through. We were on Haultain Street, near the Jubilee Hospital. I was driving; we headed this way immediately. Going down Echo Bay Road, we saw two women who matched the descriptions we'd been given. When we stopped the car, the women fled into the bush. We gave chase on foot, but they had a head start on us and we lost 'em."

"Two women walking along Collins Lane aroused a neighbour's suspicions?" I said, speaking to Ricketts for the first time. "Why? What were they doing exactly?"

"The guy who reported them said that they were just walking, but everybody knows there's a lot of money lives around here, so strangers get noticed," Ricketts answered. "The women wouldn't or couldn't give a reasonable account of themselves."

I said, "Let me see if I've got this right. You and Bradley followed the two women into the bush?"

Lightning Bradley—standing just outside the bedroom door—cleared his throat to let Ricketts know that he was listening.

That reignited Bernie's fuse. His face went very red. Going instantly into his raging-lunatic mode, Bernie lurched towards Bradley and poked his chest with a stiff finger. With ear-shattering intensity, Bernie roared, "You are suspended from duty as of this minute! If you talk to Mrs. Milton or to Constable Ricketts or to anyone remotely connected to this case without my permission, you're toast!"

The corners of Bradley's mouth sank towards his chin; his glance fell to the floor.

"You're a disgrace to the uniform!" Bernie ranted. "Give me your car keys and your notebook!"

Bradley was trembling when he handed them over.

"You're a brainless idiot!" Bernie yelled. "Now clear out of this house and wait for me in the driveway. Get out of my sight this instant!"

Bradley hurried out of the room. I usually share Bernie's opinions about sloppy police work, but Bernie was overreacting. I overcame an impulse to intervene. Bernie turned angrily towards Constable Ricketts.

"Did you hear what I said? If you or Bradley exchange a single word with each other or with Mrs. Milton, you are toast, finished. I'll shoot the pair of you down in flames! Do you understand me?"

Too intimidated to speak, the young officer just nodded.

"Okay," Bernie said, lowering his voice with an effort. "You and Bradley followed the women into the woods. Then what?"

Ricketts moistened his lips with his tongue. "We followed the two women into the bush, but they had a good start on us. To be honest, after they left the road I never saw them again. I saw something, but I don't think it was the suspects. It was probably a big bird, maybe some kind of an animal. Something. When it became apparent that we'd lost 'em, Constable Bradley thought he'd better go back to the car."

After a pause, Ricketts added gamely, "It's not fair to blame Constable Bradley entirely, sir. It's as much my fault that the women got away."

"Stop apologizing. You're supposed to be a cop, not a goddamn Boy Scout," Bernie snapped. "Just tell me what happened."

"After you leave the road, the brush is very heavy in places along there. A jungle of firs and cedars and salal bushes. Blackberry clumps everywhere. I poked around for a while after Bradley went back to the car and I ended up going down some steep ground to the beach. I guessed that the women would probably go north, so I headed that way myself. I was just level with this house when I heard a woman screaming. It was Mrs. Milton. She had just found the dead man and had fled from the house in a panic. She was in a terrible state. It took me a while to calm her down. By then I figured the suspects were long gone, so I used my cellphone to call Constable Bradley and tell him what was going on here. After Bradley showed up at the house and had had a good look at the dead man, he told me to stay with the body. 'We've got to secure the crime scene,' is what Bradley told me."

I said, "This thing that you saw in the woods. You thought it was a big bird or an animal. Can you describe it more precisely?"

"I only glimpsed it from the corner of my eye," Ricketts said after some hesitation. "Something moved very suddenly, although I didn't hear any noise. When I turned my head, all I saw was a large isolated boulder. The thing that I saw wasn't human. I don't think it was human. Seeing it kind of sudden like that, it gave me a bit of a shock. Anyway, I didn't see anything more until I reached the beach."

"Have you written up your notes yet?" Bernie asked the young constable.

Ricketts shook his head.

"Give me your notebook."

Ricketts took a small spiral-bound notebook from a pocket and handed it over.

After glancing inside the notebook briefly, Bernie said, "I'll keep this for the time being. Go upstairs and find yourself a pen and a nice big sheet of paper. Write a detailed report of this whole incident, including the things that you've already told us. Then wait for me; I'll look at your notes later and will probably have a lot more questions."

Ricketts looked sick when he went out.

Bernie looked at me and said, "Okay, Silas. Time for me to go to work."

We were alone for the first time in several minutes. I said, "The work can wait for a minute. What the hell's going on with you?"

Bernie stiffened. He leaned towards me, his chin out, breathing hard. This was a man at the end of his tether. He was ready to step over a line that would change things between us forever. His hands, dangling by his sides, balled into fists. Then all the fight drained out of him. His eyes closed, he relaxed visibly and jammed both fists into his pockets. His eyes opened. Instead of answering my question, he said, "Forget it, Silas. I'd appreciate a little help the next few days, that's all."

"Because two Native women might be involved in this mess, and I happen to be a Native? Or is there some other reason?"

Bernie relaxed, grinned, took his hands out of his pockets. He punched me lightly on the shoulder and said, "Because I need your help, pal. That's all."

That was enough.

In addition to the dead man's bed, the room's furnishings included a six-drawer tallboy, a seven-drawer oak desk and a large mahogany wardrobe. An old-fashioned washstand with a water pitcher and bowl stood in an ell beneath a small second window. A good-quality lightweight wool sport jacket and a pair of green pants, a white shirt and a pair of boxer shorts were draped carelessly across a ladderback chair standing beside the head of the bed.

I went through the dead man's pockets and found about two hundred dollars in twenties, tens and fives, in addition to a Swiss Army knife, a woman's white handkerchief edged with red lace, and a flat brass Yale key. When we checked it later, the key fitted the back door of the house. Among the items in the desk was a child's exercise book containing a multitude of names, initials, phone numbers, circled dates and a lot of writing in Chinese characters. We didn't find the dead man's wallet: there was absolutely nothing either in the room or in his pockets to tell us what his name was.

Bernie worked his cellphone while I checked the wardrobe.

A pair of freshly laundered brown coveralls, along with other pieces of the dead man's work clothing, dangled from hangers incongruously alongside a large assortment of Italian silk suits, an Abercrombie and Fitch overcoat, a couple of Harry Rosen sport jackets, shirts and designer jeans. Expensive dress shoes, workboots, and a pair of bedroom slippers stood on a shelf at the bottom. Beneath the shelf were deep wide drawers containing neatly folded underwear, T-shirts, socks and sweaters.

Bernie was staring at the corpse. "A snappy dresser," Bernie observed. "And look at the polish on his fingernails."

I grinned. "Looks like he was doing okay, for a gardener."

We heard a vehicle come to a stop outside the house. Looking out the window, I watched another snappy dresser dismount from an unmarked police-edition Crown Royal. It was Inspector "Nice" Manners. Turning away from the window, I noticed a man's highly polished black shoe partly visible beneath the blankets heaped on the floor at the foot of the bed. The shoe was a size eight with a black silk sock jammed inside it. When Bernie and I carefully moved the blankets out of the way, we found a matching shoe and the other sock.

Footsteps sounded along the passageway, and Manners came into the bedroom. The last time I'd seen him, Nice Manners had been clean-shaven. Now he was sporting an RAF air-ace moustache. He was wearing a blue blazer, a white shirt with a faint blue stripe in it, tasselled loafers, and chinos. To the casual glance, he looked like a fading porn star or a polo-playing gigolo with his best years behind him, but Manners is actually one of Victoria's senior detectives. Nice Manners is about five-ten. When I'm around, he pretends to be five-eleven. His moustache twitched when he sniffed the blood-tainted air. He said hello to Bernie, ignored me, hunkered down beside the corpse for a minute, then he stood up and put his hands in his pockets. He then looked me up and down with a smile devoid of warmth.

Bernie brought Manners up to date. "Lightning Bradley's been very helpful," Bernie observed icily, adding, "When we got here Bradley was in the kitchen, watching the housekeeper destroy valuable evidence."

Manners raised his eyebrows.

"She'd just finished washing several glasses, cups, plates and a bunch of silverware. A ton of DNA and fingerprints going down the drain, and there's Lightning, smoking, drinking coffee and telling jokes," Bernie elaborated. "What the hell are we going to do with him?"

"How about a vertical transfer? Bump him to sergeant and ship him to the Oak Bay detachment, he'd fit right in," Manners suggested derisively, articulating the popular fallacy that Oak Bay's police force consisted of sleepy underworked seat-warmers.

The cellphone in Manners' pocket buzzed. He turned his back on us and spoke to someone in a low voice. Bernie was calmer by then. He seemed neither curious nor impatient. After finishing his call, Manners pointed at the corpse and said, "He's supposed to be Ronnie Chew, a gardener, but look at his clothing. Look at his polished fingernails; if you ask me they've just been manicured."

Gravel crackling under wheels in the driveway told us that Serious Crimes was arriving.

"Get on with it, Nice," Bernie said. "Get this man's fingerprints taken ASAP, and put them on the wire. We'll need the K-9 team here as well."

Manners doesn't like it when people call him Nice. He said sullenly, "It's all arranged. Nicky Nattrass is on his way in the muttmobile."

Bernie handed Manners the exercise book that we'd found in the desk. "There's what looks like Chinese writing in this. Get it translated; there may be things we can use. I'm going back upstairs. I'll hold off questioning the housekeeper while you look around, then we'll talk to her together."

Bernie was heading for the door when he remembered something. Turning back he said, "Who's the duty ME?"

Restlessly, Manners folded his arms. This caused the collar of his blazer to ruck up behind his neck. Manners may have been conscious of this, because he put his hands back in his pockets immediately. "Dr. Tarleton," he answered. "There was a hit and run on Courtney Street this morning. The doc says he'll get here as soon as he can."

"That's not good enough, Nice," Bernie retorted. "I want the doc here now, for the body temp. I want to know what time this man died."

Taken aback by Bernie's hectoring tone and attitude, Manner's transferred his annoyance to me. Glaring at me like the god of thunder, he said gruffly, "There's something I need to discuss with CDI Tapp. You can go."

The tension and conflict existing between Manners and me had resurfaced. I didn't care; I was just glad to get out of that room. Without troubling to suppress a smile, I tramped upstairs, went outside through a pair of wide French doors, and across the gravel drive to the garage.

The first car that I looked at was Mrs. Milton's twenty-year-old Corolla. After a perfunctory search, I turned my attention to a newish black BMW sedan. The shiny car reeked of cigarettes. Its ashtray, full of half-smoked butts, might provide some useful DNA when Forensics got around to checking it. Otherwise, the car was tidy with nothing lying on its leather-upholstered seats or cluttering its dashboard. The glove compartment also proved empty except for manufacturer's handbooks. There was nothing in the car to say who owned it. I went back through the house, where I heard Bernie Tapp tearing more strips out of Lightning Bradley's hide. Crime squad detectives and forensic specialists were coming and going.

After writing some notes into my little black book, I went around to a sprawling flagstone terrace at the back of the house. Ten yards away, Mrs. Milton was seated inside a wisteria-draped gazebo, gazing into space, until she noticed that I was watching her. When I smiled, she turned away, her face registering a mixture of apprehension and aversion.

Footpaths wound through well-tended flower gardens and downhill to a landscaped lower terrace, where a large swimming pool blended nicely with the marble statues, imported Lebanese cedars and weeping sequoias that adorned the property. I followed a series of curving balustraded stairways to the beach and gazed out at the Strait of Georgia, the large inland sea that separates Vancouver Island from the British Columbia mainland.

Locally, the Strait of Georgia and Puget Sound are known collectively as the Salish Sea. The cities of Vancouver and Seattle are short ferry rides away from here. Small waves lapped the shore in a slight breeze. White triangular sails dotted the horizon. The day's warm air carried the high midsummer reek of oceanic mud and rotting fish. Horse clams, buried in the sand, were shooting crotch-high jets of water here and there. Mount Baker's immense volcanic peak rose up forty miles east, in Washington State.

Constable Ricketts had been wearing cleated-sole boots. What I took to be his footprints—visible here and there on patches of wet sand—were being erased by a rising tide. If the women that Ricketts had been pursuing had passed this way, there was no evidence to show for it by then. Standing there under the mewling cry of gulls, I concluded that Ricketts—by heading north along the intertidal zone—had guessed wrong. The suspects had either gone south or were still hiding in the bush.

I abandoned my speculations in favour of doing something concrete and used my cellphone to call headquarters. Bill Friendly was the duty sergeant that day. I asked Bill who'd reported the suspicious females.

"The caller was shy, he hung up when I asked him," Bill replied. "Call display says he was Tudor Collins. He lives at 515 Collins Lane."

"Does Collins have form?"

"No, Silas. Mr. Collins is a fine upstanding citizen. The Collinses have been in Victoria since the beginning of time. They used to own that porcelain shop on Broughton Street."

"Anything else you can tell me about him?"

Bill laughed. "Isn't that enough?"

I put my phone away. Footsteps became audible above the heavy buzz of sandflies where Constable Ricketts was coming down the stairs to the beach. When he noticed me, he turned away and began to retrace his steps. I said, "Hold it, Ricketts."

He turned, one hand on the balustrade, looking down. "Sir?" he said nervously.

"Have you made the notes that Chief Tapp asked for?"

"Yes, Sergeant."

"You told Chief Tapp that you thought the women you were chasing would head north. Why north?"

"I dunno," he said, his voice slow and abstracted, as if his thoughts were focussed somewhere else. "It was just a guess."

"I wonder if perhaps you'd noticed something. Footprints in the sand, a broken branch?"

Shaking his head, Ricketts came down the stairs.

I said, "Tell me again about that bird or whatever it was that you saw earlier."

Ricketts frowned. He didn't look me in the eye. He seemed slightly embarrassed. Seconds passed before he said, "It's strange. I don't know how to explain this without sounding foolish. I was alone in the woods. There had been no sign of the women and I was just standing quietly, waiting and listening. Suddenly I had a strange feeling that I wasn't alone, that somebody or something was watching me. When I turned around, I saw a vague shape for a moment before it vanished. Since then I've been thinking, maybe I didn't see anything. It might have been nerves, I might have just imagined it all."

"Do you think you could find the same place again?"

"I expect so, Sergeant. It's only a few hundred yards from here."

"Okay, let's go. I'd like to have a look for myself."

We started walking. Olive-green seaweed with yellowish tips mantled the offshore rocks. A wedge of majestic white swans bobbed up and down in the waves. Leaves of decaying sea lettuce littered the beach like scraps of crumpled parchment. I said, "Describe the two women that you and Bradley saw on Echo Bay Road."

Ricketts looked at me sideways, but continued to evade my eyes. "They were a couple of Indian girls. Dark or sallow skin, there was nothing remarkable about either of them. They had the same skin pigmentation as you, Sergeant, if you don't mind me saying so. They were just like the people I see hanging around the Native Friendship Centre. About 18 years old. Maybe 20. Nice looking girls, a little overweight. They might have been sisters or cousins. One of 'em was wearing a funny T-shirt. It said, *Jesus loves you, everybody else thinks you're an asshole.*"

I began to think about ravens and Tricksters.

Ricketts had recovered from his earlier shock. Smiling absently, he led me away from the shore along a ravine studded with small trees and stunted shrubs. We began to ascend an incline where the brush thinned and the floor of the ravine became a loose scree of pebbly soil covered with leaf mould and scattered patches of lichen-covered rock. Towards the top, the incline steepened precipitously; our feet began to slide. After a struggle, we reached rimrock.

Ricketts and I grabbed overhanging branches and we rested for a moment before Ricketts reached over the rim and used his free hand to part a clump of tall grass. Gazing across the rim, he said hesitantly, "I don't see it now, but I know that the big rock where I saw something strange is close by."

I dragged myself up and over the rim, and on into a patch of coastal rainforest, where access through the dense tangle of green wilderness was restricted to animal trails and to whatever footpaths may have been cleared by determined hikers. Moss draped the surrounding trees like shreds of ragged green wool.

Hearing a slight noise, I looked up through the sun-shot foliage and saw a squirrel clinging to the trunk of a big Douglas fir. The animal scampered from sight behind the trunk. After a moment, the squirrel's nose reappeared. I watched it run out along a downward-sloping branch before it leapt into space and went from sight again. The breeze had stiffened into a wind and a fir cone struck my shoulder. The cone had not fallen from the fir tree. It had rolled off a sandstone boulder.

The boulder, about the size of a small car, was partially shrouded by seed husks, fallen leaves and pinecones. I noticed an unnatural mark on the boulder's weathered surface and dirtied my hands brushing it clean. Carved into the boulder's front face were two petroglyphs, Native rock carvings that had been created by chipping and abrading with stone tools. The first was a life-sized anthropomorphic shape. A naturally occurring protuberance in the sandstone, suggestive of male genitalia, had been incorporated into the design. A second and much smaller petroglyph located below and to the left of the main figure showed a wolf, its gaping jaws held open by two pointed sticks.

Ricketts scrambled over the rimrock and joined me. Sounding vindicated, he said, "This is it. This is the place."

Vancouver Island's petroglyph sites are rarely, if ever, found away from water. Some petroglyphs are found in riverbeds and are only visible when water levels drop. Many are found on tidal beaches submerged by high tides. The petroglyphs that I was looking at had been created long ago, by a shaman or by a spirit quester seeking knowledge.

For the Coast Salish, the vision quest is a turning point in life. When our youngsters reach puberty, they endure rigorous training in preparation for vision quests alone in the wilderness. This quest usually lasts for a number of days during which the initiate tunes into the spirit world. An essential part of the process involves fasting, sleep deprivation, and immersion in icy water to the brink of unconsciousness. Sometimes, not always, a guardian animal or spirit will then appear to the seeker in the form of a vision or a dream. After his vision quest, the youngster may be apprenticed to a shaman, a carver or a hunter. The vision quest may be a part of shamanism, or more exactly, an apprentice's learning and initiation process under the guidance of a practising shaman. The shaman quest— its secrets and its search for power—is strongly related to petroglyphs because spirits—good and bad—dwell in certain boulders and trees.

"Sheesh!" Ricketts said, after looking at the petroglyphs. "What are these things?"

"Stone age rock carvings."

"They're sort of crazy-looking, if you ask me."

Ricketts was right: most petroglyphs are a bit peculiar. The creatures portrayed on them are birds, shamans, monsters and fantastic spirits. Many have overtly sexual overtones. Apart from a very few examples, the locations of which have long been known, petroglyphs are rare on southern Vancouver Island, although they are numerous farther north and on some offshore islands. To put it mildly, I was very surprised to discover a previously unknown petroglyph site half a mile from a well-travelled urban road.

Needing to take a leak, Ricketts turned his back on me and moved behind the boulder. "Holy Christ," he said. "What the hell is this?"

I went to have a look. Ricketts was standing with his dick in his hand, staring down at what at first sight appeared to be an old leather glove. Forgetting his bladder, Ricketts zipped up and bent forward. Up close, the object looked like a brown paper bag. It was about the same size and shape as a human hand. Before I could stop him, Ricketts had reached out for it. At the same instant, a heavy gust of wind roared in from the Salish Sea. Trees shook. Loose branches and other forest litter fell down from the overhead canopy. Instinctively, Ricketts and I covered our heads with our arms and crouched low. The wind continued to howl; we heard a terrific cracking noise. A big old cedar tree with two long overhanging branches was splitting down the middle. One branch fell noisily into the ravine. The old tree swayed unsteadily for a few moment and then fell towards us. The sudden effect was unnerving. Ricketts screamed. I jumped out of the way. The earth shook, and a cavity appeared where the tree's rootball pulled out of the earth. The boulder shook a little and then moved slightly. After sliding downhill a few inches, the boulder came to rest. Ricketts' panicked screams faded, and when I turned to look at him, the constable was disappearing headfirst into the root cavity. His head and shoulders were completely covered with loose earth when I grabbed his ankles and dragged him out.

Ricketts was unhurt. He rested face down for a moment, blinking his eyes and trying to regain his composure. Then Ricketts tried to get to his knees. He couldn't. Something that had been buried underground had wrapped itself around his right arm. Using my bare hands, I managed to dig him free.

Ricketts stood up with something dangling from his wrist by a leather thong. It was a sack, about the same size and shape as an ordinary supermarket shopping bag. But this sack wasn't plastic. It was made of ancient buckskin. The sack's dirty cracked leather was marked with reddish stains. I used my pocket knife to cut the leather thong away and then I carefully opened the sack. It contained half-dissolved feathers, bits of fur and skin, bones, small pebbles, a chunk of woven cornstalk and small unrecognizable decapitated animals—all of them immersed in a cauldron of clotted blood.

It was a shaman's medicine bag.

Ricketts had been fairly stoic till then, but the awful stink wafting from the medicine bag did him in. He leaned forward, holding his knees, and spewed up everything he'd eaten that morning.

CHAPTER TWO

Back at the house, I gave the medicine bag to Forensics. Lightning Bradley had already been interrogated, sent home and told to stay near his telephone until further notice.

Bernie Tapp and Nice Manners were interrogating Mrs. Milton in the gazebo when I joined them. Constable Cynthia Leach had set up recording equipment, and the session was being taped. If Mrs. Milton had been panicked earlier, no signs were in evidence by then.

Speaking with a trace of a British accent, she was saying composedly, "Oh no, my goodness, I'm the housekeeper but I don't live on the premises, because I have my own place in town. Ronnie, that's Mr. Chew, has the downstairs room. He seems like a very nice man, although I can't say that I know him very well. Ronnie's only been with us a month or two. He was polite, but his English wasn't fluent. He never had much to say for himself. He guarded his privacy. If people trespassed on the grounds, he was downright uncivil. I remember that one day when these Jehovah Witnesses came knocking on the . . ."

Abruptly, Bernie cut her off. "You're the housekeeper, and Mr. Chew was employed as a gardener. Is there any more domestic staff?"

"No, sir. Except for parties, when we need caterers and so forth."

"What about the owners? Why are they not here?"

"Mr. and Mrs. Wasserstein? Oh, they have been away in Switzerland for over a month." She smiled up at us vacuously from a bench seat.

Bernie shook his head and looked at the sky. "Are you here every day, Mrs. Milton?"

"Oh no. When the Wassersteins are away, I'm only here three days a week. Mondays, Wednesdays and Fridays. Today is Monday, of course. I generally get here about nine and I usually leave around four." After pondering for a moment she added, "I wouldn't mind putting in a little extra time. When you people get finished, Mr. Wasserstein will want things put back to rights I supp . . ." The large woman's voice faded.

Mrs. Milton's inanities had brought Manners to fury again. Without bothering to mask his impatience, he snapped, "So you got here this morning around nine?"

"I think it was about five to nine, sir," the housekeeper replied.

"Was the house locked up?"

"Oh yes, I used my key to let myself in. Everything seemed normal, at first."

"All right. Just before nine o'clock this morning, you unlocked the door and came into the house. Then what did you do?"

"Oh let me see," she said merrily, her equanimity fully restored. "I took my coat off and hung it in the pantry. Then I went into the kitchen and put the kettle on. I knew that Ronnie was home, because the house reeked of cigarettes. It was obvious that he had had company over the weekend, although he really isn't supposed to take such liberties. Mrs. Wasserstein would be furious if she found out that her gardener had been so free with his hospitality. Ronnie and some of his friends had evidently been smoking cigarettes and drinking alcohol in the lounge. Partying, I suppose you'd call it. What I did, sir, I opened a few windows to air the place out. Tidied things up a little. Collected empty glasses. Emptied ashtrays and that and took everything to the kitchen. By then, the kettle had boiled."

"And so you made yourself a nice cup of tea?" Manners said, grinding his teeth in frustration.

"I made myself a cup of instant coffee, if you want me to be perfectly accurate. I was going to wash the dirty dishes right away, but then the phone rang. I picked the phone up and said hello. But you know, I think it must have been a wrong number because the party hung up on me without speaking." Mrs. Milton's eyes narrowed to suspicious slits. "By then I was beginning to think it was a bit unusual, not hearing Ronnie moving around the place."

With knitted brows, she went on, "So I thought, well, I'll get the vacuum cleaner out and do the carpets. Make a bit of noise to let Ronnie know that I'm here. And that's exactly what I did. I was downstairs going to the utility closet, where I keep the basement Hoover. As I passed his room I saw him, covered in blood. For a minute I was frozen stiff, I couldn't move. Then I screamed. I ran screaming out of the house, because I knew that he was dead. It was obvious that poor Ronnie was quite dead."

Mrs. Milton might have been talking about the weather. There was no fright or horror in her voice.

From out in the woods came a sudden wolflike baying. Loud enough to flush birds from trees and send small animals scurrying through the undergrowth, the baying told us that Nicky Nattrass and his K-9 sidekicks had started work.

I said to Mrs. Milton, "You spoke about Mr. Chew's friends. Can you tell us who they were?"

"I'm sorry, I wasn't speaking literally. I've never met any of Ronnie's friends."

"Too bad," I said. "Okay. So you emptied ashtrays, picked up glasses and tidied the house. How many people do you suppose Mr. Chew was entertaining here last night?"

"Oh heavens, I've no idea. Three or four perhaps?"

"Those ashtrays that you emptied. What happened to all the cigarette butts?"

Mrs. Milton's merry laughter made Manners cringe. "Oh, I dumped them all into the garburator. I can't stand the smell of stale cigarette butts, can you?"

Bernie shoved his hands into his pockets; his eyes closed for a moment. "Right. Down into the garburator. You garburate stuff but you wash dirty dishes by hand?"

"Oh well that depends, sir. There's no way I'd put Mr. Wasserstein's expensive drinking glasses into a dishwasher. Or any pieces of real silverware. It would be a sacrilege. Why some of those glasses are the finest cut crystal, worth thirty or forty dollars apiece. We only use the dishwasher for ordinary cutlery and pots."

"Are any of last night's dishes still left unwashed?" Manners asked her.

Mrs. Milton shook her head; her vapid smile faded.

Manners frowned when Bernie turned to me and said, "Any more questions for Mrs. Milton?"

I asked Mrs. Milton who had hired Ronnie Chew.

"Mr. Wasserstein did, at my suggestion."

"I see. How did you and Mr. Wasserstein go about hiring him, exactly? Did Mr. Chew answer an advertisement?"

"We didn't advertise. Ronnie just showed up at the house one day. Knocked on the door and asked for a job. I suppose he must have heard that our previous gardener—that's old Mr. Tantino—had retired and guessed that we'd need a replacement."

"So you and Mr. Wasserstein interviewed Mr. Chew," I continued. "You checked his ID and put him on the payroll?"

Mrs. Milton hesitated. "Well, not quite. Ronnie began as a day labourer. I paid him out of petty cash. His work was very satisfactory. More than satisfactory. He's Chinese, you know, and they are very industrious. Ronnie knows everything about plants, pruning, soil maintenance and so on."

I smiled. "Very nice. Now. How about documents? Did Ronnie show you any references? Identity papers?"

"Ah, well no, not exactly," she answered evasively. "Our arrangement just sort of developed. By the time we realized how wonderfully satisfactory he was, Ronnie had proved himself, in my eyes at least. We were more than happy to let him work here full time and give him a room downstairs."

"Who are 'we'?"

"Well, Mr. Wasserstein and me. He was more than pleased to have a replacement for old Mr. Tantino."

"Does that BMW belong to Mr. Chew?"

"Yes, sir," she said, with a cheery laugh. "It certainly doesn't belong to me!"

I allowed myself a quiet chuckle. "So this man shows up looking for work. He's driving a late-model BMW sports car. He's wearing a nice suit and expensive shoes. He may have been wearing gloves to protect his long manicured fingernails. Weren't you just slightly suspicious when Mr. Chew asked if you were in need of a day labourer?"

Her eyes as round and guileless as before, she answered, "Well, it does sound a bit peculiar when you put it like that, I suppose."

"Just so we're clear on this," Manners interjected sarcastically, "You and your boss hired an undocumented Asian, a man with no papers, and you paid him under the table. Is that right?"

"Under the table?"

"You know what I mean. You continued to pay him cash. You never asked to see his papers?"

Mrs. Milton didn't respond.

Manners asked her to repeat her account of how she'd found Chew's body.

"Again? How many more times? And why are all these people here?" said Mrs. Milton, radiating sudden hostility and pointing at Manners, Tapp, me, Ricketts and finally at Cynthia Leach, who was all ears outside the gazebo.

Manners looked as if he had just chewed and then swallowed a whole lemon. "It's standard procedure," he snapped. "These days courts are inclined to discount important evidence when it has been witnessed by only one policeman. You have to have at least two officers present. And as for why we like witnesses to repeat their accounts, it's because people tend to forget or overlook vital information the first time round."

"Witnesses? Are you suggesting I witnessed Mr. Chew's murder? Am I a suspect? How dare you? Do you think I'm a murderer?"

Tears appeared in Mrs. Milton's innocent blue eyes. Before Manners could respond, she ran sobbing into the house. Bernie told Cynthia Leach to go after her and calm her down.

"Stupid cow," said Manners. "People like that are too brainless to live."

"Having a shitty day, Inspector Manners?" Bernie snapped. "How about trying your interrogation techniques on Tudor Collins?"

"Tudor Collins?" Manners asked, startled. "Who's he?"

"The guy who called 911, and sussed us onto the two Aboriginal women suspects. See how long it takes before your insolence reduces Mr. Collins to tears."

Flushing at Bernie's affront, Manners stalked off.

Grinning, Bernie said, "Do you think I overdid it?"

"Maybe, but there's something about this place," I said, staring at the handsome house. "It has bad vibes."

"Cut the crap. Bad vibes my ass," Bernie said, although his eyes narrowed when I told him about the petroglyph and the shaman's medicine bag.

BERNIE AND I were in the kitchen putting Ricketts through the wringer again when Nicky Nattrass came in with a newspaper-wrapped parcel clenched in the crook of his elbow. The dog master said, "A present for you, Chief. Casey's compliments."

Bernie raised his eyebrows. "Which is Casey?"

"The grey crossbreed with one droopy ear."

Bernie told Ricketts to go home, sit tight and keep his mouth shut till somebody got back to him. "I especially don't want you and Lightning Bradley swapping stories," Bernie snapped.

Ricketts went off like a lamb to the slaughter.

Nicky Nattrass placed his parcel on the kitchen table. Bernie put on a fresh pair of latex gloves and carefully removed the parcel's paper wrapping to reveal a transparent Ziploc bag. The bag contained an object about the length of a man's forearm. After staring at it for a moment, Bernie removed the object from the bag. It was heavy. At first glance, it resembled a tomahawk. The business end was a fist-sized chunk of granite, roughly cylindrical in shape, lashed to a wooden handle by leather thongs. The granite was speckled with reddish-brown stains that looked like dried blood.

"It's a slavekiller," I said, recognizing it instantly. "There was an article about these things in the *Times Colonist* a few weeks back."

Bernie's eyes widened.

"In the good old days," I explained, "before White men came along and spoiled our fun, slavekillers were used at potlatches and other Native feasts. Slaves were valuable. To show his wealth and power and to amuse his guests, a chief would sometimes kill a slave or two between courses."

Bernie said, "Kill them how, exactly?"

"Beat their brains out with a club like this one."

"Nice people, these chiefs. Think one of 'em killed Ronnie Chew?"

"No, I don't."

"Why not? I don't like coincidences, and there are a lot of them stacking up already in this case."

"Such as?"

Bernie reached into his pocket and pulled out a corncob pipe. He said after a long pause, "We can assume that two Native women are involved in this case. Then there's Ricketts' almost unbelievable story about what he thinks he saw near a Native petroglyph. We have a shaman's medicine bag. Finally, we have a Native slavekiller club. I'm no mathematician, but I know this much: The odds against that particular combination of events coinciding randomly is billions to one against."

Bernie put the corncob in his mouth and grinned. The pipe moving up and down as he spoke, he said, "So I'm asking you again, Silas. Do you think it's possible that a Native chief killed Ronnie Chew?"

"Hell no, Bernie. Anything is possible, but the chiefs that I know are all way too smart to drop a slavekiller where a dog could find it."

"Maybe, maybe not. Let me ask you this, though. Is it a Coast Salish club?"

"It might be, although slavekiller clubs were widely used. They're usually more elaborate than this one. Designs varied. Some slavekillers were made of solid stone and shaped like animals. Some slavekillers were two-headed."

"So what you're saying is, this one could be a Coast Salish club, a Nootka club or a Kwakiutl club?"

"Any or all of the above. I know it's not a nightclub."

"Or a comedy club," Bernie said.

"Or an ace of club," Nicky Nattrass added for good measure.

Bernie grinned. "Okay, Nicky. Get back to work. Give Casey a dog biscuit from me."

Smiling, Nicky went off.

Bernie looked happy. He was relaxed, smiling. Acting as he used to act. It was a good sign.

CHAPTER THREE

By the time Bernie turned the murder house over to the Serious Crimes squad, Nicky Nattrass' GMC muttmobile and several other emergency vehicles were parked along both sides of Collins Lane. Uniformed policemen and sniffer dogs combed the woods. Motorcycle cops were stopping motorists, asking questions, checking IDs and registrations, and ticketing people for not wearing seatbelts or other minor infractions. Manners fussed around, barking unnecessary orders.

Driving back to Victoria, Bernie asked me if I had any ideas about the identity of the two female suspects. It was a long shot—hundreds of Native Indians live in the greater Victoria area, and the population is constantly changing. But I told him about the two Native raven watchers I'd seen on Pandora Street a few days previously. Bernie didn't have any better suggestions, so he told me to look into it.

I asked Bernie to drop me outside the Bay building at the Fisgard Street corner. As I was getting out of the car, Bernie made a fist, pointed a stiff finger and said, "Exsanguinated."

"What?"

"Drained of blood. It's that word I couldn't think of earlier. Stay close to the phone, Silas. I'll be talking with you later."

He drove off in a hurry. I ambled south along Douglas Street.

A murmuration of starlings flew in from Vic West and settled on the utility cables flanking City Hall. Twittering gaily, the birds dumped a fresh load of guano onto the cars parked beneath them. In Centennial Square, a dishevelled middle-aged bag lady was standing on the tree-shaded grass guarding the treasures piled up on her shopping cart.

A street dealer was already doing business in the square. Wearing a T-shirt, gold chains, a turned-around basketball cap, Timberland boots and low-rider jeans that displayed the crack of his ass, he was seated on a park bench about twenty feet distant from a public phone. When the phone rang, the dealer got off his bench and answered it. The phone rang every few minutes.

Pigeons strutted. A pensioner was feeding bread crumbs to a murder of crows. Fuchsias, geraniums, petunias and bacopa dripped from the baskets dangling from Victoria's cast iron lampposts. The sun was hot.

I went into a robbery-friendly convenience store across from the square and monitored the scene from a convenient window. The street dealer was the apex of a drug-distribution triangle that also involved the bag lady and a trash bin. Every few minutes, loitering zombies hungering for a morning fix stopped by Asscrack's bench and talked business, following which they gave alms to the bag lady. Shortly afterwards, a bicycle drug mule dropped a baggie into the trash bin for the zombies to retrieve. Trade was brisk.

My car was parked on Pandora Street; I walked over there. A fat blonde with a protuberant lower lip stopped me and asked if I had a cigarette she could borrow. I used to be a smoker and I know what the craving is like. Maybe I shouldn't have, but I gave her my loose pocket change and told her to buy herself a pack.

My car is a 40-year-old MGB Coupe with wire wheels, steel bumpers and a 1798 cc engine. Ted, my personal cockney mechanic, had been trying to inveigle me into putting a 6-cylinder Buick Rover engine into it. I'd been balking at the price, and besides, the MG cornered like a Formula One Honda and it was already tuned to do a ton, easy. I got in and cranked it up, then let its 4-cylinder engine purr for a while before I engaged the clutch and drove myself across town to the Native Friendship Centre.

The two young women that I wanted to talk to weren't there. I then wandered over to the United Church soup kitchen on Quadra Street, where I asked more questions and had a free lunch. I chased down a couple of promising leads. One lead took me back across town to Joe McNaught's Good Samaritan Mission, in Chinatown.

If you have the right antennae and enough persistence, the street will tell you everything you need to know. But those girls were hard to find. By nine o'clock that night, I had visited most of Victoria's shady venues and I was still coming up dry. I went to places where criminals and dopers prowl like wolves. Places where whores and tramps gather; where mobile canteens driven by unheralded volunteers serve hot baked potatoes and cups of coffee to people with lives in terminal decline. Hoping to glean a scrap of reliable information, I listened to gossipy old tarts and shiftless informers who would say anything to earn a dollar. I was no further ahead at the end of the day than when I'd started.

The Warrior Indian Reserve is a few minutes' drive and a world apart from Victoria. Pedestrian traffic diminished after I crossed the Johnson Street Bridge and motored west along Esquimalt Road. A few minutes later, I was on home ground. With twilight gathering, I went slowly downhill past the longhouse and parked the MG beneath my carport.

A silver moon was huge above the Olympic Mountains. Blue shadows gathered like fog in the distance. A couple of fishermen were on the boat jetty, mending nets. A lone night bird screeched as I walked through my fenced private garden. After pausing to inhale the mingled fragrances of dahlias and roses, I entered my cabin. My cabin is located on the beach and it's fairly primitive by modern standards. Compared with most Native housing, however, it is palatial.

Chief Alphonse had dictated the cabin's exact location, and I built it with my own hands, largely out of rough lumber. I switched the light on and stood for a moment in the middle of the room, grounding myself by looking at the wooden tribal masks hanging on a side wall; my shelved books and LP records; an iron wood stove; an apartment-sized fridge; a kitchen sink with a single cold-water faucet. If I want hot water, I generally light my wood stove.

It was too warm now to light the wood stove, so I put the electric kettle on and opened the window curtains. The evening tide had turned and now it was falling. Colby Island was a mere shadow out there in Warrior Bay, where a dozen anchored fishboats rocked in the darkness. Clarence Immet's 26-foot wooden gillnetter had been dragged ashore, and it sat propped upright on beams of squared timber. The gillnetter had just been power-washed. Water still dripped from its hull. Tomorrow it would be dry. Then Clarence would face the dirty job of covering its bottom with antifouling paint.

Bobby Bland is one of the few blues singers ever to rise to superstardom without being able to play a harmonica, a guitar or any other musical instrument. I put Bland's *Memphis Monday Morning* record on and let his Jim Beam vocals wash over me as I looked out the window again.

Immediately below me on the beach was Chief Alphonse. Naked except for a leather necklace and leggings that jangled with small bells and deer hooves when he moved, he was dancing around a pit-fire in a counter-clockwise direction.

The chief had wrapped rice root and other bulbs in pouches made of thimbleberry leaves. Then he had dug edible roots to go along with the rice root. When the fire became hot enough, the chief had piled swordfern fronds and salal bushes on top. Potatoes, onions and carrots were laid on next, then the roots of springbank clover, Nootka lupine and Pacific silverweed. I was standing at the window, drinking Red Rose tea, when the chief caught my eye, waved me over and invited me to join his traditional feast. It had been cooking for about three hours by then. There was more than enough food for both of us, but I would have much preferred macaroni and cheese. After we'd eaten our fill, we had a sweat.

The chief was still very fit—tall upright old man with a large raptor's nose and, as usual, an eagle feather poking through his long grey braids. He went down on his knees and crawled into the sweat lodge. I turned my face away because I didn't want to look at the chief's skinny butt—not that he'd care. Once he was inside, I picked hot stones off the fire with a pair of deer antlers and dropped them into a hole dug inside the sweat lodge. The chief sprinkled the rocks with water ladled from a bucket. It was hot enough to scorch lungs inside there—heat surrounded us as if we'd entered a stove. To save my life, I opened a flap in the tarpaulin and let in some breathable air.

I broke a long companionable silence. "I saw two old petroglyphs this morning. They were carved onto a boulder hidden in the woods above Echo Bay. One of our constables stumbled across it by accident while he was chasing a couple of runaways."

"Was these runaways Coast Salish?"

"Possibly. They were young Native women. Persons of interest in a murder investigation. The constable said that he lost the women in the bush, but he kept on looking. After a while, a sudden apparition startled him. He didn't see the apparition clearly, he said. He said it wasn't human, but it could have been a bird, or an animal."

"Did you find a cave near the petroglyph?"

"No. A wind blew up and I was too busy getting out of the way of falling trees."

"Look for a cave the next time you're up there. I would."

Before I could respond, the chief said, "Them old shamans would sometimes carve a bird on a big rock, then lie on top of the carving and become that bird. Fly away. Maybe your constable saw a flying shaman."

"It's been a good day for weird sightings," I said, adding, "and there are four ravens roosting on Pandora Street right now. Two adults and two chicks."

"Te spokalwets," Chief Alphonse said portentously.

Te spokalwets: In Coast Salish, those words mean corpse, or ghost. Our old people go all weird when it comes to ravens. Every time they see a raven, or hear one calling, they expect somebody to die.

I've said it before and I'll say it again: it's a good thing there aren't more ravens around Victoria.

"And maybe you saw four ghosts," the chief said.

"No, the ravens were real," I said.

"Coast Salish dead people are all ghosts, although you generally don't see 'em because they spend most of their time in the land of the dead, Silas," the chief remarked, speaking in the calm unhurried voice of a man who knows that his words will be heeded attentively. "Mind you, though, I've seen plenty of ghosts. I saw a White woman's ghost once. Years ago.

"There were just three of us. We were fishing up Desolation Sound way. I was just a kid at the time. *Georgina Bell* was the boat's name. It was owned by BC Packers. BC Packers owned nearly every fishboat on the coast back then. It was foggy. There was no radar in them days and we grazed a rock that sprang a plank below the waterline. Lucky for us, the *Georgina* stayed afloat until we beached her on Flea Island. It took us three days to fix things."

"And that's where you saw your ghost?"

"Yes, only the ghost wasn't the worst of it. The worst of it was Flea Island's pesky fleas. Fleas got into our clothes, our mattresses, everything. We was scratched raw when the fishing season ended."

"What about that ghost?"

"I was the only one who saw it. The other two was right there with me, but I was the only one who saw it. It was a White woman wearing a black rubber raincoat with a hood that covered her head. She came out of some trees and walked straight towards me. It was pouring down with rain. I thought she was coming over to tell me something. What I was wondering was, *Where did you come from?*

"Flea Island is tiny, the size of a hockey rink if that. Anyway, at the last possible moment she veered off, and vanished. It was pouring down, but it was broad daylight. I had a good look round for her, but she wasn't there. It was a ghost that time, not a walking corpse. It wasn't scary, except she had no face. No visible face, just a black shadow beneath her hood."

"If you couldn't see its face, how did you know it was a White woman?"

"I don't know. I just knew," the chief said, adding, "As for petroglyphs, Old Mary Cooke is in Comox right now, visiting her grandkids. You'd better have a word with her about this stuff when she gets back."

CHAPTER FOUR

I used to be a sergeant on Victoria's detective squad. Now I'm a neighbourhood cop. My storefront office is located in a three-storey brick building that dates from an age when the Hudson's Bay Company still controlled much of North America. Originally, this room was a harness-shop. Sometimes when it rains, I smell old leather and saddle soap. I moved in here about seven years ago. In those optimistic days, neighbourhood law-enforcement units manned by aboriginal policemen were being hailed as bold experiments in social engineering. Once upon a time we had six neighbourhood units in this city. Mine is the only one left. A lot of police brass want to shut this unit down as well. I'm the police department's token Indian, hanging on by the skin of my teeth. Why do I bother? Because I like this job. Because I'd rather work here for nothing than earn big money at a boring job that does nothing to make the world a safer place.

People complain that I'm running a hangout for the dregs of society. Perhaps that ought to worry me too, but it doesn't. I feel quite comfortable among such people. After all, crooks, conmen, prostitutes and police officers derive from the same socio-economic group. Cops and killers have similar levels of intelligence and ability. When he isn't swinging an axe or waving a pistol the average murderer can be as charming as all get-out.

The modest office that I share with a feral cat corresponds with my lowly status. The walls are bare except for a few badly patched bullet holes, missing-kid bulletins, and two framed prints. The first print shows a young Queen Elizabeth. The second print shows the dowdy Queen after whom this city was named. Chief Alphonse sometimes jokes that but for Queen Victoria we wouldn't be Coast Salish Indians—we'd be chunks of carved wood standing outside tobacco shops. But for Queen Victoria, Vancouver Island would now be governed from Washington, DC.

My battered furnishings include a fireplace with a brass surround, a brass coalscuttle, an oak desk and a vinyl swivel chair. There's also a wooden hat tree, two metal filing cabinets, a floor safe, and a couple of chairs for visitors. I have a private washroom located down the hall. Somehow, I don't know why, a lot of people end up with washroom keys. I get the lock changed occasionally. When PC the cat is in residence, her private washroom is a kitty-litter tray hidden behind my filing cabinets. Get right down to it, there are a lot of things I don't know, including what PC does all day. I used to know what she did all night, but I took care of that by having her spayed.

At work I am supposed to be visible and accessible, so when I got to my office the next morning I opened my curtains and smiled at passersby. Next, a blue and white Crown Royal came to a stop across the street. The female police constable inside the car tapped the horn to get my attention, and then she waved me over. Running outside and dodging rush-hour traffic, I trotted dutifully across to her.

The constable was Cynthia Leach, Victoria's most glamorous cop. She has the face of an angel, beautiful lips red enough to stop traffic, blonde tresses, a flawless alabaster complexion and the kind of figure that sailors dream about during long lonely watches at sea. The last time I had seen her, Cynthia had been comforting Mrs. Milton. Sometimes I imagine Cynthia comforting me.

When I joined her, she said, "Hey, Silas. I'm in a jam. Look at this."

Cynthia pointed to the Crown Royal's left front bumper. It was slightly bent, the apparent result of a minor collision. After a deep, angry inhalation, she said, "How much do you think the repair will cost?"

I shrugged. "Five, maybe six hundred?"

"Think again. I guy I know manages a body shop, and he had a look at it. The frame's twisted. This heap is a writeoff, the body shop guy says it's not worth fixing."

I shrugged my shoulders. "So what? Traffic accidents are routine, it's not going to ruin your career. Just file a report . . ."

"Screw that, this is Lightning Bradley's car," Cynthia interrupted vehemently. "You remember that Bernie Tapp took Lightning's keys away after he was suspended?"

I nodded.

"It was my job to drive Lightning home. He yapped his head off the whole drive about what a jerk Bernie is. How he's gonna sue the ass off the department. The sleazy bastard never even mentioned the bumper." Cynthia's pale complexion was becoming darker with resentment. "I only noticed the damage a little while ago, but I swear to God I'm not responsible. What do you think I should do?"

"You don't want to blow the whistle on Lightning Bradley, is that it?"

"Well, no. Esprit de corps and all that. Stick together through thick and thin, right? Only Lightning is a prick. The idle bastard has been getting a free ride for years. It'd be a waste of time telling him to get a value system at his age."

When the light up at the Government Street intersection changed and vehicle traffic abated, we crossed to my office. Cynthia sat in a visitors' chair while I sorted through the junk mail piled on my desk. PC, had been spying on us. She came in through the cat flap immediately afterwards. PC leapt onto Cynthia's lap, nosed herself beneath Cynthia's hands for attention, then writhed and dug her claws into Cynthia's pant leg until she stroked her. Purring like an engine, PC wedged herself between Cynthia's thighs.

I sat in my swiveller and gazed up at the room's cornice mouldings, endeavouring to concentrate on Lightning Bradley's perfidies, instead of what my lucky cat was doing.

Lightning's wife, Maggie, had been lovely and smart. We couldn't believe it when, twenty years earlier, she took leave of her senses and married him. Some of us began to wonder if maybe Lightning wasn't the useless philandering shit we'd all taken him to be. Maggie was making a man out of a monkey until she was mowed down by a hit-and-run street racer and left a paraplegic. Lightning's drinking got worse, his womanizing got worse, and we all knew that behind the scenes, with Maggie in a wheelchair, things chez Bradley were grim.

I was still trying to come up with something wise to tell Cynthia when the desk phone jangled. It was Bernie Tapp. He said, "We've arrested a suspect. She's Coast Salish, so I want you here. Make it pronto, buddy."

VICTORIA'S MODERN NEW police headquarters is located on Caledonia Street. Bernie Tapp's office is on the fourth floor. When I got out of the elevator, Constable Ricketts was pacing restlessly back and forth in Bernie's anteroom.

Mrs. Nairn, a motherly secretary dressed in a green sweater and matching skirt, looked up from her computer, eyed me across her desk, smiled and told me to go straight in.

I found Bernie standing by a window, gazing across the Memorial Arena towards Mount Douglas. He said playfully, "Want to earn a little money?"

"Hell yes."

"Here's what you do. You fly to southern China, buy an old fishing trawler, the cheapest you can find. It'll set you back maybe fifty grand. Then you fill it with Chinese. Jam a few hundred of 'em into the fish holds at ten thousand dollars a crack. Ship them across the Pacific to our west coast. When in sight of land, you can either row the fuckers ashore in lifeboats or let 'em swim. Some of 'em might drown, but who gives a fuck, you'll have made a couple of million dollars. Hear what I'm saying? A couple of million for a few weeks' work."

"Ronnie Chew had a wardrobe full of silk suits that were made in Hong Kong, he owned a BMW. Who's to say he was a wetback? Maybe he flew over on China Air," I was saying, when Bernie's intercom buzzer sounded.

Mrs. Nairn said, "They are ready for you now, sir."

"Send 'em in," Bernie told her.

Nice Manners entered, followed by two female police officers and the suspect.

The suspect was dirty and she was angry, wearing a mudstained *Jesus loves you, everybody else thinks you're an asshole* T-shirt and off-the-shelf jeans. Her long black hair was mussed. Daubs of reddish mud streaked the line of her jaw. Her bare ankles were caked with filth. Glittering on her wedding finger was a platinum ring set with an enormous diamond. The diamond looked real to me. The last time I'd seen her, she'd been with another Native woman on Pandora Street, watching ravens.

Bernie was in a high good humour. The constables had patted the suspect down and emptied her pockets. Her name was Maria Alfred. She was Coast Salish, a status Indian. An identity card to that effect was found on her, along with about a hundred dollars in loose cash, a package of condoms, a tube of lipstick and a magnificent string of pearls.

Bernie gave her our usual Charter Rights spiel. Then, his eyebrows lifted, he went on to say lazily, "Listen, Maria, I want to know why you and your girlfriend ran away from the police at Echo Bay."

"It's none of your business," Maria retorted, with sullen obstinacy.

"That's where you're wrong," Bernie came back, his gaze intense. "What's your girlfriend called?"

A fleeting smile appeared on Maria's round face, but she remained silent.

"We need you to tell us your friend's name, Maria. You can save yourself some grief and tell us now, or you can tell us later. Either way, we're going to find out who she is and what the two of you were doing at Echo Bay. So do yourself a favour, and tell us. Who's the other woman?"

"I'm not saying nothing till I talk to a lawyer."

"You've been watching too much Hollywood TV, Maria. In Canada, you're re not entitled to a lawyer until you've been charged with a crime. We're just having a little exploratory conversation."

"You heard what I said. Talk to my lawyer or save your breath."

Bernie waved a finger. "So you've decided to be naughty. We have an expression for such behaviour. We call it suspicious. You're a doubtful character, which is bad enough. We don't want to add uncooperative to the list as well. So listen up: Do you know the penalty for wasting police time?"

After a beat, Maria said, "My tits will fall off?"

Bernie stiffened. "Stop playing the fool. I know you're not as stupid as you look, so tell me the truth. Why did you run away from Ronnie Chew's house, and what is your friend's name?"

Asking serial questions is bad interrogation technique. Bernie always complains when I do it.

Giving Bernie an insolent stare, Maria said, "I don't like your attitude."

"Many people don't, I'm used to it," Bernie returned with an indifferent shrug. "How long have you and Ronnie been friends?"

"I told you before, mister. It's none of your business."

Bernie raised his voice a little. "You're acting like an idiot, better think twice before your smartass cracks make things worse. Now. Let's get the ball rolling with something simple. Tell me where that diamond ring and those pearls came from."

She mumbled something incomprehensible.

"Hear that? Bernie said jocularly, to nobody in particular. "I'll go to hell, this kid is one smart shopper. The ring is probably two and a half carats, and she bought it at Wal-Mart?"

Maria shrugged.

"Ever been arrested before, Maria? Is this your first time?"

Her expression calm and unaltered, Maria used the Coast Salish word for idiot.

"Did she say something cheeky?" Bernie asked me.

"Not sure," I lied. "I don't think there's an English equivalent."

"You don't like to speak English?" Bernie asked her. "Comprenny franglais?

Maria's tongue came out like a third lip.

Things progressed like that for a while because Maria, who had never been arrested before, didn't realize how serious things were.

"Well Maria, you seem to enjoy a little fun occasionally," said Bernie, watching her with an eagle's eye. "You and your friend certainly enjoyed yourself with Ronnie Chew."

"I hardly know the guy."

"There you go again, telling stories."

"It's true," Maria said, completely at ease and relaxed. "I just met him the one time, that's all. He was nice, cute. And he wasn't mean, not like some. He had a funny way of talking that made us laugh."

"Funny? Funny's not the word that normally springs to mind in connection with men like Mr. Chew."

"He was a lot funnier than you are, I'll say that for him."

"Let's see how amusing you think this is: we found Mr. Chew's digital camera, and there were pictures of you and your friend in it," Bernie said.

Bernie reached into a briefcase sitting on the floor beside his feet, and drew out an eight by ten glossy. Tut-tutting in mock distaste, Bernie laid it down on the desk and said, "This is a blowup."

The picture came as a shock. It showed Maria in Chew's basement room. She was posed naked across Chew's bed with her knees bent, legs wide apart, smiling coquettishly without the least show of shame. One cupped hand supported her head. The other hand lay on her lower belly.

Maria pretended she wasn't interested in looking at the picture at first, till overcome by curiosity. Her reaction surprised us. Instead of embarrassed shame, or horror, she flushed with anger. "Bastards," she yelled. "That's private, see? I don't want you showing it around, hear me?"

Bernie gazed at her from under his heavy eyebrows. "Why not? You're not exactly a shrinking innocent, are you, Maria? Chew's camera is full of images like that. Quit play-acting and start talking. What have you got to say for yourself now, eh?"

"Them pictures is private. There's no law against taking private pictures of people. It's not like I was . . . You got no right, showing that in public."

"We're not the public, we're the police."

"Yeah, a bunch of fucking policemen. And this is the way you get your rocks off I guess, flashing sexy pictures around in your goddamn men's room, sniggering and leering at each other. Pulling your puds and telling jokes. Bastards!"

"This is the way things look so far," Bernie replied calmly. "You and your pal had fun and games with Chew. Then, when he was asleep, you cut his throat and robbed him."

Maria's eyes narrowed in stupefaction; her mouth fell open. "Cut his throat? What the hell?"

Bernie rose to his feet. Glaring down at Maria, he shouted, "You killed him, didn't you? Maybe it was a sex game. You may as well come clean, we'll be more lenient if you do."

Maria flinched backwards; her mouth opened but no words came out.

To everyone's surprise, Bernie terminated the interrogation. "Screw this," he said, his jovial manner returning. Turning to the two female officers, he said, "Take this woman away. Give her a good wash and some clean clothes, then you can lock her up in Wilkie Road. We'll continue this after she's had a chance to contemplate her sins. See how she rates Wilkie's nice comfy cells and institutional cuisine."

Maria appeared dazed when she was led out. After frowning at the picture for another few moments, Bernie put it back into the briefcase.

Bernie got up from his chair and crossed to the window. His grin returned when he looked outside. "That picture is just a sample of Chew's art, but just between you and me I'd rather look at chick pics than look at shit on the sidewalk."

"Are you serious?"

"Certainly," Bernie answered with a wide grin. "Chew's camera is full of it. Pictures of Maria, and her girlfriend. Twosomes, threesomes, I've never seen anything like it."

"Really?"

"Well no, not really, it's no worse than *Hustler*, but it makes a difference if you know the girl I suppose. Anyway, Silas, what's the deal here?"

"I dunno, it's too early to tell."

Restless, Bernie sat down again. "This is open and shut, isn't it? You just don't want to say anything because of the Native angle. That slavekiller club, the two Indian girls. Maria won't talk because she's guilty. Maybe it was a sex game that went wrong. Whatever. I'm betting that Maria and her friend killed Chew for the jewellery."

"Whoever it was, he or she, the killer was very very angry. Chew was almost decapitated. Is that the MO a couple of petty opportunistic thieves would use to commit an unpremeditated murder?"

"Who says it was unpremeditated?"

"Come off it, Bernie," I said. Choosing my words with care, I added, "It's time we had a talk. Man to man."

"About what?"

"You know what. How long have we known each other?"

"Ten, fifteen years?"

"Bernie, it's more than twenty years. If I didn't give a fuck, I'd keep my mouth shut, but I do give a fuck, so here goes. It's time you either took a vacation or retired. You're losing it, pal. That interview just now, for example. You cut it off before it hardly got started. What are you playing at?"

Bernie brought the corncob out again, held it in his hands, pointing it towards me like a gun. I couldn't read the expression on his face. He looked a little pale, otherwise normal. He said, "Okay, keep going."

"I've said enough. I hope you got the message."

Bernie put the corncob down on his desk. He smiled at me and shrugged his shoulders. Suddenly overcome by nervous yawns, he reached into a bottom drawer of his desk for a bottle of eau-de-cologne. He poured a little onto his hands and vigorously massaged his scalp. Still yawning, he put the bottle away.

Lately, Bernie had been using glasses for reading. He put a pair on and glanced briefly inside the red three-ring binder lying on his blotter. It was the Chew murder book—already half an inch thick.

"What's a phony Canadian birth certificate worth these days?" Bernie asked me.

Bernie's question was rhetorical. Before I could answer, he went on, "On the street, the going rate for a good fake Canadian birth certificate is a thousand dollars."

"Lord a mercy!" I said, in mock astonishment.

"Once you've got a birth certificate, acquiring a driver's licence or a passport is a piece of cake. In spite of that, forensics hasn't been able to find Chew's driver's licence, his passport or a BC Medical card. Not a single scrap of paper with Ronnie Chew's name on it. That leather notebook we found is written in Chinese characters, but it's some kind of code. Our brains branch can't figure the goddamn thing out. But, there was fifteen thousand dollars' worth of clothing in Chew's closet. His BMW is worth sixty thousand, at least. Ronnie Chew, gardener, didn't exist. He was a sham, an impostor."

"A John Doe?"

"Not quite." Bernie grinned. "We put Ronnie Chew's fingerprints on the wire. Vancouver got back to us promptly. Chew's prints are on file. The name Ronnie Chew is an alias. The murdered man that we saw on Collins Lane is a Big Circle Boy. His actual name is Raymond Cho."

Bernie looked at me. Instead of asking the question that immediately sprang to mind, I remained silent.

Bernie said, "I know what you're thinking. You're thinking that not only did Ronnie Chew never exist, it's more than probable that Raymond Cho never existed either. What exists, in all likelihood, is a mystery man with several aliases."

"So we might never know his actual name?"

"We know enough to be going along with," Bernie said, rubbing his neck. "How about a cup of coffee?"

"Sure."

Bernie hit an intercom button on his desk, spoke sweetly to Mrs. Nairn, leaned back in his chair and cupped both hands behind his head. He said, "I attended a Combined Law Enforcement Unit conference in Vancouver last month. Their east side is an ungovernable disaster. It's a drug supermarket awash in crime and violence. The CLEU told us that in Vancouver's east-side district, five percent of newborn babies emerge from the womb addicted to crank. Little League games get cancelled because junkies don't give a fuck. They dump their used needles in parks and in playgrounds where kids can pick them up and stick them in their arms to show off. Cartel enforcers are running the streets in armour-plated SUVs, popping each other with AK 47s." Bernie wasn't telling me anything new. I let him vent. "Since last year, at least four gang battles have been raging in the Lower Mainland. It's like prohibition-era Chicago over there. Innocent bystanders are getting killed as well. It's a mess. The way things are going, Vancouver Island will soon be in the same boat. Things are reaching the point where police forces are losing control using normal methods. The ordinary man on the street has no idea how weak our security system is, but we know. We know and we're worried. Victoria is worried all the way up the food chain to the mayor's office. Even Superintendent Mallory is worried."

My thoughts turned to Cynthia Leach, worrying about a damaged bumper. I said, "Are you worried, Bernie?"

"Goddamn right. I'm worried because I'm worried. It used to be I didn't take stuff personally, I didn't give a damn either." Bernie's scowl deepened. "Two months ago, on a quiet Sunday morning at about 3:00 AM, near the intersection of West Boulevard and 41st Avenue in Vancouver, an SUV boxed in a black Bentley driven by a recent Southeast Asian immigrant with gang ties. A masked man got out of the SUV and opened fire through the Bentley's windows. Two of Vancouver's finest, who were drinking coffee in a nearby McDonald's, heard gunshots and took off in pursuit. The killers got away. When the coffee drinkers went back and checked, the man in the Bentley was dead. He was Devander Raj, aged 23. Raj's assassination brought to 12 the number of gang-style killings in Metro Vancouver this year. Since then, there have been 11 more gang-style assassinations. Vancouver's serious crimes squad thinks that Raj's death and many other violent killings are linked to the murder of Ivor Wright, another gangster. You probably remember that case; it was front-page stuff for weeks. Ivor Wright was a member of Twinner Scudd's Vancouver crew. Now it's no-holds-barred open warfare. Vietnamese gangsters are involved. The Triads are involved. Gangs from Richmond and Surrey and Vancouver's Chinatown are involved. Big Circle Boys are involved."

"You mentioned Twinner Scudd, and I know the way your mind works. Do you think that Scudd is involved in Cho's murder?"

"It's possible, why not? Twinner Scudd is a Native Indian who also happens to be the biggest villain on Vancouver Island. I'm not jumping to any conclusions yet, I'm just pointing out that there's another possible Native involvement in this case. And don't forget, Silas, that Nicky Nattrass' mutts found that slavekiller club near the Echo Bay house. Face it. The Native connection is getting stronger all the time."

I thought that Bernie was talking crap, but kept that opinion to myself.

Looking down his nose at me, Bernie went on, "I just had a long phone conversation with Harry Bryce, in Vancouver. He's an inspector with BC's Integrated Gang Task Force."

Bernie had my full attention. He went on, "According to the BCIGTF, these guys are battling for turf and Raymond Cho was an assassination target. A lot of gangsters stand to benefit from Cho's death, and several attempts were made on his life before somebody finally nailed him."

"So that's why Cho moved here, to escape the heat?"

"Right. Cho moved here and masqueraded as a gardener. It was a clever ruse. Too bad for him that it didn't work. Whatever. For me, it's a serious development. A quarter of Vancouver's crimes squad detectives are tied up with gang-related issues. Victoria is already stretched to the limit, so the last thing I want is Asian hit men and stickup crews coming over here from the mainland. Knocking people off and thinking they can get away with it."

"I think I know where you're going with this now. Twinner Scudd stands to benefit from Cho's death. That's what you've been getting at. You think Cho was bumped off by a Native hit man."

Bernie took his glasses off, laid them on his desk, scratched his head and said, "Hit *man*? No, I don't think he was killed by a hit *man*. Because forensics says that there was dried semen on Cho's penis and on his lower belly. Shortly before his death, Cho was involved in sexual activity with female partners, and we know who they were because we have photographs to prove it. We don't even need DNA evidence. It's simple. Two Native girls killed Cho. Afterwards, as a little bonus to themselves, the girls helped themselves to some jewellery. For us to think anything otherwise stretches credulity beyond the breaking point. Face it. The girls might have been taking orders from somebody else. Twinner Scudd maybe. But they did it all right."

The door opened. Mrs. Nairn came in carrying a tray and put it on the desk. I poured two cups of coffee and helped myself to three chocolate chip cookies. Bernie moved the remaining three cookies beyond my reach before adding sugar to his own cup.

He put a cookie in his mouth and crunched into it. Broadcasting crumbs, he tapped the binder on his desk and said, "The Murder Book is filling up nicely. Dr. Tarleton's estimate, based on rigor and temperature, is that Cho bled to death and died two or three hours before Mrs. Milton found him. The back of Cho's head was caved in first by a single blow from a heavy object, and I'm betting that the DNA on that slavekiller club is a match for that blood in Cho's bedroom. Tarleton found a partially digested Chinese dinner in Cho's stomach. And there's more evidence, because Cho grappled with his killer. At the autopsy, foreign human skin tissue and blood was found under his fingernails.

"In addition, we have Inspector Manners' account of an interview with Tudor Collins, the guy who made that 911 call. He is a steady seventy-year-old man who has lived in Victoria his whole life. Collins knows the difference between a Native Indian and a Chinese. According to Mr. Collins, the two women that he dimed *were* Native Indians. I keep going over the same ground, Silas, because you are a hard man to convince sometimes. Look at it this way: that slavekiller club is Indian. Twinner Scudd is Indian. One might assume, given the time frame involved, and after sexual intercourse with Cho, the aforementioned Indian sex partner turned around and murdered him. So who do you think the finger is actually pointing at?"

"A giant female spider?"

My flippant remark rolled right off him. "The finger is pointing at two Native Indian girls."

"Women," I corrected him. "And that's another giant leap, Bernie . . ."

Bernie butted in. "It's a working hypothesis with a very high probability of being proved accurate."

"Do you want me to go up against Twinner Scudd?"

Bernie looked at the coffee grounds inside his empty cup as if for an answer, but apparently didn't see one. "Frankly, if Twinner Scudd is involved, I'd like to dump this whole case, but that's not an option. Because of the Native angle, I'd like to get you involved in the case. Interested?"

I felt a huge surge of relief; Bernie's insistence that the two girls had killed Cho bothered me greatly. I said, "Sure, I'm glad you asked. I'd be happy to get involved, as long as I can work out of my own office instead of headquarters."

"What's wrong with working out of headquarters?"

"Nothing. I've got responsibilities to my neighbourhood, is all. Irons in the fire that need watching."

"Fine, you are co-opted into this mess as of now. I'll square things with the front office. Poke around generally, but don't go poking yourself too far up Twinner Scudd's ugly nose. Or up Nice Manners' pretty nose. As a first priority, I need to find out who the other Native woman is and what really went on at Echo Bay."

Bernie pressed a button on his desk intercom and asked Mrs. Nairn to send Ricketts in.

The young constable looked miserable. The dark half-circles under his eyes suggested that Ricketts hadn't been sleeping much. He also appeared to have lost a little weight.

Instead of acknowledging Ricketts, Bernie opened the murder book. After scanning a couple of pages to refresh his memory, Bernie said matter-of-factly, "You look nervous, Ricketts."

"Sir? I am nervous. I'm suspended from duty, but I hope that my suspension is only temporary. I want you to know that I love my job and that I'd hate to lose it."

Bernie shook his head. "Yeah, I suppose you would," he said unsym-pathetically. "How long have you been with us, Ricketts?"

"Six months, sir."

"For some guys, policing is a soft option. Sit on your ass for 25 years. Then retire with a nice big package. Cultivate dahlias and rent yourself out on weekends to concert promoters."

Ricketts straightened even more and swallowed, his Adam's apple jerking.

Bernie went on gruffly, "This is a routine matter. A question-and-answer session to clear up some loose ends. It is all part of a murder inquiry that the department is pursuing. It is not, repeat not, a disciplinary hearing. All the same, Ricketts, if you feel threatened or uncomfortable you're entitled to have a union rep present, or a lawyer."

"I don't want either, at the moment."

"Do you have any objection to this session being taped?"

"No, sir."

"Let me know if you change your mind, okay?"

"Okay, sir."

Bernie looked at me.

I got up from my chair, went across to the filing cabinet where Bernie keeps a battery-powered recorder ready and took it to the desk. I turned the recorder on and sat down again.

Bernie shut his eyes for a long moment. Opening his eyes, he pointed a finger at Ricketts and said, "This is serious stuff, Constable. I want to go step by step through a few incidents and I want the truth. No bullshit and no omissions. The whole truth and nothing else, okay?"

"I will cooperate in every way, sir."

"Good. All right. You and Constable Bradley were in a police cruiser on routine patrol. Somebody called headquarters and reported seeing a couple of suspicious characters on Collins Lane. Correct?"

Flustered initially by Bernie's severe tone and manner, Ricketts said, "Yes, sir. When the dispatcher radioed the call, we were on Haultain Street."

"Who is 'we'?"

"Me and Constable Bradley."

"You responded immediately, you told us. What time was that, Constable?"

Ricketts reached into one of his pockets. Bernie stopped him by saying, "Don't consult your notes. I want you to answer my questions from memory."

"It was between eight-thirty and nine in the morning when we got the dispatcher's call. Maybe twenty minutes before nine. We were told to be on the lookout for two First Nations women. A pair of alleged suspicious prowlers."

"What happened next?"

"We were heading west on Haultain at the time. I did a U-turn and we ended up on Richmond Road. We winkled our way onto Echo Bay

Road and spotted two women standing near a bus stop. They answered the descriptions we'd been given. When I stopped the car, the women fled into the bush."

"Fine, you're doing okay, Ricketts. Then what?"

"We gave chase, but it was hopeless from the start. The bush is so thick along there you can't see twenty feet ahead. It was broad daylight on the road, but in some places underneath those trees it was dark enough for a Maglite. We never saw either woman again. Constable Bradley and I figured our chances of catching them were minimal. He decided to return to the car while I continued the chase."

With rising confidence, Ricketts went on, "At that time, of course, we didn't know there'd been a murder. We thought the women were at worst just a couple of suspicious prowlers. As Bradley pointed out, what were we going to do even if we did catch up with them? Deliver a stern warning?"

"True enough, that's a very good point," Bernie said formally, as if that thought had never occurred to him. "You couldn't have known that those two women would become the prime suspects in a particularly vicious murder inquiry."

Ricketts said, "Bradley went back to the car. I ended up on the beach below Collins Lane, and headed north."

Bernie frowned as if perplexed. "Why north?"

"It was just a guess, sir, a toss-up. I had no real reason to favour either direction."

"You didn't see any footprints or other signs?"

"No, sir. If I had, I'd have told you," Ricketts replied with assurance.

"Good, very good, Ricketts. All right. You headed north along the beach?"

"I headed north along the beach until I came abreast of the big house and heard Mrs. Milton. She was screaming hysterically."

Bernie's brow furrowed. He seemed a little confused. "Mrs. Milton?" he said haltingly.

"She's the housekeeper," Ricketts explained.

Maybe Ricketts didn't know it, but Bernie has a memory like a steel trap. He can recall facts and figures from cases that he was involved with 25 years back. But sometimes it is to an interrogator's advantage if the person being questioned is encouraged to think he's the smartest guy in the room. He gets sloppy and lets his guard down. Says things he shouldn't."

Still frowning slightly, Bernie consulted the murder book. "What time would that be, Ricketts?"

"A little after nine. Maybe ten after nine?"

"So what you are telling me is, half an hour elapsed between the time you got the dispatcher's call, and when you saw and heard Mrs. Milton?"

Ricketts shrugged.

"Okay, let's leave the timeline angle for now," Bernie said. "Go on with your story."

"Mrs. Milton was in a terrible state. She'd just had a terrible shock, she just kept on screaming and screaming. She was like a madwoman; it took me a while to calm her. It was several minutes before she could bring herself to tell me that there was a dead man in the cellar. I went downstairs and saw the dead man myself. It's the first dead man I've seen, but I was certain that he was dead. I called headquarters and then I called Constable Bradley. Told them where I was, what I'd found."

Bernie moved his chair back and crossed his legs. "It never occurred to you that Mrs. Milton might be the killer?"

Ricketts blinked. "Hell no, sir. She was obviously scared out of her wits. Terrified."

"Terrified, or in a panic?"

Ricketts made a bewildered face. "I'm sorry, sir. It never entered my head. Jeez. Did she kill him?"

Bernie ignored Ricketts' question. "Let me get this straight. After talking to Mrs. Milton, you phoned headquarters. Then you phoned Bradley?"

Ricketts hesitated. "It's possible I phoned Bradley first, sir. I'd just seen the dead man, I was agitated."

"By the time you called Bradley though, you and Mrs. Milton were probably a little calmer?"

"Yes, sir."

"Constable Bradley arrived soon afterwards?"

"Yes, sir. Lightning—er, Constable Bradley was the next officer to arrive," Ricketts said. "As the senior officer, Bradley told me to stay with Mr. Chew. He said we had to preserve the integrity of the crime scene so there'd be no legal issues later."

"Bradley told you to guard Mr. Chew's body?"

After pausing to reflect, Ricketts answered, "Well no, come to think of it. Constable Bradley just said to stay with the body. At the time I'm not sure that we knew who the dead man was."

"I suppose not, Constable. What did Bradley do next?"

"I don't know, sir. I stayed in the bedroom. As far as I know, Bradley was upstairs until you arrived."

Bernie made a big deal of reading the murder book. Ricketts had been standing rigidly to attention, but by then his shoulders were beginning to sag.

Bernie eyed Ricketts shrewdly. "Approximately how much time passed between Constable Bradley's arrival and when Sergeant Seaweed and I showed up at the house?"

Ricketts licked his lips. "Frankly, sir, that's rather hard to say. Time seemed to pass very slowly."

"Hazard a guess."

"Ten minutes?"

"As little as that? Think carefully, this could be important."

Ricketts ground his teeth. "I suppose it could have been fifteen minutes. Ten to fifteen minutes, sir."

"Did Constable Bradley say or do anything that might suggest, to your mind, that he and Mrs. Milton had known each other previous to this incident?"

Ricketts seemed astonished. He shrugged, and then shook his head emphatically.

Bernie slammed his desk with the flat of his hand and said, "That's a tape recorder on my desk, not a goddamn video camera. Don't nod or shrug or shake your head to me, Constable! Speak your answers out loud! Do you understand?"

"Yes, sir, sorry, sir," was Ricketts' abject response. "I'm sure it was the first time Constable Bradley and Mrs. Milton had met."

Bernie turned in his chair and looked at me. "Do you have any questions for Constable Ricketts?"

I waited till Ricketts made eye contact with me. "How long since you and Bradley partnered up?" I asked him.

"Three months, Sergeant. Give or take."

"Foot patrol?"

"Foot patrols by day, mostly downtown. Car patrols when we pull the graveyard shift."

"You and Bradley have been using one of our older-model Crown Royals. Do you usually drive it?"

Ricketts hesitated and his gaze dropped. "For the most part. Bradley drives it occasionally."

"Who was driving the Crown Royal when it was involved in a serious accident?"

Ricketts had been staring straight ahead. His face swung towards me, but he failed to meet my eyes. "Sir?"

"Were you driving the Crown Royal when it sustained an accident severe enough to twist its frame?"

"An accident? Hell no!" Ricketts said. "Who said it had been in an accident?"

"Just answer my question."

"I don't know anything about it," Ricketts said indignantly. "Before I take a car out I walk around it first. It's the standard drill. The last time I checked, the Crown Royal had a few nicks. There's a small gravel starburst on the left side of the windscreen, and that's about all."

"The last time you checked the car was when, exactly?"

Ricketts looked as if his head might burst. "The same day that we drove to Echo Bay Road and saw those women. There wasn't a fresh mark on the car, I swear."

"In your assessment, there's no question that those women you pursued were First Nations?"

"They were First Nations, all right."

I had no further questions. Bernie reminded Ricketts that it was a firing offence if he communicated with either Constable Bradley or Mrs. Milton in any way.

By then, Ricketts looked like a boxer at the losing end a fifteen-round slugfest. He said, "Permission to speak, sir?"

Bernie said, "Go ahead."

"I just want to repeat that I'll do everything possible to reinstate myself, sir, and to protect my good name."

"Duly noted," Bernie said. "That's all, Ricketts, you can go home again. You're suspended off duty with pay until this matter is settled. Stay by the phone, we might need you to come in for more questions later. Today or tomorrow."

Ricketts gave a smart salute and went out.

"Well, what do you think?" Bernie asked.

"I think Ricketts has the makings of a good officer, Bernie. Maybe you came down a bit hard on him."

"Okay, okay, I hear you, but I think he might be holding something back. And what's all this about a busted frame?"

I told Bernie about my conversation with Cynthia Leach. "I think we should impound the Crown Royal and have it looked at. Forensics, mechanicals, prints, the whole nine yards."

"All right, take care of it," Bernie said.

I picked up the phone, dialled Serious Crimes and told them what was needed.

Bernie put his feet on his desk and crossed his legs. He said broodingly, "The immediate puzzle is whether Lightning leaned on Ricketts. Asked him to lie and cover his ass."

"Whose ass?"

"Lightning's ass. Ricketts may be stupid, I don't think he's a liar."

"People lie all the time, especially children, politicians, televangelists and cops."

"Children are the worst. I have three of my own, so I ought to know."

"Televangelists are the worst. Children are bad, though. Children lie even when there's no need to lie. And that brings up something else. When are you going to waterboard Lightning Bradley?"

Bernie hesitated. "Not yet. I'll let Bradley and Maria twist in the wind for a bit. Then when they're ripe we'll bring them in separately and put the boots to 'em. We've already got a court order and we're tapping Lightning's phones. Ricketts' too. With a bit of luck one of 'em will break. He'll make a call and spill the beans. Give us something we can get our teeth into."

"When do you want me get started on this?"

"You can start right now," Bernie said. "Cho's inquest is tomorrow morning. After that it's up to you, but keep your head down. Try not to get yourself killed. Be nice when you talk to Twinner Scudd. If you need help with your neighbourhood duties, we'll find somebody to keep things going till you return to normal duties."

"If I get killed, I won't return to normal duties."

"Just remind me again. What are your normal duties?"

"I'm a neighbourhood cop. Apart from taking care of PC, I don't have any normal duties."

"Exactly, so you won't be missed. This is the deal: do a good job. If you do get killed, we'll pin a medal to your remains. Give 'em a nice send-off. Wreaths, bands playing, a few weepy girls."

I must have been scowling. Bernie said, "Okay, what's bothering you now, Silas?"

"Tell me something. Do you really believe that those women killed Raymond Cho?"

"What kind of question is that? It doesn't matter to me if they did or if they didn't kill him. That's for a jury to decide," Bernie said without hesitation. "Pay attention, Silas, darling, because I've said this before and now I'll say it again. What-I-believe-doesn't-signify. Would you like me to repeat that for you?"

"No. I think I've got it now."

"I don't have infinite time or resources to spend on this case. All I can do is try and cover the bases," said Bernie, running his fingers through his hair. "I know I've been hammering this thing to death, but just look at the facts. Two Native girls were spotted leaving the area soon after Raymond Cho was murdered. Cho was probably clubbed with a slavekiller before his throat was cut. This all leads up to certain conclusions. Whatever. I'm doing the best I can with what I've got. If what I've got doesn't work, they'd better suspend civil rights and call in the army."

"Why did you rub your head with cologne?"

"It's got alcohol in it," Bernie said, with another yawn. "It makes my scalp tingle and helps to keep me awake."

I said so long and walked downstairs. By the time I reached the basement garage, Bradley's blue-and-white was being towed to forensics.

CHAPTER FIVE

The next morning, as I was leaving my house, I found an injured pine siskin lying in my garden. Brown overall, with yellow wing bars, the tiny bird tried to fly away, but it had a damaged wing. Instead of rising into the air, it thrashed around on the ground in circles, emitting a rapid series of husky distress notes.

Wild animals don't seem to experience fear in the same way as humans. The little creature seemed more bewildered than afraid when I cupped it in my hands and deposited it high in an escallonia bush, where it would be safe from roaming cats. Bathed in a self-congratulatory glow, I took a venison chop from my fridge and chopped little pieces that I suspended from strings in the escallonia here and there. The little bird was eating breakfast when I drove to town.

I ate my own breakfast at a greasy spoon on Store Street before I went over to View Street and parked near the CIBC building. A man wearing a Bill Clinton mask was playing a saxophone on the corner, although nobody seemed to care. I went into the Bay Centre. The smell of food enveloped me as I took the escalator down to the grocery section. I bought eggs, a package of frozen Cornish pasties, a jar of Smuckers marmalade and a tin of Spam. I was trying to decide between bumbleberry pie and a pint of chocolate ice cream when my cellphone rang. It was Mrs. Nairn.

"Silas, this is urgent," she said, "CDI Tapp wants you to meet him at Lightning Bradley's house right away. The CDI has been trying to reach Bradley by phone, but he isn't answering. We know that there hasn't been any outgoing phone activity from the house during the last 12 hours. Do you know where Bradley lives?"

I knew where Bradley lived. I also knew that Serious Crimes had been monitoring his house phone and—using a frequency counter and a scanner—they had been tracking Bradley's cellphone calls as well.

I opted for the chocolate ice cream and lugged my purchases to the checkout. Time stood still while an old-timer, three customers ahead of me in the lineup, fumbled for change from a purse, one coin at a time. Time was a-wasting. I apologized to the clerk and left the store empty-handed.

Lightning Bradley's house was on a side street, a block away from Victoria's Central Middle School. When I arrived, girls wearing white shirts and grey pleated skirts were playing field hockey in the school's playing fields. The house, a small one-and-a-half storey with an attached garage, had a neglected, unoccupied look. The curtains were closed, and the grass hadn't been mowed in weeks. Weeds proliferated between the paving stones leading up to the front door.

Bernie was speaking into a cellphone when he showed up and parked at the curb. He put the phone away, and then got slowly out of his car. He was yawning when we walked up to the house together. Bernie rang the doorbell; nobody answered. I shaded the sides of my face with my hands and looked through a front window. It was dark inside, I couldn't see anything. The back door facing the school was locked.

Bernie had stopped yawning. "We're going in," he muttered.

Using my Glock like a club, I broke a side window, climbed inside, and let Bernie into the kitchen. In the day's scorching heat, Bradley's house smelled foul, and when we turned lights on, we saw a scene of utter destruction. As we slowly advanced through the house towards the living room, the extraordinarily powerful smells of spilt blood, urine and feces became unbearable. We retreated to the kitchen, opened doors and windows, wetted handkerchiefs, held them to our faces and made a second attempt to reach the living room.

The house had been thoroughly trashed. Papers, feathers and furniture stuffing was strewn everywhere. Fine suspended particles filled the air. Drawers had been pulled out of cabinets, and their contents dumped onto the floor. Cushions, pillows and mattresses had been slashed. Carpets had been drawn back to reveal bare boards. Cabinets had been dragged away from walls; hollow metal curtain rods had been taken down and searched. The toilet's tank lid lay in small pieces on the bathroom floor. Photographs had been removed from their frames. But that was all incidental. We only half-noticed such things at the time, because the woman we found in the lounge took our minds off everything else.

It was another grisly bloodbath.

The woman was fastened to a fake-leather recliner by yards of duct tape. Her blue woollen dress and the recliner she sat in were drenched in blood, as was the carpet beneath her. Flies buzzed around the corpse. More duct tape had been wrapped around her head, covering her mouth and anchoring her arms to the chair. She had been badly beaten. Her face and body were swollen and bloated beyond recognition, but a folded wheelchair leaning against a wall and the corpse's muscular arms and useless, atrophied legs told us that this was Bradley's wife, Maggie.

Maggie's fingernails had been ripped out. Her dress had been slit open down the front, exposing her sagging breasts and her groin area. And Maggie's glistening entrails. Gripped by primeval dread and disgust, I touched Maggie's skin. It was still warm, and rigor had not yet commenced; she had been dead less than three hours. The scene was so ghastly that for a few seconds I experienced involuntary skin-crawling sensations.

"The guy who did this is a maniac," I said unnecessarily. "A stark raving lunatic."

We went out to the backyard together; children's laughter echoed distantly in the school playground.

When Bernie finished phoning Serious Crimes, I said, "I'd like to know where Lightning is."

Bernie took a deep breath. "Think he did it?"

"Not a chance."

"He might have done it," Bernie insisted, his face flushed. "Lightning's job was on the line and it must have preyed on his mind. He might have gone over the edge. If he did, I'm responsible."

"That's crap, Bernie. You're talking nonsense."

Bernie's head snapped back as if I'd slapped him. After that we barely spoke to each other until Serious Crimes showed up minutes later.

Bernie laid down the law. "We've got to keep the lid on this business," he told everyone sternly. "A complete silence, I want the press kept out of it as long as possible."

I didn't see any particular need for it, but I didn't argue. Bernie turned his attention to the foot soldiers, some of whom were already stringing yellow Crime Scene Police tape around the house.

When I got home, I removed every stitch of my clothing, put it in a garbage bag, and secured the bag with a twist-tie. Then I went out to the backyard shower and scrubbed myself with deodorant soap until my skin felt raw. The smell of death was in my mouth and in my nostrils; I couldn't wash it away.

CHAPTER SIX

First Woman—who brings rain to Vancouver Island—had been smiling instead of weeping for weeks, and Victoria was hot. It was two in the afternoon, and I was hot. My office was hot. The city was hot like August in Tucson is hot. Last week, CFAX's weatherman told us that Victoria's present climate is the way it was in northern California 50 years ago. I'm beginning to believe it. Local farmers are ploughing up their potato fields now. Planting grapevines and calling themselves vintners. People grow peaches instead of apples in their backyards.

I looked at Pandora Street through a slat in my closed office window blinds. A narrow bar of bright afternoon light spilled inside. A fat bald taxi driver, hunched over his steering wheel like a Buddha as he waited for the traffic lights to change, was casting lascivious eyes at a young prostitute, skinny as a desert rat, who was lurking outside Swans pub. A street-person of indeterminate sex was collecting discarded bottles and cans from a garbage gobbler. I brought out the office bottle, braced myself with a stiff one, and started looking through the Raymond Cho murder book.

According to the ME, Raymond Cho had been murdered approximately two or three hours before Mrs. Milton discovered his body. When screened, the bloodstains on the slavekiller club did not match Cho's DNA. The blood in the medicine bag—as I could have told them—was that of wild animals and birds, not humans. Forensics had found traces of cocaine in Cho's room and in his BMW, along with numerous fibre samples and many disparate samples of human hair. Ultraviolet light had revealed bloody size ten shoe prints leading from Cho's bedroom and down the corridor to the staircase. Lightning Bradley wore size tens. Nice

Manners had seized several pairs of shoes from Lightning's house, one pair of which, when examined under ultraviolet light, showed traces of blood. Bradley's uniform had been found in the house and, when examined, it too had tested positive for cocaine.

The crime-scene bunnysuiters who had unearthed Cho's smut-filled digital camera had also lifted a complete set of Lightning Bradley's fingerprints from the inside of Cho's BMW. In addition, traces of cocaine had been found in Bradley's Crown Royal.

Bradley's future—and Ricketts'—was looking increasingly bleak.

After another drink, I used my desk phone and called Fred Halloran at the *Times Colonist*. Fred was out, but I tracked him down at Pinky's. I told Fred that if he'd wait for me, I'd go over and buy him a drink. Fred was a newspaperman who had me to thank for a couple of scoops; it was time for him to return the favour.

The sun had moved even closer to Victoria by then. I was wet under my clothes by the time I had walked the several blocks to View Street. The sun blazed above the rooftops. Wisps of steam rose from manhole covers; the sky pressed down like molten lead. Half a dozen Harleys were parked outside Pinky's—a hole-in-the-wall bar. Rotating gaily up on Pinky's flat roof was something new: a red neon pig driving a purple neon motorcycle.

Pinky's has low ceilings, bad-smelling air, and is furnished with the kind of seedy mismatched oddments that marginal restaurateurs pick up at fire sales. Rock music poured out of giant speakers. Bearded bikers with jail-tatted arms were drinking beer at tables set around a small dance floor. Female patrons dressed in clothing suitable for hanging around on street corners after dark lounged here and there. Fred Halloran sagged against Pinky's bar clutching an empty glass. Thin and sixtyish, with a gloomy expression, horn-rimmed glasses and ill-fitting dentures, Fred wore a brown fedora and a scruffy beige raincoat that had been out of fashion since the Beatles left Liverpool. I sat on a stool and asked Fred if he expected rain.

"Jeez, this weather," Fred mumbled.

Pinky's Irish beer slinger—a red-haired, red-nosed, beer-bellied functioning alcoholic named Doyle—was behind the bar picking his teeth with a plastic cocktail fork. Doyle wore a Guinness apron, a starched white collarless shirt with the sleeves rolled up, and black pants supported by wide green suspenders.

"Glory be to God, it's the filth, so it is," said Doyle to me. "And here a fellow was telling me only half an hour ago that you'd been swept to your death down a drain, so he did."

"And the best of Hibernian luck to you too, Doyle. I'll have a cheese-burger and fries, a pint of Fosters, and give that ink-stained wretch over there whatever he's drinking."

"Oh, you're a great man for the drink, Silas. A double Scotch will set me up nicely, so it will," Fred Halloran responded in a fair imitation of Doyle's rough Belfast patter.

Doyle shouted "Cheese and fries!" through a hatch behind the bar, poured the drinks, set my Fosters in front of me and slid the Scotch to Fred along a bar scarred and burnt by yesteryear's untended cigarettes. Doyle then leaned against the bar's back counter and resumed work on his upper molars.

Fred stopped ogling a long-legged woman across the room. With his glass tilted slightly in his hand, he eyed me over the rim and said, "Here's looking up your old address."

"I seem to recall that you covered the crime beat in Vancouver before you moved to Victoria."

"I was a reporter on the *Vancouver Province* in the sixties. Those were investigative journalism's glory days," Fred said wistfully. "Jack Webster and Jack Wasserman were the writing stars back then. Ben Metcalfe and Doug Collins were doing great columns as well. They're all gone now."

A mirror behind the bar gave me a good view of the whole room. I watched a dishwater blonde come in. She had freckles across the bridge of her nose and had once been very pretty. Now she was emaciated and twitchy; the lids covering her blue eyes were at half-mast.

Doyle edged closer. He removed the cocktail fork from his mouth, eyed the blonde speculatively, and said, "There'll be a hot time in the old town tonight, begorra."

I was already sick of Doyle. An empty table had come up beside the dance floor. I picked up my drink and said, "Okay Fred. Let's you and me go and sit over there."

The bikers who had used the table before us had left empty glasses and crumpled Dorito packages in their wake. Terri Murnau came over to clear up and swish a damp rag.

Terri is my age, about 40. A good-looking waitress, Terri was wearing a Che Guevara T-shirt that she must have purchased in a weak moment. She had either switched to wearing loose-fit jeans, or was losing weight. The skin raccooning one of her eyes showed purple beneath its makeup. I asked Terri to bring us another round of drinks.

After Terri went away, I said, "I expect you still know your way around Vancouver, Fred. You'd know all about the Big Circle Gang, I suppose."

Fred had been slumped in his chair. He straightened up and returned my gaze warily. "I know a bit. Why do you ask?"

"Casual interest," I said—sharing secrets with newspapermen unnecessarily is a mug's game.

"Baloney, your nose is growing." Fred dropped his voice to a confidential whisper. "Come on, strictly off the record?"

"There's nothing," I lied. "If anything comes up you'll be the first to know."

"A few years back, I did some investigative journalism on gang activity for the *Vancouver Province* which the wire services picked up," Fred said, awakening fascination showing on his face. "After my stories went to press I received a few threatening phone calls. Such calls are part of the territory and reporters get used to them. Still, those particular calls made me nervous. I'm glad to be in Victoria now instead of on the mainland. To be honest, just talking about those mobsters makes me nervous. What do you want to know, exactly?"

"What you can tell me about the Big Circle Gang?"

Fred looked at me directly; his dark glasses emphasized his facial pallor. "I thought you were going to ask me about Twinner Scudd. You're involved with the Raymond Cho murder investigation, right?"

The speed with which secret information is transferred from police headquarters to the Fourth Estate never ceases to amaze me. "I'm just a neighbourhood cop."

"A neighbourhood cop who bailed from the detective squad. You never got around to telling me why."

I hunched my shoulders. "I enjoy what I'm doing now. Working with street people. Setting my own hours and my own agenda."

Fred sipped a little whisky. "The Big Circle Boys, or Dai Huen Jai, are brutes first and last. It's not strictly accurate to call them a gang. The Big Circle Boys are a loose network of interlinked cells usually consisting of ten members, led by a so-called Big Brother. The head of the organization, if there is in fact a head, is rumoured to live in Hong Kong. The Big Circle Boys originated on the Chinese mainland. They first showed up in Vancouver in the 1980s although it was several years before they made a blip on police radar. The Big Circle Boys arrived via Hong Kong, travelling on false passports. Raymond Cho may have been a Big Brother."

Fred stopped talking when Terri delivered our drinks, along with my burger and fries.

"What are these things?" I asked, pointing at the interlocked straw-like objects covering my plate.

"They're waffle fries," Terri replied. "What do they look like?"

"They look like deep-fried hairpieces," I said. "I hope the chef didn't fry 'em in Brylcreem instead of cooking oil."

Terri sauntered away.

I said, "Okay, Fred. You talked about a leader who may or not exist. But the Big Circle Boys didn't appear out of thin air."

"The Big Circle Boys arose out of China's Red Guards—a paramilitary arm of the Cultural Revolution who murdered intellectuals and the upper classes during the Mao Tse Tung era. The very mention of their name put the fear of God into people. After Mao died, the Chinese People's Liberation Army stamped the Red Guards out. Viciously. Many Red Guards were killed by firing squads. Some were tortured and then buried alive. The rest were locked up in prison camps outside Canton City. On maps, Canton's prison camps were shown inside a big circle—hence the name. A few prisoners managed to escape. Some escapees ended up in Hong Kong. Afterwards a few came to Canada posing as refugees. They are all very hard men."

I tasted my burger. After two bites I pushed the plate away.

Fred popped one of the waffle fries into his mouth, grimaced, washed it down with Scotch, and said, "Ten years ago there were about fifty Big Circle Boys in Vancouver, there are probably a lot more now. However many there are, the Big Circle Boys are alive and well and operating in Vancouver. They're into every kind of mischief. Drug trafficking—primarily heroin brought in from the Golden Triangle. The Big Circle Boys have also branched out into cocaine and BC weed. Prostitution, gambling and massage parlours. Loansharking. Extortion. Human smuggling. Vancouver is a big city; there's plenty of muck to wallow in."

He sipped a little more Scotch. After a pause he said, "All due respect, Silas, but if you check any of this with Canadian Security and Intelligence Services, or the Mounties, I'd advise you to take anything they tell you with a dose of salt. Their take on Asian gangs isn't reliable."

I asked him why.

"Several reasons. By and large it has to do with language. Most CSIS cops and Mounties are Canadian-born high school graduates. Their first and usually their only language is either English or French. Many big-time Canadian gangsters were born overseas. They conduct their business in Mandarin or Vietnamese or Russian. What do you think happens when English-speaking cops try to infiltrate Urdu-speaking gangs?"

"I think they could end up with their feet in buckets of concrete."

"Or worse. CSIS and the RCMP are actively recruiting foreign-language speakers, but at present they mainly rely on paid informants."

Fred finished his drink and licked his lips. I offered him a refill. To my surprise, he declined. We shook hands. Fred buttoned his raincoat up to the neck.

Nature abhors a vacuum. As Fred went out, an alley cat slinked into view from behind a small stage at the back of the room. She's known on the streets as Candace, but the name on her birth certificate is Hilda Mullins. If Candace weighed ten pounds instead of a hundred, I'd put a rhinestone collar around her slender white neck and keep her in my office as company for PC. After scanning the room, Candace made a beeline to my table. Her face has coarsened slightly since I first knew her, although she still has very good bones. She was wearing her business suit—a slinky black cocktail dress with a low-cut top and six-inch stilettos.

Putting both hands on my table and leaning towards me, smiling as if she meant it, Candace gave me a chance to admire her new implants before saying huskily, "Remember what I told you the last time I saw you in here?"

"No, but I remember what I thought. I thought that you were bad news, but that you had a beautiful ass and nice legs and that your figure was lovely. In fact, it's lovelier than ever. When you pull your shoulders back like that, your nipples point straight up."

"What I said, Copper, is there was a time when they didn't let Siwashes inside places like this."

"They've amended the Indian Act since then. Besides, I'm not Siwash, I'm Coast Salish. Would you like a drink?"

"A drink will do for a start, but what I really want is to get laid. It'll set you back two hundred. Cash or VISA. Special deal because I like you."

"You've got VISA now?"

"Certainly. In my business you've got to keep up to date. My ass isn't the only thing that moves with the times."

I don't want to know what had been in the mouthful of cheeseburger I'd just eaten, but whatever it was had taken my appetite away. I raised a hand for Terri.

"Christ, I love big cops. I'm so horny my pants are wet, I can hardly wait," said Candace with a theatrical moan. "Let's go over to my place and get it on."

Candace was an unapologetic hooker, but at that moment, strangely enough, I was half-deluded into thinking she meant it. Even hookers, I suppose, tell the truth about sex sometimes. I sat there, mute and slightly aroused although, I've never had commercial sex and I wasn't about to start. When Terri arrived, I gave her a twenty and said, "I'm leaving now. Candace can have whatever she wants, as long as it comes out of a government-approved bottle. I'll settle with Doyle the next time I come in here."

Candace looked disappointed. I was too, in a bizarre way, because until things had cooled off between us recently, I'd been enjoying a very satisfactory love life with a woman called Felicity Exeter. But Felicity had ignored my last few calls, and I didn't know why. Weeks had passed since we'd seen each other. But I don't pay for sex. So I left Pinky's, walked half a block and stood outside Peacock Billiards for a minute, trying to remember if I'd ever told Felicity that I loved her. Maybe when I was drunk, which wouldn't count. Felicity had told me that she loved *me*, more than once. Perhaps she'd gotten over it, and I was no longer the person who used to matter to her.

Looking north along Douglas Street, I pondered my next move, wondering whether it would be a good time for me to brace Twinner Scudd. I decided it wasn't.

The sky was clear. The city was hot, noisy, bright. Victoria is a port city and a favourite tourist destination, especially for Americans who love the usually cheap Canadian dollar. The downtown sidewalks were a blur of colour because a French aircraft carrier had just dropped its anchors in Royal Roads. Sailors on shore leave and local girls with sun-bleached hair strolled back and forth, flirting and enjoying themselves. Skateboard kids were doing crazy matador acts between moving cars and taxis. Street buskers and jugglers and ice-cream sellers were all cashing in.

I spent the rest of the day snooping around, trying unsuccessfully to get a line on who Maria Alfred's companion might have been. About nine PM I picked up my car from the lot and detoured through Chinatown, noticing its garish coloured lights, chop-suey cafes, and the gaudy imported wares displayed in shop windows. When a red light stopped me at Fisgard and Government I had time to notice a bicycle-rickshaw parked on the street outside Wong's Cafe.

I derailed thoughts of the rickshaw I'd seen in the Wasserstein house and began to wonder what secrets lay hidden behind the red-painted doors and silken curtains that abound in this ethnic neighbourhood. The rickshaw kid had legs like Arnold Schwarzenegger. He got on his bike and started pedalling before the light changed, slowing motor traffic down to Store Street. Where he turned right, I turned left. I winkled my way onto the Johnson Street Bridge, and went home.

Instead of brushing my teeth and going to bed, I poured myself a drink, found a dead fly on my windowsill, took it outside and said hello to pine siskin. He seemed happy to see me, and hopped out of the escallonia bush onto my hand when I offered him the fly. Afterwards I sat in my garden, thinking about the secret life of birds, and Maggie Bradley, with the siskin's background chatter a pleasing accompaniment to my ruminations.

CHAPTER SEVEN

Acoroner's inquest into Raymond Cho's death opened at the Blanshard Street courthouse at 11:00 AM. After hearing about a hundred words from Detective Inspector Manners, the coroner adjourned the inquest pending further evidence, much to the dismay of the ink-stained wretches, the idlers, the pensioners and all of the other irregular sad sacks that fatten their shrunken lives on courthouse misery.

Manners stood down from the witness box and exchanged a few private words with Bernie Tapp. Bernie and I then left the courthouse together and stood on the sidewalk. Dark thunderheads were massing over the Sooke Hills. A majestic bald eagle was devouring something small and feathery on the courthouse roof. In the sky above the eagle, a pair of bereft thrushes screeched piteously.

Nice Manners came out of the courthouse, got into a waiting patrol car, and was driven off.

Bernie is one of those fidgety pipe smokers constantly patting his pockets for matches or tobacco pouch or reaming dottle from the pipe's bowl with a pocket knife. He was going through another pipe-filling, tobacco-fiddling routine when a taxi drew up nearby. Bernie and I watched as Terri Murnau got stiffly out of the taxi, paid the driver, and then limped slowly up the courthouse steps. Terri hadn't been limping when she'd served Fred Halloran and me at Pinky's Bar.

Bernie said. "I'm going to grab a cup of coffee. You coming?"

"Can't, I've a couple of things to do."

"You do that, but don't bully your expense account too much," Bernie said amiably. Puffing smoke like a steam train, he began a slow locomotion towards the Fort Street Starbucks.

I re-entered the courthouse. The corridors were jammed with conmen and crooks, and with their natural prey: the frightened, the cheated, the confused, the old. Barristers wearing black jackets and pants, white shirts with wingback collars and flapping white neckties, strode purposefully around at $500 an hour.

Terri Murnau was leaning against the wall outside courtroom five with most of her weight supported on one leg. She was heavily made up, but not heavily enough to conceal the puffiness surrounding both of her eyes. She looked exactly what she was. An attractive middle-aged battered woman wearing a charcoal-grey pantsuit and black flat-heeled shoes. We exchanged smiles. Terri's shoulders covered up the court calendar posted on a board behind her, preventing me from seeing what kind of legal or domestic trouble she might be embroiled in.

I said, "Everything under control, Terri?"

She regarded me contemplatively for an instant. "I'm getting a grip on it," she said noncommittally.

British Columbia courts go easy on wife beaters, unfortunately, and Terri probably knew it. I told her to give me a call if she needed anything, and continued along the marble corridors to the BC land registry office.

Generally, the land registry office is busy; there's usually a lineup. That morning, for a brief period, I was the only customer. I showed a woman behind the counter my police badge and asked to see the conveyance on Ernest Wasserstein's Echo Bay property. A copy of that document arrived promptly. The deed was simple enough. Ten years earlier Ernest Wasserstein had purchased his house, fully furnished, for nine and a half million dollars. I also discovered that Collins Lane had been gazetted in 1873.

Well, that was interesting.

By the time I returned to courtroom five, Terri Murnau had gone. I examined the court calendar posted beside the courtroom door. Regina vs. Murnau was being heard before Judge Hilda at that very moment. By then, it was a little before noon.

Something was nagging me. I went back to my office and ran a computer check on Ernest Wasserstein. He was a Swiss national with two convictions for fraud in Canada. Thoughtful, I locked up my office, strolled across to the Broughton Street parkade where I'd left the MG, fired it up and drove out to revisit the Echo Bay scene of incomprehensibly violent murder. Traffic alternately raced and crawled.

Echo Bay's village clock was striking two when I stopped at a corner grocery to buy myself a cold drink. Getting out of the car, I noticed the Mai Thai Restaurant. Forgetting my thirst, I went into the restaurant instead. Heavy cooking odours. A Help Wanted sign in the front window. The curtains were closed and the lights were off. After going in out of the day's bright sunlight, it took a minute for my eyes to adjust to the gloom.

An agitated elderly Asian woman came fluttering out of the kitchen, waving her arms and trying to shoo me back outside. "Close till six please," she said, speaking English in a heavily accented voice. "Restaurant close please, come back later please."

When I showed the woman my police badge, she gave a stifled cry and fled from sight through a bead-curtained doorway.

I sat on a stool and gazed at the display of domestic wines and Thai beer stacked behind the counter. Silence reigned until another Asian woman appeared. She was about twenty, exuded tranquillity and looked like the first woman's granddaughter. Her black hair had yellow streaks, and she was wearing a blue silk shirt and slim-fit jeans. She regarded me seriously, although her narrow gaze seemed slightly unfocussed. I thought, *she's worried.*

Smiling, she asked tentatively, "Is there something I can do for you, sir?" I asked her name.

"Tania Sundaravej," she answered. "That was Granny you were talking to just now. She said you're a policeman. There's nothing wrong, I hope?"

Her voice was well modulated, Canadian.

"I'm looking for someone who lives nearby and might possibly be one of your customers."

"This business has been a going concern since I was five years old. We have thousands of customers."

I paused. The inquiry was in its early stages, and we were still playing things close to the chest. I wondered whether it was safe to use the dead man's name. What was I going to say otherwise? That the man I was interested in was Chinese, about thirty? A man who dressed well, drove an expensive late-model German car? That description fitted thousands of people. I grinned at her. "This is confidential. His name is Ronnie Chew. A Chinese man, about thirty. He's apparently well-to-do. Drives a nice Beemer, wears very good expensive clothes."

Her smile became radiant. "Oh Ronnie, sure. Ronnie was in here on Saturday night, late."

"Alone?"

"He was with a couple of friends, I served them myself. Wait a minute."

Tania put on glasses with bottle-glass lenses, reached beneath the counter and brought out a register, but couldn't find what she wanted. She said, "It's crazy in here on Saturdays. Generally, Ronnie books a table when he's coming." She took her glasses off and turned the book 180 degrees so that I could read the page. Ronnie Chew's name wasn't there.

"Ronnie must have just walked in at the last minute. It's lucky we had a free table." Tania pointed vaguely to a table in a far corner of the room. "Minnie was hostessing, she put him over there."

"What time would that be?"

"It must have been close to eleven. We stop cooking at midnight, and the bar closes at one. Ronnie and his friends were among the last people to leave here."

"Do you know who Ronnie's friends were?"

"No, I've never seen them before. Two girls."

"Tell me about them?"

"They were two Indian girls, yeah. A bit rough around the edges if you know what I mean."

"I know what you mean. I'm an Indian too."

Tania's face fell. She put her glasses on and saw me clearly for what was evidently the first time. "Oh hell," she said. "No offence, but I'm blind as a bat when it's shadowy like this, even when I'm wearing glasses."

"Were you wearing glasses on Saturday night?"

"Sure, most of the time. I can't function without them really, but I'm vain."

"As you were saying. Raymond's friends were a couple of Native Indian women."

"Well, yes. One of them even asked me if there was a chance of a server's job going. I tried to put her off. Maria, I think she called herself. I told her we didn't need a server right now. In fact, we're always on the lookout for staff, only Thai food is a specialty. We can't use servers unless they know our menu and our way of doing business. She wouldn't have been a good fit." Tania smiled disarmingly. "I hope you're not gonna put the thumbscrews on me for being honest."

"How did Maria handle rejection?"

"She was okay with it. Told me she already had a job, but was looking for a change. She wrote her phone number down on a paper napkin and asked me to give her a call if something came up. Before you ask, I threw the napkin away. But I remember where she said she worked. It was the Ballard Diner."

It was a rarity, but for a change, Dr. Tarleton's autopsy had been wrong. Ronnie Chew didn't die with a belly full of half-digested Chinese food. It had been Thai food.

I DROVE FROM the Echo Bay village to Collins Lane and came to a stop outside Tudor Collins' wrought-iron gates. A long curving driveway ran from sight between glades of ornamental bushes and deciduous trees. I pushed an intercom button located on a stone gatepost. Before the intercom squawked, enough time passed for me to look around and notice a closed-circuit television camera aimed on the gates from a nearby tree. I told the intercom who I was and badged the camera. More time passed till there was a metallic click, and the remote-controlled gates swung wide. I had driven a hundred yards up the driveway when a man appeared with a spaniel at his heels. The Collins house wasn't fully visible, but a couple of elaborate brick chimneys rose above the treetops. I got out of the car.

The man was white-haired, of medium stature. I knew that he was over 70 years old, but he looked younger. His brown eyes were alert and direct. I badged him again and asked if he was Tudor Collins. He nodded. Before I could get a word in, he said categorically, "If you're here to ask me more questions about those two girls I'll tell you exactly what I told Inspector Manners," he said, a slight note of irritation in his voice. "They were Native Indians, the same as you are. They weren't Chinese, or Japs. They weren't East Indians."

"How can you be so positive?"

"Two reasons. First, because of the way the girls looked. Second, because of the way they spoke the English language. I've lived a long time. When I was a little boy before the war, Indians had a regular summer camp on the beach below Collins Lane. The women dug clams and picked berries while their men were out fishing in canoes. They were real canoes too. Carved cedar dugouts, not this plastic crap you see now. When the women weren't busy with something else, they'd be weaving fancy baskets. They'd bring clams and baskets up to the house. My parents always bought something. I've still got some of those baskets. I showed 'em to a dealer one time. He couldn't wait to get his hands on 'em, but I'll never sell. They're souvenirs of a vanished age, right?"

"If you like that sort of thing."

Collins smiled at a memory. "Back then, English was the second language for many Natives and they had a peculiar way of pronouncing the English letter S. It's hard to describe, but it sounded as if they'd sort of swallowed the word when it was halfway out of their mouths. Slurred it, kind of. The word 'yes,' for example, comes out sounding sort of like 'yeshul.' You don't hear that peculiarity so much now as formerly. When you do hear it, you know that you're listening to somebody who learned to speak English in a place where there were few White people. An isolated reserve, say."

"I was born on a reserve. Do I swallow my Ss?"

"No you don't, because I expect you live in town and were educated in White schools. Am I right?"

I nodded.

"That's a relief, I'm glad somebody believes some of the things that I say, because I've been starting to wonder."

"What do you mean?"

"You're the second policeman I've spoken to."

"You're referring to Inspector Manners?"

"Yes," he said. "And before him there were those customs people."

Customs people?

Instead of pursuing that topic immediately, I said, "Collins Lane was gazetted over a hundred years ago. You folks have been here a long time?"

"We have. My ancestors bought this land from the Hudson's Bay Company in 1867. A hundred acres at ten shillings an acre. Shillings, mind you, not dollars. It should have cost us more, but the property wasn't considered agricultural back then. Too many trees and rocks. We don't own that much property now, worse luck. My dad managed to hang on to it all until the dirty thirties, when money became tight. Unfortunately, after all those years, Dad couldn't come up with the taxes. In 1938, 90 acres reverted to the Crown."

"The Collinses must know all about that petroglyph, then. The one at the head of that ravine?"

Collins' eyes narrowed immediately. I knew that I'd broached an unwelcome topic. I also knew why he'd be anxious.

"I don't want to talk about it. Is this a murder inquiry or a fishing expedition, because I thought it was already settled. Mrs. Milton let the cat out of the bag when I saw her on the lane yesterday. She told me that those two Native women cut that Chinaman's throat," Collins said, his face registering disapproval. "I knew there was something fishy about him, too. I mean, there he is, a gardener. Live-in help earning the minimum wage. The man can hardly speak English, and yet there he is, driving around in a 60-thousand-dollar car. No wonder the customs people flagged him."

"Customs people? I don't understand. What are you talking about?"

"Bureaucrats!" said Collins, with a disparaging snort. "Another case of the right hand not knowing what the left hand is doing. It's less than a week ago since they were here. Customs and immigration inspectors. Two men. Standing where you are standing now, asking their nosy bloody questions. They were trying to trace a Chinaman. Wanted to know where he lived and so on. When they gave me his description, I told them that the man they wanted was probably Ernie Wasserstein's gardener."

Collins gazed at me expectantly.

I nodded. "Did they tell you why they wanted him?"

"Of course they did, I would have kept my mouth shut otherwise. They told me he was one of those illegals. People who come out from China packed like sardines in fishing trawlers. Hundreds of 'em jammed below decks. The minute the trawler docks, the illegals clear off, disappear, clutter up the country. Why don't you bureaucrats combine forces for a change? Work together instead of protecting your own turf?"

I stared at him without speaking for a moment. By then Collins had begun to annoy me, and it probably showed. He went on lamely, "Actually, I wouldn't want Wasserstein to know that I blew the whistle on his man. It would create bad blood between neighbours."

"You said there were two immigration inspectors. How did they identify themselves?"

"They didn't. But I know how to size people up. I took them at their word."

"What did these men look like?"

"What did they look like? They looked ordinary."

"Mr. Collins, this might be very important, so I want you to think back carefully. Were these men tall, short, well-dressed, what?"

Collins scowled at a memory. "They were a couple of functionaries in dark suits. One character was swarthy, short, as wide as a door. About fifty years old, with a ridiculous comb-over. He let his partner do the talking."

"Did you tell Inspector Manners what you've just told me?"

Collins shook his head. "It didn't occur to me to do so at the time."

I nodded absently, because I was thinking of something else. It was Collins, probably, who had gone to the trouble of camouflaging the petroglyphs with leaves and dirt. And I knew why. He didn't want the general public—especially First Nations people—to know anything about the petroglyphs, because if they found out and made a stink, the BC government would undoubtedly declare the property a heritage site. Collins' acreage would be whittled down further.

I said, "We'll need the tapes from the CCTV camera monitoring your front gate as evidence. I'll take it with me now."

"Sorry, officer, no can do. I can't oblige you because the camera broke down ages ago and I have never bothered to get it fixed. It was mostly for show, anyway. We had a burglary here two years back. The burglar bypassed the camera and came over the fence instead of climbing the gate. He didn't get anything because my dog sniffed him out, raised an alarm."

"Are you planning to leave town during the next little while, Mr. Collins?"

"Not that I know of."

"Good," I said. Raising my voice a few decibels I added, "You'll be hearing from us again. In the meantime, Mr. Collins, I advise you very strongly to keep this conversation and any comments about policemen, immigrants and Canada Customs strictly to yourself."

He seemed offended. I was getting back into my car when he screwed up his courage and said sullenly, "And before you leave, here's another thing. How about cracking down on these speedsters? There was another crash on Sunday morning. A driver ran right off the road. Drunk probably, lucky he wasn't killed."

Collins was still scowling when I backed the MG away.

THE MURDER HOUSE was still surrounded by scene-of-crime-tape. I had expected a guard to be posted on the property and was mildly surprised to find that there wasn't one. The house was locked. After poking around in the usual places, I found a front door key stashed under a potted geranium. When I let myself in, the door swung closed behind me. I spent a couple of minutes admiring the Chinese rickshaw that was parked in the vestibule.

It was a wooden, runner-pulled, two-wheeled work of art covered with about ten coats of red lacquer, beautifully inlaid with mother-of-pearl flowers, birds and pagodas. I told myself that one of these days, I was going to find out how that rickshaw got there, and why. The Inuit kayak standing in the corner was an ancient bidarka. Built of bones and sinews and sealskin, of a type rarely seen outside a museum. That single yellow driving glove was still on top of the table. Instead of returning the key to where I'd found it, I dropped it into my pocket.

Every curtain in the house was closed. It was cool and dark inside. I went back to the MG and got a Maglite. With the light in hand, I combed the premises from roof to basement—something several members of the crime-scene squad had already done more than once.

In collecting its evidence, Victoria's forensics squad had concentrated its efforts on the house's front vestibule and hall, its kitchen, lounge, the basement staircase, and along the downstairs hallway that led to Cho's L-shaped bedroom. Fingerprint samples belonging to several individuals had been lifted from all of those areas. Cho's fingerprints predominated. Other fingerprints had been attributed to the housekeeper, and to Maria Alfred. I assumed that some of those still unaccounted for belonged to Maria's female companion. Some fingerprints had been smudged in a manner that, according to our experts, suggested that one or more individuals had moved around the house wearing gloves at about the same time that Cho met his death.

The house was well maintained. Given its antiquity and its proximity to the ocean, the place was reasonably fresh inside. Many disparate hair and fibre samples had been collected from Cho's bed, from his bedroom furniture and carpet, and from a downstairs laundry room. Forensics had taken away Cho's blood-soaked duvet and bedsheets, along with broadloom carpet and loose rugs. I searched Cho's bedroom and the downstairs washroom thoroughly. Where they had been exposed, the floorboards were covered with dark reddish dusty stains.

Cho's white Ikea washroom cabinet contained a man's razor, shaving cream, a package of ibuprofen tablets, a few bars of soap, toilet rolls and the like. I poked my fingers into cans of talcum powder and jars of cream. I opened the top of the tank, drained it, and looked inside. Nothing except rust stains. Forensics had taken away the male clothing previously hanging on the back of a chair and in Cho's wardrobe. The tallboy's drawers were empty. Used towels had been removed from hampers to be checked for bodily fluids and hairs. Bunnysuiters had cleaned drain traps from sinks to check for hairs and bits of human tissue. A dirty job, but some people get paid to do it.

Thoughtful, I went up to the ground floor and helped myself to an apple from a cut-glass fruit dish that was standing on the dining room table. I was eating the apple when I heard a car approaching the house. Its engine slowed, then stopped in the driveway. Somebody knocked on the vestibule door. I left the apple core on the table and walked quietly into the lounge. After thirty seconds, the knock was repeated. Another pause ensued. I heard the tinkle of splintering glass, followed immediately afterwards by a metallic click.

I was no longer alone in the house. Somebody had broken in. I concealed myself behind the lounge's heavy velvet curtains as the intruder's confident tramp went through to the kitchen and down the basement stairs. I took my shoes off. Walking in stockinged feet, I went quietly downstairs, stopped partway along the passage, and rested with my back to a wall. Farther along the passageway, sounds indicated that the intruder was opening drawers and moving things around in Cho's bedroom. Electric light showed in the chink between Cho's door and its frame. I opened a door on the opposite side of the hallway, let myself inside a dark utility room, and waited in its doorway. A month seemed to pass before a figure appeared in Cho's doorway holding something shiny in his hands. Unrecognizable in the darkness, he grunted, and backed into Cho's bedroom again. Holding the Maglite like a club, I moved carefully towards Cho's room.

The figure reappeared almost instantly and a pistol roared. In a rain of bullets, I flung myself back into the room I'd just vacated and mentally recounted the shots I'd heard. Six, I thought. Guessing that if he'd used a revolver it might now be empty, I grabbed a bottle of liquid soap from a shelf and threw it into the hallway. That brought the gunman from his lair, but a click from his revolver told me his gun was empty. The dark figure of a man with a scarf covering the lower half of his face was trying to reload the revolver when I hurled myself at him. We grappled and fell down together, me underneath. Him with his knee in my groin. When we hit the deck, the pain in my balls was almost paralyzing. He swung the empty revolver at my head. I twisted aside and swept a kick at his knees. My kick missed. A blow intended for my head struck my left arm above the elbow. I rolled away across the carpet as the man came towards me. I was trying to climb up his legs when he hit me with the revolver again. This time the blow fell on my upper back. I managed to get my arms around his waist and throw him off balance. He chopped the back of my neck with his gun. I kneed him somewhere. Gasping, he tried to throw me off, but I held on until we crashed to the floor. His breath smelled revoltingly of garlic and rotten teeth. The revolver had fallen and was a few feet from my left hand. When I reached for it, pain radiated down my arm all the way to my fingertips. The intruder lurched away, grabbed his revolver and ran upstairs. After a while I crawled into Cho's room and looked around. I was reaching for my cellphone when the intruder's car engine coughed into life.

My cellphone wasn't in my pocket. It had fallen out while we'd been wrestling. By the time I found it and called headquarters, the car had gone from hearing.

NICE MANNERS WAS the first officer to appear in my painful field of vision. He found me sitting in a soft leather lounge chair with my feet raised up on a padded ottoman. Openly scornful, he wasn't very sympathetic when I told him I'd been kneed in the balls.

"Why the hell were you here in this house?"

"Bernie has already told you that I've been seconded to this case."

"Yes, he did, and I tried to talk him out of it. We can manage quite well without you."

I didn't say anything.

Manners said, "What the hell were you looking for, anyway?"

"More importantly, who was the intruder, and what the hell was *he* looking for?"

"Go on. Make a guess."

"Maybe it was a killer, revisiting the scene of his crime."

"That's quite possible," Manners said reluctantly. "But if so, why?"

Exasperated, I shook my head. I didn't know. Worse, I couldn't even describe my attacker except to say that he had bad breath.

"The trouble with you, Seaweed, you're not much of a sleuth," Manners said, narrowing his eyes to make himself look scary, "Why don't you go home and stop making a nuisance of yourself?"

That was the smartest thing Manners had said to me all year.

I staggered upstairs with my legs wide. My balls were killing me. I got as far as the front hall before the need to sit down became imperative. But there were no chairs there. I was about to plant myself down on the oak table when I noticed that the yellow glove had been removed.

A uniformed constable was manning the front door. I called him over and said, "Go downstairs and tell Inspector Manners I need to talk to him. Tell him it's urgent."

The constable hurried away. Manners showed up ten minutes later. By then, I was feeling a little better. I told Manners about the missing yellow glove.

Instead of speaking, Manners cupped his right elbow in his left hand and flicked his mustache with his fingers. He was thinking. His thoughts however, were too important to be shared with me. After a long minute, he turned on his heels without a word and went back downstairs.

I drove home, swallowed a couple of Tylenols and had a lie-down Later, I phoned Bernie Tapp. When he answered, I brought him up to date regarding the yellow glove, the Ballard Diner, Tudor Collins and the Mai Thai restaurant.

"Why are you talking funny? You sound winded."

"Because of my balls."

"Quit bellyaching. If it was really bad you'd be lisping," Bernie said unsympathetically. "Serious Crimes is stretched to the limit. Can you take care of the Ballard Diner angle for me?"

"Okay," I said, hanging up.

Outside, waves broke whitely on the beach, trees whispered. I went out into my backyard, and swung myself into a string hammock. I was trying to forget my aching nuts when pine siskin leapt from the cherry bush onto my chest and began his sweet serenade. I was telling myself that things could be worse when my eyes closed.

CHAPTER EIGHT

The sun had blazed around behind my cabin, and I woke up in the shade. The crown of the split-leaf maple that I'd planted in the garden two years earlier was a lacy mass against a blue sky strewn with small white clouds. My balls had calmed a trifle, but I had a backache from lying in the hammock too long. I was wondering whether to risk swinging down off the hammock to the ground and finding out whether I could walk or not when I became aware that I had company. Old Mary Cooke was sitting on a patio chair with a table at her right hand, looking as usual like a mound of Goodwill clothes in a floppy black hat and layers of skirts and coats. She smelled like clothes-dryer lint. She was over a hundred years old. Her face was as wrinkled as a dried apple, although her hedge of silver hair was still threaded with black.

"Feeling better?" she asked me in her very gentle voice.

"A little."

"You've got a bit of bird crap on your shirt, but it'll brush off after it dries."

"So it will."

"Somebody kicked you in the balls, right?"

"How did you know?"

"Because you've been moaning and cradling your nuts in your sleep," she said without smiling. "Does it hurt like hell?"

"It's more of an ache than a hurt."

"I keep being reborn a woman. I don't think I've ever been born as a man, so I don't know what having balls feels like. When balls get hurt, do they ache like toothache?"

"Nothing aches like a toothache, unless it's a bad earache."

"Earache is bad," Old Mary said, nodding her agreement. "I used to get a lot of earaches, back in my abalone-diving days. My mother used to pour warm codfish oil in my ears to make it better."

"Wait a minute," I said. "Can I get you something from the house? A drink? Maybe a sandwich? I've got some venison left."

"I don't need nothing right now. Thank you, Silas."

After couple of very careful stretching exercises to loosen the kinks in my spine, I rolled off the hammock, staggered inside my cabin, took out a bottle of Schweppes ginger ale, a tray of ice and a pint of Seagrams from the refrigerator, and mixed myself a stiff drink. Five minutes later, feeling better, I went back outside.

Old Mary appeared to be asleep, but her dark hooded eyes opened when I sat opposite her at the table.

I said, "Do you know Echo Bay?"

Old Mary Cooke chuckled. "I've known Echo Bay since it was called Su'qu'imish. The name got changed after White people settled on land up above where we used to pick summer clams. Everybody calls it Echo Bay now, except for a few old rememberers like me."

"There's two rock carvings on a boulder at the brow of a ravine overlooking Echo Bay. The first carving shows a life-sized human skeleton. The second carving, below and to the left of the main carving, shows a wolf with its jaws held open by sticks."

A shadow passed over the old woman's face. Maybe a minute went by before she said, "A long time ago there was a village at Su'qu'imish. Long before my old folks' time, there was a year-round village at Su'qu'imish. Now in them olden days there was a young Su'qu'imish boy went out on spirit quest looking for seawolf power. His father had sent him out. His father said to his son, 'If you don't eat too much and you keep yourself clean by swimming, seawolfs will come to you, salmon will come to you, whales will come to you, because you don't smell. Take sharp sticks in case seawolfs come.'

"When that young boy came back after swimming, his father said, 'Did you get seawolf power?' The young boy said 'No.' The boy's father sent him back out to look for seawolf tamanhous again. This time, when the boy washed himself clean and dived in with his pointed sticks, a big seawolf swam by. When the seawolf opened its mouth to bite him, that boy put his pointed sticks in the wolf's mouth so it couldn't bite him.

"Right afterwards, the boy noticed an old white-haired man sitting on the beach with a bunch of dentalia beads. Lots of dentalia. And this old man said to the young boy, 'This is all the seawolf power you'll get, it's just this dentalia. Help yourself. When you get married you'll have a son, that son will look like a White man. He'll have white hair and white skin and pink eyes.'

"Well, when that boy got home his father said, 'Did you get it?' I got it, the boy said, and showed his father them dentalias. The father said, 'Okay my son, you done okay. You can have yourself some wives.' So the boy uses some of them dentalias to give a potlatch and get married and buy slaves and food. He was a man now. He kept on that way till there was no dentalias left. Then there was this child born to one of the man's slaves. It must have been bad seawolf tamanhous the man had, because the child born to him was a White child, with white hair and pink eyes. None of that man's wives or slaves gave him any more children."

When Old Mary left, I hooked the garden water hose up to my home-made outdoor shower gizmo and treated myself to a long icy soak. Feeling slightly more human, I put on a pair of stonewashed loose-fit jeans, a pale green shirt with a white stripe in it, and a pair of blue and white Nike sneakers. Drove back to my office.

PC treated me with her customary indifference, but she warmed slightly when I refilled her water bowl and gave her half a can of Thrifty's premium flaked tuna. I took out the office bottle, poured myself another drink and turned my swiveller towards the window. Outside, a bedraggled woman in a rain-shrunken wool coat was approaching people with her hand out.

The phone rang. It was Lightning Bradley. He said breathlessly, "I'm in a mess. I don't know which way to turn. Maggie's dead."

"We know she's dead. But the question is where the hell have you been hiding? We've been looking all over for you."

"I need help, Silas."

"I know you do. It's time to come in out of the cold, help us get this mess sorted out."

"It's not that easy. I'm scared."

"No wonder. But instead of talking to me on the phone you should come in. Talk to me and talk to Bernie."

"Screw that, I don't care about goddamn Bernie. I've got my time in already. I've spent years watching assholes like Tapp and Manners climb the goddamn ladder, stepping on my goddamn shoulders and lifting themselves up. Well, them cocky bastards can go screw themselves," Bradley said, his voice rising and falling with emotion as he spoke. "It's not what you think. The reason I'm in trouble has nothing to do with that screw-up on Collins Lane. Well, maybe a little bit. The thing is, Silas, I'm at my wits' end. I'm in a mess that I don't see no way of getting out of. So how about it?"

"You know the drill, Bradley. If Bernie Tapp finds out you called me, you'll be in a worse situation than you are already. You'll probably drag me down with you."

"What happened to your guts? I thought we were pals, Silas," he said. "Haven't we always got along?"

Instead of replying, I had a little drink.

Lightning said, "I've got to talk to somebody, I've just got to. There's more to this than . . . I'm talking about maiming and killing people. More lives are at stake if I don't get some help."

"Okay," I said wearily. "Spell it out for me, what's the problem?"

"It's not that easy. I can't talk on the phone, we've got to meet face to face," Bradley was saying when the phone went dead. I thought I'd lost him until moments later, when he said urgently, "My life is in your hands, pal. You've got to come over here. Please come over here."

"Where are you?"

Instead of replying, he groaned.

"If I don't know where you are, how am I supposed to find you?"

"I'll find you," Bradley said, hanging up.

Call display told me that Bradley was in town. I phoned Telus. After the usual runaround, I was put through to a competent supervisor who told me that the number in question corresponded to a public phone located at the Ross Bay Cemetery end of Dallas Road. I called headquarters and left a message for Bernie Tapp, who was at a meeting.

The bedraggled woman was still on the street when I closed my window blinds and left my office. She stumbled towards me, high and disoriented, dirty and bare legged, her face contorted with misery. She was about 40 years old and wouldn't live to see 45. I gave her a dollar and tried to put her, and Bradley, out of my mind as I strolled towards the Inner Harbour.

Deep-fry odours lured me down to a waterfront pier at the foot of Broughton Street, where young entrepreneurs had converted a couple of steel shipping containers into a fish and chip shop. I paid eight bucks for a sackful of halibut and fries. Munching steadily, contented as a cow in clover, I ambled south along wooden docks crowded with summer tourists. To my right, beyond a small boat marina, the harbour lay smooth and green. Highrise apartment buildings and hotels loomed upright, casting shadows in the breathless air. Leaving the boardwalk, I passed through a small green park and an area of busy restaurants and shops on my way back to Pandora Street, got back to the office, and had a nap.

About six o'clock, I took out the office bottle, had a little drink, and allowed myself to worry about Lightning Bradley. I was still agonizing when Bernie Tapp showed up.

He said without preamble, "Forensics found something interesting in Raymond Cho's BMW."

"Such as?"

"Traces of cocaine, and a complete set of Lightning Bradley's fingerprints. It doesn't end there, either. Forensics also found cocaine traces in Lightning's Crown Royal."

Instead of telling Bernie that I already knew all that, I said, "Lightning phoned me this afternoon. I called you right after but you were at a meeting."

"What time did you call me?"

"Two, three hours ago. Lightning told me he was in a jam. He wants to meet me, and talk. He asked me to keep it confidential. I told him I would."

"Good boy. In murder cases, strategy trumps privacy every time," Bernie said. "When do you meet?"

"He's gonna call me, let me know."

I went on to tell Bernie about the conversation I'd had with Tudor Collins.

"Fine, I think we should follow that up," Bernie said, a grin splitting his face. "Let's go for a little drive."

Talking strategy all the way, Bernie drove us across town to the Titus Silverman Memorial Recycling Depot.

Little had changed since Titus Silverman had been murdered, one year previously. Now owned by Tubby Gonzales, Titus' former chief lieutenant, the recycling depot operated out of a flat-roofed utilitarian building located in an industrial area adjacent to one of Victoria's minor navigable waterways. Scruffy binners were trading bottles and cans for cash at tables on the sidewalk in front of the depot. Abandoned shopping carts lay everywhere. We parked next to a tarpaulin-draped car in a churned field littered with shards of glass and scraps of jagged metal. Clumps of grass and a few scraggly bushes shook in a light summer breeze. A small muddy incline sloped down to the Gorge waterway's mucky green waters.

We tried to enter the depot through a back door marked NO VISITERS—TRASPASSARS KILLED, but it was locked. I kicked the door a couple of times. Nothing happened, so I kept kicking until the judas hole opened. A voice told me to fuck off. I showed my badge. When I tried the door handle again, it wasn't locked. We went in.

Inside, surrounded by mountains of cardboard boxes, five men and a woman were playing Texas Hold'em at a felt-covered octagonal table. Bernie and I went past the gamblers without creating a ripple of interest. Bernie shoved open an unpainted wooden door, and we went into a small, square, windowless room with unpainted gyproc walls, a concrete floor with a square of brown furry carpet on it, and the kind of furniture appropriate to a recycling facility. This was surprising. The office *could* have been furnished like Louis the Fifteenth's drawing room, because, according to Victoria's drug squad, the Gonzales outfit was buying two keys of cocaine a month from Vancouver, cutting it to make six, selling it down the line to their street dealers and pocketing about eighty thousand dollars every month.

Today's was my second visit to this office in less than a year; nothing much had changed in the meantime.

Sitting behind a desk poring over a dog-eared jerk-off magazine was a Mexican. The thin hair on the top of his head was worn in a farcical combover. His name was Tubby Gonzalez. He had bad breath and the consummate liar's frank unwavering gaze. It focussed on me as I entered and took his measure. Gonzalez was somewhere between forty and fifty years old, on the short side and a little overweight. His shoulders were probably no wider than an ordinary door. On the desk in front of him, overflowing with butts, was a hubcap that he was using as an ashtray.

History continued to repeat itself when I said, "Remember me?"

"How could I forget?"

"This is Chief Detective Inspector Tapp."

Gonzales smiled, but his eyes were dead cruel and cold. They were the eyes of a vicious hoodlum. A flicker appeared in their murky depths, and then they coiled into darkness again.

Bernie did the talking. He said, "When's the last time you took a trip down Collins Lane?"

After a nicely judged pause for suspense, Gonzales said, "Is that supposed to be a riddle? The only trip I've taken lately is down Memory Lane."

Nobody laughed. Gonzales' excessively insolent manner remained intact, but sweat had appeared on his otherwise unruffled brow. He wasn't as calm as he pretended to be.

"Things are going smoothly since we dug Titus Silverman's body out of Goldstream Park, are they?" Bernie asked him. "Recycled cans to China, empty bottles to the glassworks, cocaine to Government Street."

"Another riddle? Coke to Government Street? I haven't the least idea what you are talking about. Even if I did know, which I don't, I wouldn't be dumb enough to tell the fuzz."

Grinning, Bernie sat down at a chair in front of the desk. I folded my arms and tried to look tough.

Bernie made a big production of smoothing his healthy head of hair with the flat of his hand, and then said, "I think you should start wearing a hat, Tubby."

"My name's Tomas, not Tubby."

Bernie said, "Weather like this, Tubby, with lots of damaging UV rays pouring out of the sky, it's bad for the naked scalp. You think that dinky comb-over is going to protect your skin from malignant melanoma?"

Gonzales gave him a brooding look from beneath his heavy dark eyebrows. "Are you trying to frighten me, Inspector?"

"Chief Inspector, and no, Tubby, I'm trying to be helpful," Bernie retorted. "If you had been wearing a hat when you and one of your sidekicks masqueraded as customs inspectors on Collins Lane last week, and if you'd been using breath mints when you attacked one of my officers, we might not be here now. You could have saved yourself this interrogation and a shitload of aggravation."

"That's ridiculous. I've got better things to . . ."

"Cut the crap." Bernie leaned forward. "Those Collins Lane mansions have CCTVs up to their ying yangs. We've got time-dated pictures of you and your buddy, talking to people. The pictures are grainy black-and-whites, but it's you all right. Tubby Gonzales. To back things up, what we'll do is, we'll put you in a lineup with a few more other ugly Latinos, and let our witnesses point you out. Witnesses who will testify that you told them you were with Canadian customs and immigration. That's a serious offence in itself, but there's worse to come."

Gonzales tried to read Bernie's expression, but he was keeping it blank. Bernie was lying. Collins' CCTV camera didn't work, but the lies were effective. Gonzales opened his mouth, swallowed some air, but wisely decided to keep mum.

Bernie said, "Where were you late Saturday night, early Sunday morning?"

Gonzales' expression seemed frozen, but shifting currents moved in his eyes. He said, "Me and my girlfriend went to the pictures, the seven o'clock show. Eighteen bloody dollars for two tickets. Then we get to endure fifteen minutes of goddamn Toyota commercials before the show starts. After the picture ended, me and her had coffee and dessert at a cafe downtown. Then we went home to bed."

"The pictures, eh? What show was on?"

"*Slumdog Millionaire*. It's a drama, on at the Odeon. I wanted to see Leonardo Di Caprio in *Body of Lies*, but she told me that if I let her have her own way, I'd have a different promise to look forward to after I took her home, so I gave in," Gonzales said, beating a little rat-a-tat-tat on the desk with his stubby fingers. "I seem to recall putting the ticket stubs in my pockets, I've probably still got 'em."

"I think you've probably got ticket stubs, but they won't be yours, because you weren't at the pictures, were you?"

Gonzales smiled.

Bernie said. "Have you read today's paper?"

Gonzales thought for a moment before he shook his head.

"There's a story on the front page that you might find interesting. Sunday night, the man you were looking for on Collins Lane was brutally attacked and murdered. You had means, motive and opportunity so just remember this, Tubby. We'll be back. Don't leave town without telling us first."

CHAPTER NINE

I drove over the Johnson Street Bridge to a mixed industrial-residential area in Vic West. Boatyards, corner grocery stores and dreary crackerjack houses stood intermingled with marine-electronics shops, propeller shops and the like. Roads inclined up from the harbour like ladders. The day had dawned hot and humid, but it was a little cooler down near the water.

The Ballard Diner turned out to be a greasy spoon squeezed between a Shell station and a boatyard. The vehicles parked on the loose gravel in front made it look like a car wrecker's yard. I parked my MG between a rusty Ford Tudor and a mint condition '55 Chevy Bel Air. I noticed that the diner's front door opened outwards and that it was loose in its frame. The lock was a good one. A spring-mounted bell jingled when I entered.

The diner was jammed with blue-collar longshore types. Johnny Cash poured his heart out from a jukebox. Country music for men who went down to the docks and worked on ships. I sat down at the counter next to an elderly unshaven dockrat missing half his front teeth and wearing a Canucks cap and khaki dungarees. The diner's windows overlooked a harbour bustling with workboats and yachts. I had plenty of time to admire the view, because the counterman/cook had his hands full.

The Coho car ferry was leaving for Port Angeles. A passenger-catamaran was inbound from Seattle. Tied up at the Ogden Point terminal was a massive multi-decked cruise ship as tall as the Empress Hotel. Maybe the diner's cook hated the view though, because his mouth was tight and he had misery written all over him. Stiff and gangly, he wore a collarless white dress shirt with rolled-up sleeves and a blue apron. He moved arthritically in orthopedic shoes, and I surmised that extracting information from him would be an uphill job. I ordered bacon and eggs, hash browns and whole-wheat toast, and sipped a cup of very good strong coffee while he prepared my breakfast. His unhurried economy of motion, perfected over many years, was a treat to watch. I wondered whether he'd learned his trade in the navy. He looked old enough to be a Korean War vet.

I was wearing civilian clothes. When the opportunity arose, and without making a fuss about it, I showed him my badge and said, "When you have a minute, I need to talk to you."

"I ain't got a minute."

"Mister, you need a waitress."

The old-timer sitting next to me chuckled.

The cook put my breakfast down in front of me before saying, "My waitress hasn't come in yet. She didn't come to work yesterday neither."

"That'd be Maria?"

The cook gave me a thoughtful look, but didn't reply.

"Give me her phone number," I said. "I'll call her for you, tell her how much you miss her."

The cook straightened up and looked me in the eye. After a great show of deliberation, he said shrewdly, "I don't give out my employees' phone numbers or personal information."

"How about giving me some HP sauce to pour on these excellent hash browns?"

"No HP? That's a tragedy," the cook said. "I'm working here on my own since five this morning and it's been a long day already. Maybe I'm losing it."

"I'd still like some HP sauce."

It came eventually, but by then I'd finished my breakfast. The diner remained crowded, otherwise I might have taken the cook into a back room and resorted to threats. Even though I knew that threats probably wouldn't work, because he seemed savvy enough to know that I couldn't force him to cooperate. I couldn't even search his premises without papers and, if I tried it, the police board would put me out to pasture. As long as he minded his own business, the cook/counterman was safe.

When I went out, the elderly customer followed me. He had a lined grey face and washed-out watery eyes. His back was stooped. He walked with a cane and a forward-leaning lurch. He had a greasy neck, unlovely nose hairs, and a cheerful grin.

I was unlocking the MG when he came up and said, "I heard you talking to Buster. You're a cop, I seen you show Buster your badge. Am I right, or am I right?"

I leaned back against the car door and put my hands in my pockets. I didn't say anything.

"I hear cops pay for information sometimes."

I smiled, wondering whether I'd hear something useful.

"I got a room nearby," he went on, speaking with many hand gestures. "I'm in and out of the diner all the time. Buster is always close-mouthed, but he's worse since Maria ran out on him."

"Good help is hard to find."

The old guy found my comment amusing. When he finished chortling, he said, "Yeah, that waitress was a pretty little thing. Indian kid, popular as all get out."

"If you've got something other than idle gossip to tell me, say it."

"Sure I've got something, that's why I'm talking to you. I've got something that maybe you can use."

His grin widened. He had my undivided attention. He gazed at me expectantly as I brought out my wallet and peeled off a twenty.

He made a grab for it, but I held it out of his reach.

He said, "I'd tell you for nothing if I had the dough, but I have a hard time making it on my lousy pension."

"For twenty bucks I want more than chitchat."

"I know what you want."

"Do you have Maria's address or phone number?"

"No, I don't. I got something better than that."

The old-timer's name was Colin Topham. He lived in a decrepit boarding house near Spinnaker's pub. I drove him over there. His room was up two flights of worn uncarpeted stairs. The whole house was fetid with the curdled odours of fried food and of clothing that had ripened on smelly bodies. Using a key dangling from a string looped around his neck, Topham unlocked a door and let me into a small room cluttered with a black-and-white TV, a sagging vinyl sofa, an unpainted pine table and two mismatched wooden chairs. Yesterday's dishes soaked in a sink full of greasy water. The room's single narrow window was jammed shut. It was hot enough to roast clams in there. Topham didn't seem to mind the lack of air, but I did. He looked aggrieved when, after a struggle, I managed to get the window open.

When that house had been built, the window had afforded sweeping views of tree-covered hills, sawmills, Esquimalt Harbour, shipyards and docks busy with steamships loading timber for Europe. Now the window looked out on a sea of houses and commercial buildings.

Topham brought out a photo album and placed it on the table. When he had found what he wanted, he put his finger on the page and closed the album to prevent my seeing what was in it.

Topham said, "So what about it, mister? How much money are we talking about?"

Poverty, not greed, made his face suddenly ratlike and sly.

"Twenty," I said, giving him a mean-eyed stare.

Topham opened the album. It was a disappointment. Instead of photographs, the album contained dozens of amateurish pencil drawings.

"That's Maria," Topham said proudly. "See the way the light comes from over her left shoulder and makes kind of a halo around her face? I sent it to a magazine, it's what you call a life study."

Topham had the best of the bargain. Raymond Cho's digital camera had provided all the photographs of Maria that we could use. Topham's cookie-cutter sketch showed a square-faced girl. To me it was completely useless. But I felt sorry for the old guy, so I gave him the twenty, shoved the drawing in my pocket, wished Topham good luck and went back down the stairs.

Along the street from Topham's house was a corner store. I went in to pick up the day's newspaper and idly checked the shelves: groceries, soaps, shampoos, Aspirin, soft drinks, potato chips and Cheezies.

Baking soda, metallic scouring pads and butane lighters. A crackhead's holy trinity, but not much needed nowadays when dealers sell ready-made crack. Mix a little soda with a hit of coke, add drops of water, fire it up with the butane lighter, let it cool enough to crystallize and you've got yourself a pipeful. If you stick a chunk of scouring pad in the stem of your pipe, it will collect some of the vapours. Fire up the scouring pad later for a weak hit when the jitters set in.

The woman minding the shop was a cheerful black Jamaican wearing a muumuu. Wide-hipped and narrow-shouldered, she surmised that I was a stranger in town. She had no prejudices against Natives, and had a room at the back I could rent for 20 dollars a day. Less, if I took it by the month.

The Collins Lane murder had already been shunted to the fourth page.

I went home and called Bernie, told him I'd struck out at the Ballard Diner.

"What do you mean, struck out?"

"The guy who runs the diner wouldn't co-operate."

"You should have leaned on him. Withholding evidence from police is a crime."

"The only way to eliminate crime is to legalize it," I observed philosophically.

"So I've heard, but don't worry your little pointed head about it," Bernie said tersely. "I'll get a search warrant."

That sounded good to me. I spent the day wandering around town. Then I went home and had a long afternoon nap, because I was expecting a long, busy night.

CHAPTER TEN

The ringing phone woke me up following a long complicated dream involving feral cats and a roll of barbed wire that I forgot almost entirely the moment my eyes opened. It was Bernie Tapp. He said, "Bad news, Judge Numbnuts turned me down when I applied for a warrant to search the Ballard Diner."

"Now what?"

"Damned if I know. Plan B, I guess."

There was a long silence, after which Bernie grunted and hung up.

I got off the bed and walked around restlessly. My mind swirling with bad ideas, I mixed myself a rye and ginger with plenty of ice. Swigging occasionally, I cleaned myself up at the kitchen sink, applied deodorant, swallowed the rest of my drink, brushed my teeth with Colgate instead of having another drink, and then I got dressed in a black cotton shirt, and charcoal grey loose-fit trousers. Black socks. Attired like that, in the proper arena, I could pass as a small-time wannabe drug dealer, fink, petty crook, or as a standard-issue small-town semi-tough long-haired asshole. It would also make it harder for people to see me in the dark. According to my good Chinese Rolex, it was ten-thirty. From my open window, the onshore wind was pleasingly cool. White surf, boiling onto the beach, broke the surrounding darkness. The Milky Way sparkled above. Somewhere in the night, an amorous dog was broadcasting its lament. I knew how he felt because I felt the same way. I always do when I haven't seen Felicity Exeter for a while. Enveloped by shadows, trying not to think about Felicity, I went out to the MG.

NANAIMO'S IS A private nightclub located in a former union hall half a mile from the Ballard Diner. I didn't know the Native bouncer guarding Nanaimo's front entrance, but he reminded me of a heavyweight coal miner that I used to know. The bouncer wore a cheap three-piece black suit and he spoke with a voice thickened by years of overindulgence in duty-free cigarettes. A gold chain dangled from his vest pocket. His white shirt had a celluloid collar. His large square head was as bald and as shiny as a sea-washed pebble. Black hairs sprouted thickly from his ears and nostrils, and from the backs of his large square hands. With a droopy nicotine-stained Fu Manchu moustache and highly polished black steel-toed boots, at first glance he looked to be a figure of fun, but menace lurked in his dark eyes. I paid the club's twenty-dollar membership fee and scribbled a pseudonym on a membership-application form. After patting me down for concealed weapons, the bouncer waved me on through.

Interior decorators had stripped the union hall of the honest working-class ambience it had once possessed. Instead of lecterns, a proscenium arch stage, patriotic flags and photographs of labour martyrs, I was confronted by a retro-style '80s disco with strippers' poles, dancers' cages, and a lit-from-below glass dance floor. The patrons noisily milling around that night were the usual mix of men who longed to be successful property developers and girls who wanted to star in movies opposite Brad Pitt. Pill pushers roamed, preppy Uplands chicks flaunted their first tattoos for disinterested loggers, crooks, oilpatch roughnecks, and a local poet wearing brown corduroys and a black turtleneck holding hands with a Japanese fraud who slaps paint on canvas with floor mops at ten thousand a pop.

Cocktails were twelve dollars, draft beers were seven-fifty.

Clubbers were coming and going in and out of a billiard room, two bars, an illegal cigar lounge, and a private room labelled *The Landlord's Snug*. The Pet Shop Boys were performing inaudibly on one big flatscreen television. Prince was eating a microphone on another big screen.

A pair of wide French doors gave onto an open-air deck. I sat at the deck's last remaining empty table, and rested my elbow on a wooden railing. I was admiring the builder's yard next door when a waiter attired like the bouncer arrived. Another Native hard man, he had wide cheekbones, narrow eyes, and thick dark hair trimmed closely to his head. I ordered a double Chivas over ice with water on the side. Victoria's lights twinkled in the darkness.

A woman sitting alone at a table adjacent to mine introduced another permutation into the chess-like game that I was trying to play that night. Her eyes were a very deep blue. She was about 40, with long wavy black hair, wearing a white dress made of smooth clingy fabric. The martini glass on her table contained a cranberry-coloured liquid. She had the regal manner and bearing of someone born to money and she looked out of place, sitting alone in a club. She looked the way Gina Lollobrigida looked back in the '50s. She caught me admiring her, or maybe she didn't after all, because her deep-blue eyes bored a hole right through me. On her face was the taut passionate expression you observe on people who are navigating life-altering events. Disastrous illnesses or divorces, for example. You see much the same look on heroin junkies late for a fix. I finished my first drink. When the waiter came over again, I ordered another Chivas and asked him what the woman at the next table was drinking.

"Cosmos," he said.

"Is she a regular here?"

"I've never seen the lady before."

"Give her my compliments, and ask her if I may buy her another Cosmopolitan."

The waiter did so. After glancing at me coldly, the woman fished inside a small leather handbag, brought out a small thin white rectangular object, and handed it to the waiter. The object looked like a business card, but it could also have been a tiny heat-sealed cellophane bag stuffed with fine white powder. The waiter slipped the object into a pocket. She and the waiter exchanged a few quiet words, after which the waiter looked at me, and raised his shoulders a trifle to let me know that I'd struck out. As he left the patio, the waiter brushed past a man who was standing in the doorway.

It was Tubby Gonzales. After glancing around and seeing that all the tables were taken, Gonzales turned away without noticing me.

The waiter returned to the patio with two drinks on his tray. He placed one of the drinks on the woman-in-white's table and said something that made her laugh. Still grinning, the waiter delivered my drink. "The lady is a little amused. She thinks you must be short-sighted. She thinks you mistook her for a pick up."

"A reasonable assumption, unless she's waiting to meet someone."

"A woman like her, that's almost a certainty." His grin faded as he added, "Maybe you have the wrong idea about her occupation, my friend. The first time we find a hooker working the club, we boot her ass out the door. The second time, we boot her ass out the door and break her legs." He walked away.

I gave it ten minutes. Nobody had joined her, so I stood up and spoke to her. I said, "I beg your pardon, ma'am. Please forgive me if you think that I insulted you, because it wasn't intentional. I am a stranger in a strange land."

She acknowledged my existence with a slight nod, but continued to gaze out towards the dimming horizon. She was quite slim and beautiful.

After a beat I sat down again and tried to ignore her. She waited a few more minutes to let me know that my existence wasn't important, but afterwards she gave me a speculative look and remarked in a voice no louder than necessary, "I suppose many people tell you that you are very good-looking. I expect you get all the girls you want?"

"Oh, come on."

Her voice was as soft as thistledown. "I must say that nobody would mistake you for a stranger in these parts, although maybe you're Haida or Tsimshian. I'm not an expert on BC's Native tribes."

"I'm Coast Salish, so at least one of your assumptions about me is correct. The word Nanaimo derives from Snuneymuxw, a Coast Salish word which means meeting place. Before the Dunsmuir coal mines were developed, a lot of my people used to live in Snuneymuxw. Traditional Coast Salish territory stretches all the way from Seattle northwards as far as Cape Mudge. I happen to live in Victoria."

"I happen to live in Qualicum Beach. Most of the time that is," she responded with slightly more warmth. "My grandfather was an architect. He designed some of James Dunsmuir's buildings. He designed this building too. It used to be called the Ginger Goodwin Memorial Hall."

I spread my hands. "Then we have something in common. When James Dunsmuir arrived here from Scotland, a century and a half ago, Native Indians told him where to find Vancouver Island's coal."

"I know they did, and more fool them. Dunsmuir parlayed his coal mines into a knighthood, and into one of the largest fortunes in the British Commonwealth."

She looked over my shoulder. Her date had just shown up. Tall and good-looking, about thirty years old, he had longish black hair and a detached, almost feline manner. He had on a Hawaiian shirt, cargo pants and deck shoes. He looked at me, scowled, and then turned to the woman and said, "Is this guy bothering you?"

She said wearily, "Oh, Larry. Please don't start that again."

She rose to her feet and said to me, "Thanks for offering to buy me a drink, it was very kind of you, another time perhaps. Now I have some business to attend to. Goodbye."

Trailed by the newcomer, she went out. I finished my drink and left the deck's relative quiet for the club's noisy main room. In there, it was standing room only by then. The waiter who had served my drinks was tending a cash register. I said, "Hearing loss must be an occupational hazard. How do you put up with it?"

"There are no conditions of life to which a man cannot accustom himself, especially when they are accepted by everybody else."

"Nicely put."

"The words are Tolstoy's, sir, not mine."

"That woman. What's her name?"

"I have no idea, my friend."

"How about Larry, her hunky boyfriend?"

"Larry Cooley? Oh yeah, he comes around here occasionally."

"I'll pay my tab now."

"Interesting concept, this club," I added, as he rang up my bill. "Glum instead of glitter. Native waiters in three-piece suits instead of hotties in shorts. It's working, though. The owner must be an original thinker."

"He is original in many interesting ways."

"Who is he, by the way?"

Evidently this was a touchy subject; the slight warmth that had been in the waiter's eyes plunged to zero as he handed me my bill. I owed him about thirty dollars. I gave him two twenties and told him to keep the change.

"Come in again sometime," he said, instead of answering my question. "Maybe you'll have better luck with women."

A half-remembered Tolstoy quotation flitted into my mind, but I couldn't remember exactly how it went. I thanked him in Russian: "Spasiba."

"Pozhaluista, sir."

As I turned to leave, I noticed Tubby Gonzales standing at the bar. I grinned at him, and went out.

CHAPTER ELEVEN

By then it was late enough for the business that I had in mind. I drove a quarter of a mile and parked the MG in a back lane off Esquimalt Road. I put a few items from the MG's toolkit into a canvas sack and toted it along dark narrow streets to the Ballard Diner. The diner had closed for the night, but its inside and outside lights had been left on. Gravel crunched beneath my feet as I approached the diner's front door. Using a two-pound hammer and a tapered steel punch, I drove the pins out of the door hinges, dragged the door open, and went inside. I had a Maglite and thought about turning the diner's lights off while I poked around, but decided against it. If any reasonably observant patrolman cruised past on his regular beat and noticed that the lights were out, he'd stop and take a closer look anyway.

The diner's records were stored in an unlocked drawer underneath the lunch counter. It took no time at all to find the file containing Maria Alfred's local address, along with her Social Insurance Number, her date of birth, and other information. Suddenly, I remembered the Tolstoy quotation that had eluded me earlier. It was: *Pure and complete sorrow is as impossible as pure and complete joy.*

A gruff male voice said, "Hold it right there, pal, you're under arrest. Police is on its way."

A lightweight rent-a-cop was standing in the front doorway, tapping his left hand with a nightstick held in his right hand. He was wearing a wrinkled blue uniform with the words Marlowe Security printed across the front of his jacket. He looked pleased with himself.

When my brain resumed its normal functions, I said, "Under arrest for what?"

"Whadda you think, you dumb bastard? Breaking and entering for a start. Stupidity."

"Not so fast, I own this place. The Ballard Diner belongs to me."

The rent-a-cop's grin faltered. "Since when?"

By then, the bleep-bleat-bleeps of approaching police sirens were shrieking in the night.

I reached across the counter, picked up a pepper shaker and said, "Pay attention please. Buster sold the diner to me last week. Look, my name is on this shaker."

When the poor idiot leaned in for a closer look, I shook an ounce of seasoning into his eyes and leapt backwards beyond his reach. Howling, temporarily blinded, he thrashed towards me, his arms flailing, but by then I'd jumped over the counter. He tried to follow as I went outside. In his half-blinded state, he tripped over a stool and measured his length on the floor. Those sirens were louder now. Red and blue flashers winked as two police vehicles banged into sight around a corner two blocks away. Resisting a strong temptation to run, I walked out onto the unlit rubbish-strewn wasteland behind the diner. Next to invisible in my dark clothing, I stepped across a double set of railroad tracks and put uphill distance between myself and the diner, until I was brought to a stop by a brick wall crowned with razor wire. I skirted along the wall to my left until I reached a wet ditch separating a warehouse from an RV storage yard. The storage yard was fenced and well lit. I continued uphill. A bum asleep inside a wooden crate groaned when I tripped across him in the darkness. After a while, I came upon a row of 1890s brick-built houses with fenced back yards. I went through a garden without waking any dogs and got clean away.

CHAPTER TWELVE

Safely back in my car, I tried to think of something comic to tell Bernie Tapp if Internal Affairs knocked my door down and arrested me for burglary in the middle of the night. Blue-and-white cruisers were more numerous than prowling cats when I drove back to Nanaimo's. By then it was about two AM.

Rave noises poured from the club's windows and from the open patio where I had been sitting earlier. Before getting out of the car, I took my Glock from its clip beneath the MG's dashboard, and stuffed it into my belt. The bouncer who had patted me down for weapons the first time was still on duty. He recognized me. This time he just waved me straight through.

Nanaimo's alcohol-and-drug-fuelled drama had kicked up a notch. Girls who a year or two earlier had been playing with dolls were washing down ecstasy tablets with kamikaze shots. Stockbrokers, visiting firemen, and lone-wolf sailors blowing their pay while they sought less-than-eternal love were revealed spasmodically beneath the club's pulsating strobe lights.

The waiter who had served me earlier was beside the counter. He said, "You must be a glutton for punishment."

"What's that supposed to mean?"

"Are you still waiting for the woman in white?"

"That might be nice, but she gave me the brush-off. I'm here to see your boss."

"I'll see if he's in his office."

"No need, I'll find my own way."

"The boss doesn't like unannounced visitors."

I badged him and said, "I'm a police sergeant. Policemen don't do announcements."

The waiter's eyes widened.

"And here's another thing," I said. "That pimply kid standing near the stage is dealing Ecstasy."

"What's a rave without rave drugs?" the waiter replied. After placing a glass of milk on a silver tray, he picked it up and said, "Follow me, sir."

"I'll follow you if you add a Chivas and water to that tray."

Smiling slightly, the waiter did so. I trailed him up a flight of stairs and along a crowded balcony to an unmarked door. With the drink tray expertly balanced on one hand, the waiter knocked. A shadow dimmed the judas hole set in the door, and then the door opened on silent hinges. The woman in white came out. Her eyes were narrow, her lovely mouth was tight with anger. Watching her stride away along the balcony and down the stairs, I concluded that she hadn't even noticed me. Her ass was spectacular in the white clingy dress she had on. I followed the waiter inside. He placed my Chivas and the glass of milk on the manager's desk, and exited with the silver tray under his arm.

Twinner Scudd's office reminded me of a butcher's shop. It was about twenty feet by fifteen, lit by fluorescent tubes. The room's smooth plaster walls and ceilings were coated with glossy white paint. Scudd was standing with his back to an open window behind a big white desk with a white marble top. Half a dozen high-end white moulded plastic chairs were scattered here and there on the room's white ceramic floor tiles.

Scudd's bodyguard was a pierced and tattooed thug named Eddie Cliffs. Cliffs was another Native, and I'd brought him down for pandering, once. Eddie Cliffs scowled menacingly until Twinner Scudd pointed to the drinks on his desk, whereupon Cliffs came over and put the glass of milk in Twinner's hand. After a slight hesitation, Cliffs handed me my drink and returned to his station by the door.

Twinner Scudd was a fat Native Indian from up Desolation Sound way. His thick black hair was buzzed close to his scalp. His face was the colour of olive oil. He wore a dapper white suit, a white T-shirt, and white shoes. His eyes were invisible behind dark glasses.

"So, Seaweed. How long's it been?" Scudd asked as he sat behind his desk.

I sat down, rolled a little Chivas around my tongue. "Five, six years?"

"It's been eight years," he said in a voice of subdued menace. "Eight years since you guys busted my Saltspring grow-op."

"Baloney," I said negligently. "I'm not interested in busting back-country grow-ops. Besides, Saltspring Island is Mountie country. I had nothing to do with it."

"Somebody blew the whistle, and a lot of serious people think it was you."

"Serious? The same people probably think that the earth is flat and that the moon is made of green cheese. When I go after you, Twinner, it won't be for growing BC bud, it'll be for something serious. Murder, for example."

I couldn't see Scudd's eyes behind his glasses, but his fat shoulders straightened at the word "murder."

I went on, "After the formality of a trial, the outcome of which will never be in doubt, we'll bolt you up and you'll never see daylight again. There's a cell in a Supermax with your name on it. You'll sit inside a rubber cube for the rest of your days. You won't hear another sound except the sound of your own screams. You'll never set eyes on another human being. Your food will be shoved through a slot in a door. There'll be no books for you to read, no TV to look at. You'll be stark raving mad in a year, or less, because you'll know we'll never let you out."

Scudd said, "The jail that can hold me hasn't been built."

I threw back my head and laughed. Eddie Cliffs lurched forward and grabbed my shoulder. Before I could do anything about it, Scudd waved a lazy hand and Cliffs backed off.

To me, Scudd said, "Cliffy's got a short fuse, best you don't mess with him. You're still the cocky bastard you've always been, but when you're on my turf, you better watch your manners. Start throwing accusations of murder around, and Cliffy's likely to lose his temper, drag your head off by the roots."

"And you can tell that moron Cliffy something. Tell him that if he touches me again, I'll break his heart."

Cliffy started moving. By then I was ready. He ran towards me, his arms wide, yelling. Maybe he was expecting me to throw a punch, but I didn't. I have too much respect for the fragile little bones in my hands. Instead of breaking them on Cliffy's thick head, I aimed a kick at his balls. My kick missed its target and landed on his left knee instead. Howling with pain, Cliffy leaned forward. I grabbed him by the hair and brought up my knee simultaneously. Cliffy's nose exploded into a brilliant ball of blood as he collapsed. I put my foot on his throat. I said, "Listen, Cliffy. If you move a muscle, I'll crush your larynx. You'll suffocate to death, right here on this floor. It'll be the last move you ever make. Savvy?"

Cliffy made a gurgling sound. I interpreted it as an assent. I went back to my chair and watched him. Twinner seemed amused. After a minute, Cliffy managed to get to his feet. He went out of the room, trailing blood.

I said to Twinner, "Where were we before we were so rudely interrupted?"

Twinner smiled. "We were talking about murder, as I recall. Just remind me. Who am I supposed to have murdered this time?"

"A Chinese guy from Vancouver."

"There are lots of Chinese guys in Vancouver. Nothing personal, but I hope them slant-eyed fuckers all stay over there."

"His name was Raymond Cho. He was a Big Circle Boy."

"Oh yeah? But I didn't kill no Chinaman, because Chinamen ain't no threat to me."

Standing up and waving a finger in my face, Twinner added more forcibly, "Around here, I'm the boss and don't you forget it. There was a woman in my office just now. She was trying to shove me around too. The bossy little cow even had the nerve to threaten me, till I showed her who was running this show. Before you flap any more gum, keep this in mind: Cliffy's gonna get better, and he's gonna be mad. I could get Cliffy to blow you away. You'll end up in a landfill somewhere. Nobody would know, nobody would shed a tear, you'd be forgotten in a week."

I moved slightly in my chair. Then I took my Glock out and laid it gently on the desk. Twinner Scudd's eyes widened and his patronizing grin faded. Slowly, he sat down again.

I said, "Think you're a hard ass, Scudd? Tell you what, let's play a little game. Let's see who can pick that gun up first, aim it and shoot a hole in the other guy's head."

At that moment, fortunately perhaps for me, Scudd wasn't in the mood for games. He placed his hands flat on the desk, well away from the gun. I put the gun in my side pocket, where it made my jacket sag but was in easy reach if I needed it in a hurry. I said in a neutral voice, "It must be very annoying for you. You build up a nice little illegal monopoly, then complete strangers ride into town. Try to steal a piece of your action."

"What illegal monopoly is that?

"I'm talking about your giant share of Vancouver Island's cocaine trade. You or one of your associates killed the Chinaman because you thought he was going to horn in."

Scudd took his dark glasses off, dabbed his dark eyes with a white handkerchief and then put his glasses on again. He said, "This is interesting. Tell me more."

"Well, it's a rough business, wholesaling illegal drugs. But you've been in the business for years and you've learned how to cope. We know that you came to an arrangement with the Hell's Angels and that you have split the business fifty-fifty from Nanaimo northwards. Apart from a little penny-ante stuff, Victoria and the whole of the South Island has been your drug domain almost exclusively. Until now, that is. Today, there's all kinds of people horning in."

Scudd slowly raised his hands from the desk, sipped a little milk, and said, "For instance?"

I said, "The Big Circle Boys. The Red Scorpions. The United Nations Gang. Tubby Gonzales."

Scudd laughed. "What a crock. Red Scorpions? Are you kidding me, they're a bunch of fucking nitwits. Headbangers who can't find their asses in the dark. Tubby Gonzales is a personal friend of mine, for chrissake."

"Lucky you. I didn't know Gonzales had any friends. And by the way, the dead Chinaman was a fancy dresser with a yen for naughty girls. You may have read about him in the newspapers."

"There's a lot of fancy dressers with a taste for naughty girls, but I don't read newspapers. I don't even watch much TV. All I do is count the money this club is earning for me, every cent of it legal. You have the wrong idea about me, Seaweed, because in spite of what you think, I am a changed man now. I am a solid citizen. I've turned over a new leaf. Given up my life of crime, because it's easy to make money legally. Income tax auditors check my books every year. A bunch of pen pushers with smelly armpits, dandruff and cheap suits. Sometimes they beef about my expenses, but when they come sniffing around, I tell Cliffy to feed 'em hamburgers and all the liquor they can drink. Free of charge, so we don't get any serious hassles. Besides, if I do get hassles, Cliffy leans on people. Otherwise I claim racial discrimination and invoke the Residential School Defence. It works every time."

"You never went to a residential school. You were born on Quanterelle Island. You went to school at Surge Narrows."

Scudd grinned.

I said, "I'm looking for a missing woman. She was friends with a woman called Maria Henry. Maria was born on Quanterelle Island too."

"Yeah, Maria, my hot little kissing cousin. Somebody told me that Maria's enjoying life at Wilkie Road jail right now. Have you accused her of murder as well?"

"Right now, all I want is to talk to Maria's friend."

"Well, Seaweed. I can't help you there."

"I'd just like to talk to her, and I'm certain that you know the woman I'm talking about. The next time you see her, tell her that. Tell her that I just want to ask her a few questions. She can phone me at my office, anytime." I stood up. "In the meantime, Twinner, try to behave yourself. I think we'll meet again real soon."

"I can hardly wait. In the meantime, Seaweed, be careful you don't shoot yourself playing with guns. That's a job I want to do myself." Scudd's jaw tightened. "Do you want me to put that scotch you just drank on a tab, or will you pay for it downstairs?"

I took money from my pocket. Dropped it on Twinner's desk. Went out. Cliffy, outside on the balcony, holding a bloody rag to his nose, gave me a mean slit-eyed glance before he rejoined his boss. Five minutes later, I was downstairs, watching the action, when I saw Tubby Gonzales again. The Mexican was arm-in-arm with a girl girl half his age. She looked drunk. Gonzales appeared to be enjoying himself. I kept my eyes on them for a couple of minutes before he and the girl went out together. If I'd been smart, I'd have left the club then and there. Instead, I went into the *Landlord's Snug*, where I had another Chivas. The smell of Havana cigar smoke hampered my appreciation of the scotch, so I paid the bill and visited the men's room. It was unoccupied, except for a stooped old attendant who was mopping the marble floor tiles with intense concentration. I wondered if the old boy had been called to mop Twinner's office yet.

To my left were four toilet cubicles. To my right was a long black granite counter with six white porcelain washbowls. Gold-plated plumbing fixtures. Stacked cotton napkins instead of paper towels. The space dividing the toilet cubicles from the washbowls was about four feet wide. In an ell were four urinals. The old guy finished his work on the floor and went out. I was alone, lathering my hands with the club's scented liquid soap at one of the washbowls when the door opened. Looking up to the mirror, I saw Eddie Cliffs and two of the club's wide-shouldered bouncers come in.

Cliffs had a large plaster across his nose. He leaned against the door to prevent anyone else from entering the washroom. "Hello, smart guy," he said, in nasal tones that made him sound like a cartoon character. "It's showtime."

There wasn't enough room between the cubicles and the counters for the two goons to stand side by side. The bouncer who looked like a coal miner was putting on a pair of black leather gloves. All three men were facing me in single file, which skewed the odds in my favour. As long as the goons didn't crowd me backwards into the ell, where the floor space was wider, I was in pretty good shape for a showdown.

The coal miner's fighting technique wasn't highly developed. Like Cliff, he was another rusher. Rushing at your opponent is efficient if your opponent is a powder puff. I'm not. The coal miner wasn't very obser-vant. Otherwise he might have wondered what was weighting my jacket pocket down on one side. When he charged, I was ready. Instead of back-ing up, I took the Glock from my pocket and slashed the air with the gun in a 90-degree roundhouse swing. As the blow connected with the coal miner's face, I stepped aside. The coal miner's head stopped moving for a moment, but the rest of him kept going. Spewing teeth, he slid feet-first to the end of the room, where he crashed against a radiator and lay inert.

One down. Two to go. I was starting to enjoy myself, and I didn't hesitate. Holding the Glock by the barrel, I swung it at the second bouncer's head. He put his arm up to block the Glock's descending arc. There was a loud snap as his forearm broke. He screamed. My second blow missed his head, but it smashed his collarbone and sent him flying backwards against Cliffs. Cliffs had been trying to get out of the washroom, but when the second goon fell against him, his escape route was blocked. By then, solidarity had reached its limits in that former union hall. I stepped on the second goon's chest, grabbed Cliffs' shoulder, and turned him around to face me. He was trying to explain something about my huge misunderstanding of the situation when I head butted him.

Three men down. Down and out.

Butting Cliffy's head left me feeling slightly dizzy. My ears were ringing. I felt better after splashing my face with water and cleaning spots of blood off my jacket at a washbowl. After dragging Cliffy and the goon out of the way, I went out of the washroom.

By then, the club's former ambience had undergone a subtle and almost imperceptible change. Nanaimo's was still crowded, but instead of the former rave scene, there was an eerie calm. People had stopped dancing and had gathered in small groups of five or six people. I thought initially that a lingering adrenaline rush was leading me to misread the situation. But there was more to it than that. Something unusual and dangerous was going to happen. The collective unconscious had picked up on it.

Then all hell broke loose. The patio erupted into a ball of fire. The club's strobe lights, and every other light in the club, winked out. Flatscreen TVs and speakers went dead. Flames, rapidly expanding from the patio, blocked the club's chief emergency exit. Mass hysteria set in; pandemonium ensued. Screaming helplessly, people were trampled underfoot as everyone rushed for the front door. I was carried along in the crush. After an interval, a few emergency lights clicked on to augment the red-yellow glare spreading throughout the building. In moments, the wall adjacent to the patio was completely ablaze. The hundred-year-old wooden structure burned fiercely. As it became heated, ancient varnish and paint first bubbled, and then sloughed down the walls to the floor in thick viscous waves, like volcanic lava. When the flames reached the ceiling, they spread outwards. By then, fierce crossdrafts were broadcasting airborne fragments. Burning drapery and plastics spread flames to the remaining walls. The noise was tremendous. People were shouting "Out! Get Out!"

Hemmed in by the crowd, I was carried helplessly along towards the front door. An opening designed to accommodate two or three people at a time was being jammed by a panicked herd. I managed to fight my way out of the crowd and make my way back to the washroom. Flames followed me inside till I slammed the door shut. Light streamed into the washroom through a broken window. Cliffy had gone, as had the guy with the broken arm. The coal miner was still tits-up on the floor against the radiator. I dragged him upright and managed to shove him partway through the window before someone outside gave me a hand to drag him the rest of the way.

Instead of climbing out the window, I went back into the club. By then, it was almost entirely engulfed in flames. Superheated air began to scald my exposed skin. The roar of conflagration rendered every other sound inaudible. Then, fifteen feet from where I was standing, I saw a black figure trying to drag itself across the club's burning floorboards. Insanely, I took a step towards it. Something hot and heavy fell from the ceiling and bounced off my head and shoulder; my hair was burning. I backtracked to the washroom. A fireman had poked his fog-nozzle through the window. Bathed in a cool moist mist, I climbed outside. The fireman turned his fog-nozzle on me.

CHAPTER THIRTEEN

Morning sunlight brought me awake at about eleven o'clock. I got out of bed. My head-butting forehead throbbed with pain. I switched the radio on. CFAX's big news was the Nanaimo's arson disaster. Three people were dead, 20 survivors were in hospital.

Still half asleep and groggy, my eyeballs immersed in what felt like a greasy vaseline scum, I called Bernie Tapp and told him about last night.

"You were inside the club when the fire started?"

"Yes. Moments earlier I'd been talking with Twinner Scudd."

Bernie grunted.

I said, "In addition, I found out where Maria Alfred lives."

"You found out, hey?" Bernie said sarcastically. "I suppose you were walking along the street, noticed a bit of paper lying in the gutter. Picked it up and guess what? It had Maria's name, address and phone number written on it."

"That's about right, actually. I am one lucky dude."

"The fire marshal says the Nanaimo's fire was a definite arson. Who do you fancy for it?"

"Ordinarily, I might suspect somebody like Tubby Gonzales, except Twinner Scudd told me that he and Tubby are buddy buddy right now."

Bernie had a sudden coughing fit. When it subsided, he said throatily, "Maybe we should bug Twinner's house."

"Twinner doesn't live in a house. He lives on a hundred-foot yacht. It's called the *Polar Girl* and when he's in Victoria he keeps it in that marina just south of the Johnson Street Bridge."

Bernie had another coughing attack. He grunted something unintelligible.

I said, "What?"

Bernie said, "Somebody dialled 911. Reported that a brazen long-haired First Nations thief robbed the Ballard Diner last night."

"No kidding? Do you want me to check Maria Alfred's house, do it yourself, or send Serious Crimes?"

"Go ahead, do it yourself but keep me posted. Serious Crimes is working overtime as it is, and I'm up to my armpits." He added. "Did you get hurt last night?"

"A few little bruises and burns. Nothing much."

"Well, you take care of yourself. Like I said, I'm up to my armpits, I can't afford to lose any more men."

I hung up and called the same number by hitting the redial button. This time, I spoke to the drug squad, and asked Sergeant Bondat to tell me the latest drug-war rumours.

Bondat took a deep angry breath and then went on to tell me something that I already knew. He said, "Tomás Gonzales and Twinner Scudd are battling for market share against dealers from Vancouver. Now we're hearing that the Big Circle Boys are moving in. The Red Scorpions have been sending their people across too, setting up dial-a-dope operations and recruiting local small-time punks. We've been rounding up these idiots like cattle. Most have priors for drug and weapons possession. They're wannabees with jailhouse attitudes and big showoff RS tattoos. The kind of cheap punks who'll slash complete strangers just to show their friends how tough they are. They're so dumb they don't even know that they're cannon fodder for the big players. They are expendables, dupes, fools. Mugs programmed to take all the risks and deflect heat away from the bosses. Their biggest moment comes after they're dead, when they get the big funeral, the black granite tombstone, and Mommy telling the TV cameras how wonderful her loser son was to his family and other loved ones. Loved ones? Shit."

Bondat sounded bitter. He went on, "When the Red Scorpions fade to black, another bunch will try its arm. It never ends."

I put the phone down, looked in the mirror and examined the burnt remnants of my ponytail. I'd been wearing my hair down to my shoulders.

It took me several minutes in front of a mirror with a pair of scissors to make a half-decent job of trimming it above my collar.

Mr. Siskin seemed to be doing okay. When I went outside, he gave me a song and I gave him a ball of suet. Feeling better, I drove downtown to my office and checked my voice mail. Nothing. After giving PC her breakfast, I went next door to have my own breakfast at Lou's Cafe.

Lou is full of surprises. He is a small angry man with a bandit moustache, and I think he's bald, but I've never seen him without a hat on. That day he was wearing a red Turkish fez with a golden tassel. I was wearing 30-dollar wranglers, a Harley-Davidson T-shirt and blue Nike running shoes. My head was concealed beneath an NYPD baseball cap.

I knew that Lou had fought alongside Tito during the Second World War, but what he hadn't told me until that morning is that as a university student in Budapest, Lou had majored in mathematics. Bottom line: Lou had just finished reading Benoit Mandelbrot's book on Chaos Theory. The way Lou described it, civilization as we know it is on the verge of collapse. Mandelbrot's proofs involve global warming, hedge funds, money markets and black swans. It was completely over my head.

After Lou's lecture and another cup of coffee, I dropped some bills on the table and took a leisurely stroll along Victoria's tree-lined sidewalks for five or six blocks before cutting across the gardens in front of the Empress Hotel.

My forehead was feeling better when I sat on a bench overlooking the Inner Harbour. Bikers and in-line skaters whizzed past. A slight breeze spanked the waves. Two boys out on the water were teaching themselves how to sail a plywood dinghy. Tourists and locals were out in droves. The causeway was busy with pedestrians admiring the yachts moored at the Empress marina. Lovers passed by arm-in-arm. Ferryboats and yachts came and went. A pair of ravens warbled and tumbled beguilingly. Apart from a kilted bagpiper standing underneath a tam-o'-shanter, playing mournful dirges, things were quite pleasant.

The boys were demonstrating their skill at falling off the dinghy into the water when Victoria's Royal BC Museum opened at ten o'clock. I showed my police badge and homed in on a section devoted to Vancouver Island's coal-mining industry. The information that I wanted was contained inside a free brochure. An architect called Peter Gregory Mainwaring had designed the Ginger Goodwin Memorial Hall.

An elderly stranger confronted me as I was passing through the First Nations' exhibit on my way out. "Are you a docent?" she asked me rather abruptly.

I shook my head.

"You look very familiar," she said accusingly. "Are you certain that I haven't seen you in here before?"

"You've probably mistaken me for someone else," I replied in a less than accommodating voice, because my interest had been piqued by a glass showcase that contained a heavy chunk of granite sculpted to look like a ferret. Its two pairs of feet were shaped like wedges, and set disproportionately close to the ferret's head. It was a Tsimshian slavekiller club.

I left the museum, crossed Belleville Street, walked down Government Street to Langley Street, and went inside Alfredo's barbershop. Alfredo's is a two-chair operation, although one of the chairs has been surplus for ten years. Unisex beauty shops have been brutal to old-fashioned haircutters. Alfredo Bertinelli is a sorrowful-looking man with a black moustache, a formal manner and an Italian accent. He was sitting in the surplus chair listening to grand opera.

I said, "Ever noticed Clark Gable's hair in *Gone with the Wind?*"

Alfredo reluctantly diverted his attention away from Jussi Björling and Robert Merrill, who were singing Bizet's *Pearl Fishers* duet.

Alfredo said, "Mama mia! It's Silas Seaweed."

"Mama mia?"

"I'm Italian, people expect it. How long have you been standing there?"

"Since yesterday. I hate to intrude on your fantasy, but I just asked you if you'd ever noticed Clark Gable's hair in *Gone with the Wind?*"

Bizet's music and those marvellous voices were making Alfredo's eyes liquid. "I've noticed Clark Gable's hair in *Gone with the Wind*," he declared. "I've noticed William Powell's hair in *The Thin Man*."

"William Powell's hair in *The Thin Man* looks too much like Fred Astaire's hair in *Royal Wedding*. I don't want to look like a debonair hoofer, I want to look like Clark Gable."

"Everybody does. But I'm a barber, not a magician."

I waited.

"One Clark Gable coming up," he said, dabbing his streaming eyes with a blue handkerchief, "although your hair is a bit darker than Gable's was."

It was a fifteen-minute job that took an hour. We heard Amelita Galli-Curci's version of the "Bell Song" from *Lakme*, and Enrico Caruso's *La Boheme* arias. My haircut might have taken all day if another customer hadn't come in. Alfredo's prices were prominently displayed. He charged 16 dollars for a standard haircut; seniors got a four-dollar discount. He wanted five dollars for trimming beards, and 20 dollars for a hot-towel shave. I've never had a barbershop shave in my life. Alfredo swung my chair 180 degrees till my back was to a wall mirror, and held a hand mirror in front of my face. I said hello to the shorthaired stranger seated behind me, and gave Alfredo a twenty. He hesitated over the change—I left the shop before he could charge me the seniors' rate.

Walking up the Fairfield slope towards the Blanshard Street courthouse, I noticed another massive new condo rising up to shoulder the sky near the Strathcona Hotel. Minutes later I was in courtroom number seven, watching Mickey Haggerty go down.

A greasy vicious rat, Haggerty had beaten a fellow drug addict to death with a length of two-by-four. The two men had been in a tussle about who deserved the last suck from the crack pipe they had been sharing. Murder was Haggerty's crowning achievement in a criminal life that had escalated from street trafficking, petty theft, burglary, robbery and aggravated bodily harm.

When I had arrested him for the murder, six months earlier, Haggerty was still standing over his victim with the two-by-four in his hands. Back then, Mickey Haggerty had weighed about ninety pounds. He was six feet tall and he had been wearing a dirty T-shirt, shorts and flip-flops. He had terminal-stage AIDS, Hep C., syphilis and gonorrhea. Now he was wearing a borrowed brown suit and a white shirt. Prison grub, regular medications and abstinence had put a bit of meat on his bones. Haggerty even had a certain swagger. He had pled down from Murder One to Murder Two. His sentence was a mere formality. Haggerty was in either case a dead man walking. He would be sleeping in potters field within five years or less. When Judge George asked Haggerty if he had anything to say before the sentence was passed, Haggerty asked the judge to give him a cigarette. The judge declined, whereupon Haggerty told the judge to go and piss up a rope. The judge appeared to be having difficulty controlling his emotions when he handed Haggerty 25. And that was that. As they were leading Haggerty down the steps, he noticed me standing in the gallery and gave me a wink.

I went out into the lobby and walked the crowded corridors to the land registry office. This time there was a lineup. I had to wait fifteen minutes before being served. As before, I showed the clerk my badge to save myself the customary search fee. I asked to look at the documents relating to the Nanaimo's nightclub property. The property was owned by someone called Penelope Grace Mainwaring. Well, well, I thought. Things were getting curiouser and curiouser.

CHAPTER FOURTEEN

D owntown Victoria's urban odours of hot oil and burnt rubber diminished as I drove north. Subdivisions and new streets flanked the Trans-Canada Highway until the Helmcken Road Hospital fell behind and I took the View Royal exit. After a couple of miles of country blacktop, I entered a green valley lying between the foothills. Another half a mile brought me to the long unpaved road that leads to Felicity Exeter's farm. I turned left, rattled across a cattle stop, followed twin wheel ruts across smoothly undulating pasture land dotted with grazing sheep till I parked the MG beneath trees near a barn.

I gave a start when I saw my face in the rear-view mirror. I was unshaven and my hair was standing on end. Thanks to last night's escapade, my eyes were red and there was an angry bruise along the line of my jaw. I got out of the car and leaned against it. Miniature potted cedars flanked the curving drive that wound up to Felicity's house. To the right there was a tennis court and a swimming pool. Music played above the sound of happy voices. The house's front door stood wide open.

Felicity came outside the house, shaded her eyes against the sun and peered towards me. Wearing a clingy, sheer low-neck black sweater, a short black velvet skirt, and high-heeled, pointy-toed boots over bare legs, she was worth looking at. I was burning to make love to her. When I came out of the trees and walked towards her, she stepped backwards a little. Her usual welcoming smile was absent.

Her face inanimate, she said without any particular warmth, "You've had a haircut."

"Yes, I have. Do you like it?"

"Not particularly, no. And I'm sorry, Silas, but I've got Wilderness Preservation Committee people here, and I'm sure you wouldn't find them very amusing." She switched an artificial smile on. "There's a woman in the kitchen will give you a drink if you ask her. Otherwise, darling, if you don't mind helping yourself, you know where the bottles are kept, don't you?"

She was turning away when I said, "Hold it a minute."

Felicity turned back. Hands on her hips she said, "Yes, master?"

"What's up? We haven't seen each other in ages and all you do is tell me to help myself to a drink?"

"Face it, sweetie. Drinks are more important to you than I am, sometimes."

We didn't kiss. She returned to the house. Wondering about the impression I had made on her, I went past the unpopulated swimming pool into Felicity's kitchen. I was pouring two inches of Bacardi rum into a cut-glass tumbler when my cellphone buzzed. It was Bernie Tapp. He said, "What are you doing right now?"

"Chasing sheep in a farmyard with the rich and famous. In a few minutes I'll be going to . . ."

"No, you won't, pal. You're going out to Wilkie Road prison. I'll be there waiting for you, so get cracking," Bernie said, hanging up before I could object.

A man swaggered into the kitchen carrying an empty glass. He was wearing a hacking jacket, a Hathaway shirt and cavalry twill trousers. He had the rugged good looks and assertive self-confidence that one associates with Second World War tank commanders and Arabian deserts.

He assumed that I was hired help. "Felicity's meetings are fun, but talking is thirsty work, so how about pouring me a drop of that Scotch?"

It was rum, but I didn't tell him that. After tasting the drink, and remarking on its funny taste, he went out without thanking me, but at least he didn't offer to give me a tip.

Felicity's voice reached me as I was crossing the field to my car. "Idiot," she said fondly. "Where do you think you're going now?"

"Bernie just called me, I can't stay."

"See me later?"

I grinned at her.

CHAPTER FIFTEEN

Wilkie Road prison looks like a Scottish castle. It is place where unpleasant things can happen to people in secret. An arched stone passageway as dismal as a catacomb led Bernie and me through cavernous halls lit by tiny barred windows. Additional crypt-like passageways branched off into darkness. Barred stairways descended to grim cellars. The prison, reeking of ammonia and mould, rang with hollow, distant-sounding voices. Bernie and I know our way around in there, but it's easy for first-time visitors to get lost. Somebody coughed. Peering up in the gloom, I saw a spiral staircase ascending to a sort of pulpit, behind which a turnkey's pale blurred features gazed down at us from a height.

Bernie's eyes had lost all their warmth. "We're here to interrogate Maria Alfred," he said.

Without a word, the turnkey pushed a buzzer. A male guard appeared promptly and conducted us to a cell. "We call her Tightlips," the guard declared officiously, unlocking the cell's heavy iron door. "Talking with her is a waste of time, you won't get nowhere with her."

Maria's own clothing had been taken away, and now she was wearing an orange prison-issue jumpsuit. She looked well scrubbed, and her cappuccino-coloured complexion was unblemished. The whites of her dark doelike eyes were clear. She had a pretty but not beautiful face and an air of being drugged. Her wrists were manacled to a belt around her waist. Her ankles were tethered together by a short chain. Stooped and subdued after her hours in solitary, with long black hair concealing most of her face, she looked like someone expecting a whipping. Her cell was a plain concrete windowless cube containing a stool, a lidless toilet, and a stainless steel sink. No bed. No mattress.

Bernie Tapp faced the guard and said with deceptive calm, "Who ordered these restraints to be put on?"

"Nobody, I put them on myself," the guard answered. "It's standard practice."

"Take them off."

"That's not my responsibility," the guard replied imperiously. "Chains are usual when violent prisoners are to be moved. You'll have to . . ."

"Who do you think you're talking to?" Bernie growled, as a look of fury appeared on his face. When the guard still hesitated, a grunting noise emerged from somewhere deep inside Bernie Tapp's heaving chest. The guard caved, undid the chains and let them drop to the floor. Raising her head, glancing timidly at Bernie and me for the first time, Maria absently massaged her wrists.

"All right," Bernie snarled, still angry, "let's go."

The four of us formed a little procession—the guard punching a number code into wall-mounted keypad security devices as we went along. The prisoner shuffled along behind him. Bernie and I came last. The interview room was another cell. Lit by three bare 100-watt light bulbs, it had a grey acoustic-tile ceiling and bare unpainted concrete-block walls. The cell contained a wooden table and three wooden chairs. A tape recorder was mounted on a shelf below a large mirror. The cell's ceiling-mounted CCTV camera looked like a sprinkler head.

Bernie asked the prisoner to sit down at the table. After some hesitation, she did so. Bernie and I sat opposite to her.

Bernie said, "Is your name Maria Alfred?"

She nodded without speaking, looking past Bernie instead of at him.

"You might remember us. I am Chief Inspector Tapp. The officer in here with us is Sergeant Seaweed. We're investigating a murder and we have a problem. We think you can help us to sort this problem out. We'd like some co-operation this time, Miss. You have Charter Rights, you don't have say anything. But what we want, Miss, is for you to answer some simple questions. For a start: Who are you, what's your name?"

As anticipated, a few hours in Wilkie Road had softened her up. "You already know my name."

"That's right. But we are recording this interview and we need you to state your name out loud."

"I want a lawyer," she said, her distrust palpable.

"Of course you do," Bernie answered cheerfully. "In the meantime, we just want to clear up a few little things: Your name, for starters. Little details about where you live, your age, your occupation."

"So when do I get this lawyer?"

"You'll get a lawyer soon enough. In the meantime, let's address the business at hand. Look, Miss. You may not wish to talk to us, and we understand that, only we want to talk to you. We like to communicate properly, clearly and at a simple level of understanding so people know exactly where we're coming from. You probably think we're trying to trick you in some way. Nothing could be further from the truth. Let me tell you something. We know a lot about you already. We know for instance that your name is Maria Alfred and that you are a waitress at the Ballard Diner. Your employer speaks very highly of you. He misses you very much. Your job is waiting for you when we get this mess sorted out. Okay?"

The suspect replied in Coast Salish.

Bernie looked at me.

I said, "Picture two kneeling men performing an act that, until Pierre Elliott Trudeau became prime minister, was contrary to the code of criminal justice."

"You want me to go and get screwed, is that what you want?" Bernie said, grinning across the table at her. "Believe me, Maria, I get screwed on a daily basis. Not actually, of course, just metaphorically. You are trying to screw with me now, but it's a bad idea, believe me."

She asked me what metaphorically meant.

"It's a way of describing things that are not literally true," I replied in English.

"I'll fuck you," she said to me in Coast Salish. "You're one of us, right? Tell me how I can get out of here, and I'll do whatever you want. I'll fuck you till blood comes out of your eyes."

I pursed my lips at the graphic mental image that Maria's words had conjured up. "The way to get out of here is to be sensible and answer the chief inspector's questions," I explained. "Tell the truth and don't try to be clever."

"What's she going on about now?" Bernie asked me.

"Nothing much. English is her first language, she knows what you're saying."

Bernie tucked his chin into his collar and stared at her through his bushy eyebrows. "A few days ago, Miss, you and another woman visited a house with a man called Raymond Cho, where you murdered him ..."

"Bullshit, that's a complete crock," Maria said.

Continuing as if he'd never been interrupted, Bernie said, "It's a private house on Echo Bay. We know that you were there, because we have pictures and because you left fresh fingerprints all over the place. We found them in the kitchen, in the vestibule and in the lounge. Fingerprints don't lie."

Maria stared down at the table.

Bernie gave her a few seconds to absorb that information. He went on, "Cho's body was taken to the Jubilee Hospital where it was autopsied. Samples of human tissue were found beneath Cho's fingernails. When you were strip-searched before your incarceration, Maria, deep unhealed scratches were noticed on your behind and on your lower back."

Maria thought for a minute and then said, "All right. Ronnie likes his girls on top. He was a bit rough, though. Got carried away I guess. He ripped my ass with his nails when I was riding him, but I didn't notice it at the time. He did the same thing to Ruthie."

Bernie had been looking half asleep during the previous few moments. The name *Ruthie* brought him wide awake.

He grinned satanically. "Yes, right. Maria. It's time for you to tell us a little more about Ruthie."

Maria's hand flew to her mouth—a habit with her when taken unawares. "Did I say *Ruthie?*" she said unconvincingly. "I don't know what I was thinking of. It was a whatchamacallit. A slip of the tongue."

"Baloney, you're not an infant and neither are we. Do yourself a favour. Tell us about your friend Ruthie."

"Not without speaking to a lawyer first."

Bernie sighed, because Maria proved adamant. He asked her many questions but, initially, he skirted around the details of the murder. Concealing from a suspect what is already known about a crime gives investigators an edge. After more of Maria's stonewalling, Bernie decided to jolt her a little. First, he leaned back until his chair was balanced on two legs. After gently rocking back and forth for a time, he said calmly, "Let me tell you something. When you and your girlfriend Ruthie arrived at Raymond Cho's house, he was alive. Now he's dead. Somebody first knocked him out with a club and then slit his throat."

"A nice guy like him, why would anybody want him killed? What for?"

"That's what we're here to find out. We don't care who used the club. It's nothing personal with us. What we generally do in cases where there are two prime suspects, is we go easy on whoever co-operates first and gives us useful information."

The corners of her mouth turned down. "Prime suspects? Who's a prime suspect?"

"You obviously are one. Your friend Ruthie is another."

"And you are peddling horseshit."

"You're a liar and an idiot," Bernie yelled suddenly, standing up and leaning across the table with his weight on his arms, a ferociously intimidating look on his face. "I've a good mind to throw you back in that cell and let you rot in the dark. Raymond Cho's dead. He was murdered and you, you little twerp, you did it."

"My God, my God, I can't believe this bullshit."

"Bullshit? Horseshit? I'm telling you the truth. Raymond Cho is dead. He was murdered. You and your friend are prime suspects. We found the slavekiller that you clubbed him with."

"Slavekiller? Clubbed?" Maria said, her lips trembling. "You're just trying to scare me, set me up."

After glowering at her for half a minute, Bernie sat down again. He said with deliberate slowness, "One of our suspects is going to use her brains. If she's got a lick of sense, she's going to tell us how and why Raymond Cho died. She'll co-operate with us, because we are willing to make a deal. The suspect we make the deal with will get every consideration. The one stupid enough to keep her trap shut will be charged with murder. It'll be an open-and-shut case. Do you understand what I'm getting at? The one who is stupid enough to be uncooperative with the police will be charged with murder. She'll be taken before a judge and jury, and she will be found guilty. Guilty of murder. She will spend 25 years in prison before she becomes eligible to apply for parole. The chances are that she will never get parole. She will die in jail. It'll probably be a place like this one. It won't be any fun at all, I can assure you. How do you think a jury's going to react when the prosecutor tells them that your blood and skin was found under Cho's fingernails? Do you think that a jury will believe that you got those scratches playing games? Are you a halfwit? That evidence is proof positive that you killed him during a struggle that ended in his death! So who's going to talk? You, or Ruthie?"

Maria's expression of baffled innocence faded, and she broke into tears. Bernie didn't let up. After another half-hour of unsuccessful threats lies, and formulaic interrogation tricks, Bernie turned to me and said, "Okay, it's your turn."

I pasted a neutral expression on my face and said softly, "Maria. Look at me, please."

Still shocked into speechlessness after Bernie's rough handling, she bowed her head and looked at the table instead.

I said, "Maria Alfred. We are policemen trying to find out exactly how and why a man ended up dead in a house on Collins Lane. It's in everybody's interest that the truth comes out. You need to listen carefully to what we say. Do you understand the danger that you're in?"

Tears squeezed between Maria's eyelids and slid slowly down her cheeks. Until that moment, she had struck me as being someone who, instead of dealing with life's ugly realities, preferred to shut her mind to them.

I felt sorry for her, but was careful not to let my feelings show. I said sternly, "We think you can tell us how Mr. Cho was murdered, and by whom. You were either acting alone or in concert with your friend, Ruthie. Pay attention Maria, for God's sake. You've been locked up for a bit already. You've had a little taste of what jail can be like for a woman. Think of what you'll be giving up if you persist in this foolishness. You'll never get married, have children or put a pretty dress on. You'll never go out dancing with boys. It doesn't have to be that way," I continued, as tears ran unimpeded down her face and dripped onto the table. "You can either go to jail or you can go back home. Marry a nice man and live a normal life. It's your decision."

"I don't know nothing about no murder, honest."

"You must know something. All of the evidence points that way."

"It was my friend must have done it, Ruth's the one you want," Maria sobbed. "We were just having fun. I didn't do nothing to hurt nobody."

"Ruth who?"

"Ruth Claypole."

"Good girl," Bernie said. "That's the spirit, now you are using your head. Just tell us what happened in your own words."

"Screw you!" Maria screamed, her eyes burning with hatred. "Get the hell outta here, I won't say another word with you in the room, you shit-eating bastard."

Shaking his head, Bernie said in a kindlier tone, "Forget it, Maria. It's my job to be here."

As if alone with me, whispering, Maria said, "The three of us was just partying, fooling around. I only went along for the ride."

"What is your relationship with Ruthie?"

"We went to school together," Maria said reluctantly. "We been best friends all our lives. She must have killed him."

"Did you and Ruth Claypole grow up on Quanterelle Island?"

"That's for me to know and you to find out."

"Finding out shouldn't be too difficult. Did you see your friend kill Mr. Cho?"

"No!" Maria replied furiously. "We was all in the lounge room of Ronnie's house, having drinks. It was a living room sort of, but that's what Ronnie called it, a lounge room. We was all three of us pretty loaded. Ronnie had big stash of reefers. We smoked a couple. He offered us blow, but my friend and me have seen too many people get burned. We don't touch nothing except the odd reefer and especially not blow. I must have been pretty drunk to do the things I done in them dirty pictures. Jesus. Then I left Ruth and Raymond to it and I went upstairs and back to the lounge room. You know what Raymond and my friend were doing in his bed. I don't have to tell you what it was they was doing. I was left on my own for a while, so I looked around the house for a bit. Later on I walked along the beach to try and clear my head. I'd had a little too much to drink and that. When I got back from my walk, Ruth was taking a shower. I figured Raymond was having a snooze. Raymond had told Ruth that he wanted to screw us both again, a threesome, I don't know where he got the energy. Cialis I think, maybe rhinoceros horns, who the hell knows what them guys take. Jesus. But we decided to clear out before he woke up. We found the keys for his Beemer and tried to start it, only it wouldn't go. It had some kind of anti-theft gadget. We didn't know how it worked. We couldn't figure it out. There was no phone in the house either, to call for a taxi, so we was forced to walk."

Bernie had been sitting motionless, studying her. He said brusquely, "How long have you been acquainted with Ronnie Chew alias Raymond Cho?"

Rage came into her eyes. "Fuck off! You can fuck right off!" she screamed. "I ain't fucking talking to you."

I gave her a few moments to calm herself. "Please answer CDI Tapp's question."

Panting with rage, she said, "What question was that again?"

"How long have you known Ronnie?"

"Ronnie? We didn't know him at all, we just ran into him in a club."

"What's the name of this club?"

"Nanaimo's."

"Excellent, you're doing well. So, you met him in Nanaimo's?"

Maria nodded. "It was a Saturday night. Me and my friend we were in this club. Me and my girlfriend Ruth. It was full of Japs, Chinks and ragheads. All of them drunk and throwing money around. We didn't know nobody there till this guy Ronnie, he invites us to sit at his table and have a drink with him. We didn't argue. He ordered a bottle of fancy red wine for us. We'd hardly had a taste of it before trouble starts. Ronnie was drinking brandy shooters and he was half pissed. Everybody had been having a ball. Singing and dancing and that. Next thing a fight starts. Guys are losing it and going crazy. Glass is breaking. People are screaming and hiding under tables. I ran for the door, everybody's panicking and screaming. In the rush, me and Ruth got separated. I guess the next thing I remember I'm outside on the street trying to flag down a taxi, because cops is showing up already. Then, before I could bag a taxi, Ruth shows up along with Ronnie. His car is parked down there somewhere. He had a nice car, a Beemer; he took us to his car. We got in and he took off like a goddamn jackrabbit. Ronnie was so scared, he was trembling. He said guys was out to kill him. He was a target he said. At the time, I thought he was just, you know, pretending. Showing off like, trying to make us think he was a big shot. We didn't care.

"Ronnie acted like he had money. He invited us to go with him to a party. He'd been half-drunk before, but now he was sober and he was scared. Shit-scared. He kept telling us that guys was out to get him, but I swear we thought he was bulling us. A party sounded okay though. Next thing we know, we're in the Beemer on the road. We went along for the ride. Ronnie calmed down a bit, but he asked us not to leave him on his own. He needed company, he said. He said he'd give us presents if we kept him company because he was rich, loaded. So we stayed with him.

"When we got to Ronnie's house, we found out it wasn't going to be no real party. Just the three of us in this house. I never seen nothing like it in my life. It was a palace, not a house." Maria's voice trailed away.

"You're doing fine, Maria. Keep talking, tell us what went down."

"No goddamn way. I've said enough."

"You'll have to tell us sometime," I persisted. "They'll keep you locked up until you do."

"I won't tell you nothing."

"Where is Ruth?"

"I won't tell you nothing about her! Ask her yourself. You won't get no help from me."

"You and Ruth have been friends for a long time?"

"All our lives. We went to school together."

"Which school would that be?"

After thinking the question over, Maria said reluctantly, "That'd be Surge Narrows School."

"That's better," I said. "Use your head, Maria, and come clean about the rest of it. Basically, we think you're a nice girl. We know you didn't kill Cho out of pure maliciousness. You had the means and the opportunity, but what was your motive for killing him? *Why* did you do it? Did somebody tell you to do it? If so, tell us who this person is. Tell us now, it'll be very much to your advantage when you're taken before a judge and jury. So to repeat. Why? Tell us *why* you killed Ronnie Chew, alias Raymond Cho?"

"What are you talking about? I'm telling you. I told you already. I don't know nothing about no killing."

"You told me that three people were in the house. You, Ruth Claypole, and Mr. Cho. Do you seriously expect us to believe that you didn't know that Mr. Cho had been murdered?"

"I don't know nothing about it. The last time I seen him he was alive, for chrissakes!"

Bernie stepped in and said in a soothing voice, "That's all right, take it easy. You've been very good. It's just . . . Try to see it from our point of view. There are three people in a house. A person dies and one of the people with him pretends she knows nothing about it?"

"I never saw Ronnie dead. I keep telling you, he was alive the last I seen him."

Bernie said, "Maria. You say that there were just three of you in the house that night?"

She nodded.

"I want you to cast your memory back to the time Raymond Cho was killed."

Maria's face fell. "What are you talking about? How many times before you bastards will understand I don't know nothing about nobody being killed."

Upset and apparently confused, Maria burst into sobs. I resisted a strong temptation to pat her shoulders and speak comforting words. Even Bernie seemed affected.

"Just a couple of things more," Bernie said in a kindlier voice. "Take it easy, Miss, we'll soon be done . . ."

"Goddamn, you're trying to make me say things that aren't right and put words in my mouth," she cried. "I ain't saying no more till that lawyer gets here."

"Tell us why you ran away from the house, first," Bernie said patiently.

Shaking her head, staring down at the table, she said in a low voice. "We took a few things as souvenirs. Ronnie said he'd give us presents. Me and Ruthie ain't hookers, but we thought we'd earned 'em. I took a ring and a pearl necklace."

"Then you murdered him," Bernie said flatly.

Maria leapt to her feet. "Bastards," she cried. "Bunch of lying cheating pigs. I'm not saying nothing no more, that's final."

Bernie switched the tape recorder off. By then I'd modified my opinion of Maria. She could have ratted on her friend and waltzed, which counted for something.

When we left the interrogation room, the guard was waiting for us.

He led Maria through a barred gateway and locked it. Smirking, speaking from behind the safety of the bars, he said, "I told you. Didn't I tell you guys that you wouldn't get nothing out of her?"

That set Bernie off again. Dangerously unbalanced when his hair-trigger temper is aroused, his face the colour of a beetroot, he reached for the gate and shook it.

I said, "For Christ's sake, Bernie, get a grip of yourself." Bernie stiffened, but he didn't say anything. By the time we left the jail, he was his jovial self.

We had gone to the jail separately. Bernie followed me back to my cabin in his Interceptor. I brought a bottle out and we had a few drinks, talked things over.

"Maria's no killer, her friend did it," Bernie said "This is nice Scotch. Is it single malt?"

"It's Chivas Regal. I don't think either of them did it."

"Listen to me, Silas. If I find a dead guy with puncture wounds to his neck, I look for a fucking vampire. If I find a guy with his throat cut, in a room where a little while earlier he'd been playing hard-core sex games with a couple of girls, I concentrate on the girls. It's complicated I admit. We don't have all the answers, but we have some of the answers. To add to our existing headaches, the stains on that slavekiller weren't blood. They were some kind of chemical, Forensics haven't identified them yet."

I smiled indulgently.

"I suppose, being Indian and all, you can afford these fancy brands because they're duty free," Bernie said, shoving his empty glass across for a refill.

"And not only booze. If I flash my status card I can load up on duty-free gas, groceries. Duty-free cigarettes are so cheap I'm thinking of taking up smoking again," I crowed, filling his glass up. My smile fading, I said, "I saw people pushing drugs openly in Centennial Square a couple of days ago."

"Yeah, we know about it. Rope a dope. The only thing we don't yet know is where they're getting product. We think Gonzales is their supplier and one of these days we'll find out for sure."

I nodded.

"There's been a development," Bernie said. "Vancouver told us more about Raymond Cho. Their story is that two months ago, Raymond stole two million dollars cash from his own mob."

I DON'T KNOW what time it was when I stripped down, cleaned myself up at the kitchen sink and put on fresh clothes, but it was probably two in the morning, perhaps a little later, when I got to Felicity's house. The lights were all on; the front door wasn't locked. Somebody had done a good job of cleaning the house though—there was no remaining evidence of last night's party.

Felicity was alone, lovely, asleep. Flaked out on a couch in the lounge. I was close enough to her to smell the subtle perfume she was wearing. Longing built up inside me like an electrical charge, but I didn't want to wake her so I went into the kitchen, found a half bottle of Pinot Grigio, poured an inch into a glass and drank it. When I went back to the lounge, Felicity wasn't there. She was in bed.

"Hello, Silas," she said, the barest suggestion of tremor in her voice. "Kiss me, Silas."

I took my clothes off and got in beside her.

CHAPTER SIXTEEN

Victoria's residential and commercial belt has been expanding rapidly in recent years. After a few twists and turns, I was happy to leave Douglas Street's heavy traffic behind and turn onto Burnside Road. More miles of quiet farms and woodsy calm brought me to Jinglepot Road. Scarcely better than a lane, the Jinglepot winds up over a slope in the foothills and along a ridge. It was five degrees hotter up there than downtown. The air smelt faintly of burning sage. The place I wanted was a modest pre-war bungalow. Screened from the road by tall poplars, it had blistered paint and curling asphalt roof shingles. Off to the right, half-overgrown by blackberry bushes, was a low concrete building that looked like a military gun emplacement. The bungalow's unkempt lawn was dotted with cedar lounging chairs, kids' tricycles, a baby buggy and several multicoloured balls. I left my car at the side of the road.

Afternoon sunlight streaming through the poplar trees created moving patterns on the cracked cement pathway leading up to the bungalow's front door. I pasted a Fuller Brush man's smile on my face and knocked. After a long interval a middle-aged woman wearing a headscarf and paint-spattered overalls opened the door.

Looking a trifle flustered, she said, "Are you here about the room?"

I flashed my police badge. "Good morning, ma'am. No, I'm not here about the room. I am Sergeant Seaweed, Victoria PD. I'm here about Maria Alfred."

"Maria," the woman said, her tentative smile fading. "She's my tenant. I haven't seen her for a few days."

"And you are?"

"Jenny Victor."

Before I could get a word in edgewise, she went on with growing indignation, "The thing is, we need Maria's rent money to make our mortgage work, and she's in arrears. My husband and I bought this house six months ago. It's a bit of a wreck, and we're renovating. But it's hard, you know, because he has a full-time job in town and the way the price of building materials keeps going up ... We think Maria's taken off without paying us what she owes."

"When's the last time you saw her?"

"Oh I don't know," she said unhappily. "Last week I guess."

"If you don't mind, I'd like to take a look at her room."

"Well, I suppose ..." Mrs. Victor was saying when we heard a slight thudding noise followed immediately by a child's wails.

Throwing up her arms in consternation, Mrs. Victor retreated indoors. I followed her along a hallway into a kitchen at the back. A cute two-year-old with a mane of blonde curls and a rosebud mouth had fallen off a chair while trying to climb onto a table. Mrs. Victor swung the sobbing infant into her arms and began to walk up and down, patting the infant's back and making shushing noises.

Mrs. Victor seemed physically inert. Worn out at 40-something. She seemed slightly too old to be the child's mother. When she remembered my existence, Mrs. Victor pointed to a door that opened off the kitchen and said, "Maria's room is down there."

I went down a steep flight of steps into a dingy low-headroom base-ment with exposed ceiling joists and wall studs. Half-stooped to save my head from injury, I groped around in semi-darkness until I found another door, opened it, located a light switch, and turned it on. Nothing happened until, after more blind groping, I located a lamp set on a low bedside table. It lit up when I turned it on. Floorboards creaked above, where Mrs. Victor was pacing back and forth.

Maria Alfred's rented room was only about twelve feet square. It was evidently a recent addition to the house. The room's gyproc ceiling and walls were a bilious shade of yellow; the linoleum floor was bumpy. The furniture consisted of a single bed covered with a white candlestick bed-spread, a single bamboo chair with a yellow cushion, a chest of drawers and a circular picnic table with a matching plastic garden chair. A cheap wooden desk placed beneath a wall-mounted mirror doubled as a dressing table. A folding Chinese screen concealed a built-in closet empty except for wire coat hangers. The drawers had been cleaned out. A metal waste-basket contained nothing except discarded tissues. The room was clean, and the floor appeared to have been recently waxed. After thinking, I removed the drawers from the desk. When I did so, a photograph that had been wedged behind one of the drawers fluttered to the ground. It showed a group of twelve girls standing outside a country schoolhouse. I turned the photograph over. Girls' names were written on it in immature pencil lettering. One of the girls was Maria Alfred. Ruth Claypole was another.

I put the photograph in my shirt pocket and went back upstairs. A well-tended vegetable patch that would have gladdened any gardener's heart bloomed nicely in the backyard. There was no sign of the infant. Mrs. Victor was filling a bucket at the kitchen sink. She squirted some liquid detergent into the bucket, and then turned towards me, folded her arms and leaned back against a counter.

"Satisfied?" she said, with a kind of resigned fatalism. "Find what you wanted?"

I handed her the photograph. "I found this in the desk. Recognize anyone?"

Without hesitation, she pointed to Maria and said, "That's her."

"Recognize anyone else?"

After a long look, Mrs. Victor shook her head.

I said, "Maria has done a runner, obviously."

"Of course she has. Now we're faced with the expense and trouble of advertising and interviewing tenants all over again. Maria was only with us two months. It's pathetic. You try to do the right thing, and this is all the thanks you get."

"When Maria moved in, I suppose you got her to sign a rental agreement?"

"Well, no," Mrs. Victor replied with awkward self-consciousness. "I guess we never got around to it."

"You didn't check with Maria's previous landlord, ask to see references?"

"Well, no," she said reticently. "Not that I remember. We took Maria on trust. She seemed all right to us."

"So you don't know where she came from, where she lived before?"

"We never talked much, come to think of it, because we didn't have much in common. I have an idea she came from one of the islands up Desolation Sound way. Maybe Quanterelle Island. That's about all I can tell you."

Steam rose from an electric kettle. When the kettle clicked off automatically, Mrs. Victor turned towards it. Speaking with her back to me, she said in a nervous voice, "I'm making myself a cup of instant. Excuse me if I don't offer you one, but I'm a bit rushed. If there's nothing more, I'd like you to leave now."

I leaned back against the table, put my hands in my pockets, and said rather sternly, "Maria's room has been stripped. Am I supposed to believe that she came in here while you were out of the house and took her things away?"

"Yes," Mrs. Victor replied reluctantly. When she turned to face me again, her glance slid away and her cheeks reddened.

I waited. Mrs. Victor's shoulders slumped, and she covered her face. "We were keeping Maria's stuff in lieu of rent," she began to say, and then she started to cry. Tears squeezed between her eyelashes. "It's so hard, you don't understand. Everything's going wrong. The house, my husband's job. I'm sorry."

Feeling like an asshole, I said roughly, "Show me where you put Maria's stuff."

Stooping, her arms folded across her narrow chest, she led me to a backyard shed and flung the door open. Maria Alfred's possessions had been stuffed into two large orange garbage bags and were lying against a wall along with miscellaneous garden tools.

Without saying anything, I picked the bags up and put them in my car. I felt miserable; even the sky was clouding over. When I got behind the driving wheel, I glanced at the house. Mrs. Victor was watching from a window.

Cops know that people lie all the time. You get to expect it from everyone—not just villains and psychopaths, but from people who go to church on Sundays. Lying to cops is standard practice.

I went back to the house and knocked. Mrs. Victor opened the door about six inches, enough to show me her nose and eyes, red from weeping.

I hardened my heart and said sternly, "You're sure that I've got everything?"

"Everything. You've got everything. I swear, we weren't going to steal it."

"Thanks, and good luck with renting your room. Next time, I advise you to get your tenant to sign a rental agreement. Standard forms are available free from the rentals branch office on Wharf Street. Check people's references too, and make sure the first month's cheque doesn't bounce before the tenant moves in. If everybody was honest, Mrs. Victor, my job would be superfluous."

Sometimes, I really hate being a cop.

It was raining by the time I got back downtown.

CHAPTER SEVENTEEN

The desk phone was ringing when I slung the orange plastic garbage bags into the corner of my office. Taking my time about it, I then picked up the mail littering the floor beneath my letter slot and put it on the desk. When I opened the window blinds and looked out, it was still raining. The mail was mostly junk. I wasn't ready to start poking through the garbage bags just then. To deflect my thoughts, I cracked the office bottle and poured myself a drink. Felicity thinks I drink way too much, and she's probably right.

PC emerged noiselessly from behind the filing cabinet. After stretching and yawning, she assumed a sphinx-like pose, looked towards me and meowed. PC has me properly trained. As she required, I quickly finished my drink, took my glass and PC's stainless steel water bowl out to my private washroom, rinsed them both, filled the bowl with fresh clean water, put it back where it was supposed to be, and then I opened a can of Thrifty's white tuna and dumped the contents into PC's stainless steel food bowl.

PC was having dinner, and I was building an origami beetle out of multicoloured junk mail when the phone rang again. I picked it up. A familiar voice said, "Silas? Silas Seaweed?"

It was one of the neighbourhood crazies. "Yes, Fran," I said politely. "This is Silas."

"Do you know where Bowker Creek goes under the road at St. Ann's?"

"Ye-es."

"Oh, I am pleased," Fran said. "We're having a get-together under the big willow tree. There'll be hot dogs and coffee. June 14th, two o'clock. Mark it on your calendar."

"Sorry, Fran. Today's the 15th of August."

"Oh dear, are you quite sure?" Fran said, putting down the phone.

PC had gone out. I poured myself another drink, put on a pair of rubber gloves, and then briefly inspected the contents of the garbage bags. It was mostly clothing. I didn't see any documents or personal information. So much for that.

I stood by the window and looked down Pandora Street towards the abandoned Janion Building, seeing its boarded-up windows and bird-shit-spattered facade. It was raining harder than ever by then and a bit early for the evening stroll, but a wizened forty-year-old floozy wearing a blonde wig was already tottering back and forth in a tatty white blouse, fishnet stockings and leather skirt. Then the door opened. Cynthia Leach strolled in. I admired her porcelain skin and lovely blue eyes as she took her cap off and put it on my hat tree. Posed entrancingly, she tossed her head back and ran her fingers through her short blonde curls.

"Nice Manners wants you," Cynthia said, hitching a fully loaded equipment belt up her shapely waist.

"I know, I've got call display."

"You don't like him very much, do you Silas?"

"Do you?"

"I like him more than you do, obviously. He's not bad-looking, either."

Feeling a slight pang of some emotion that, if I'd been fifteen years old, I might have diagnosed as jealousy, I said, "It's not Manners that I hate, exactly, it's his type. He's the kind of guy who wakes up every morning and pastes this certain expression on his face. The one that says 'I'm big and great and I'm important. You are a piece of shit.'"

Cynthia gave an indifferent shrug. "Have you heard the latest?" she asked, carelessly resting one shapely buttock on the corner of my desk. "City council is thinking of stopping drivers from renewing driving licences until their parking tickets are paid."

"I know that too. The army of Right is on the march, the forces of Evil are in full retreat."

"There are a couple of garbage bags in the corner."

"Yes, I know."

"Do you know everything?"

"I know that a ghost moved into this building recently."

"My God," she said, staring at me. "I've just noticed. What's happened to you?"

"Haven't you been paying attention?"

"You look different."

"Every day and in every way I'm getting worse and worse. Somebody tried to roast me alive the other night."

Realization dawned in her eyes. "You were in Nanaimo's when it was firebombed?"

"Right."

"But you look ... your face seems thinner for one thing. Are you losing weight?"

I shook my head.

Cynthia gave me a long, penetrating look.

Flushing noises emanated from my private washroom. With Cynthia at my heels, I ran from the office, tore down the hall and unlocked the washroom door. It was unoccupied, although water from the last flush was still swirling in the toilet bowl.

"Will you please explain what's going on?" Cynthia asked.

"Search me. All I know is, there's no possible way that a human being could have flushed that toilet and escaped down this corridor without being seen. This isn't the first time it's happened."

Cynthia sniffed. "Lucky you didn't find a woman in there, or you'd be in big trouble."

Footsteps sounded as Nobby Sumner, the building superintendent, came downstairs from his roof garden, lugging a desiccated potted ficus. I asked him if he'd noticed anybody near my washroom. Nobby shook his head.

Cynthia followed me back to the office. Cynthia was going on and on about male insecurity and rights-invasion when she reached into the junk mail still remaining on my desk.

"What's this?" she said, bringing out a large, cream-coloured envelope. She held it to her nose, sniffed and said, "Hmmmmm. Expensive. It's patchouli, I think."

"Let me guess. It's a property developer looking for investors."

"Let's find out," Cynthia said bossily, ripping open the envelope and drawing out a deckle-edged card.

Her jaw dropped open. "It's from P.G. Mainwaring," she murmured in reverential tones.

"P.G. Mainwaring?" I said, grabbing the card.

Printed on it were the words in copperplate: P.G. Mainwaring invites your attendance at the Mainwaring Memorial Lecture, 7:30 PM, August 14, Empress Hotel. RSVP.

"August 14th. Pity, that was yesterday. I didn't know you moved in such exalted circles," Cynthia opined enviously. "How does a deadbeat like you happen to know the likes of P.G. Mainwaring?"

"P.G. Mainwaring?" I said guardedly. "I've never even heard of him."

"Idiot! Men don't drench letters in patchouli. P.G. isn't a guy. They say she owns a thousand apartment buildings."

"Who says?"

"Everybody. You'd know that yourself if you read the business section occasionally, instead of the funny pages."

Cynthia and I were cheek to cheek, looking at the card together, when the door banged open and Lightning Bradley marched in. "You two look very cosy," he said with a knowing smirk.

Lightning looked thinner than before, haggard. He threw the burning stub of the cigarette he was smoking into the cold fireplace and added with a suggestive leer, "Am I interrupting something?"

Cynthia groaned, stood up and put her cap on at a jaunty angle.

I said, "Are you driving, Cynthia?"

"Yes, why?"

"Would you mind dropping those two garbage bags off at Serious Crimes?"

"About your washroom," she said quite seriously. "Technically, you may be dealing with a poltergeist. Ordinary ghosts don't possess physical attributes. That's why they walk through doors instead of opening them. Ghosts certainly can't flush toilets."

Well, she was wrong there. When they want to, Coast Salish ghosts can do many strange things.

Cynthia said, "After you get rid of Ugly, Silas, just lock yourself in, close the blinds, take a couple of Aspirins, and have a long nap."

"You don't get it," I said.

"Damn right I don't," Cynthia said. Her expression changed. She said animatedly, "My God! I just noticed. You've had a haircut!"

"Twenty bucks at Alfredo's."

"You wuz robbed." Cynthia blew me a kiss, picked the orange sacks up and carted them off without saying a word to Lightning. Looking through my window, I watched her lug the sacks across the street and into the back of a blue and white Ford. A puff of black smoke escaped its exhaust pipe as she revved the car's big V8. Cynthia glanced over, saw me looking, and made a funny face. I watched her drive past Swans Hotel, turn right onto Store Street, and go from sight.

Lightning threw himself into a chair and was reaching inside his tunic for another cigarette when he noticed my frown.

I said unsympathetically, "You are under arrest."

"What for?"

"Conduct unbefitting. Suspicion of murder. There's a BOLO out on you, for God's sake."

"Serious Crimes sends Be On the Look Out notices for jaywalkers, so who gives a damn?" Putting both hands into his pockets, Lightning added, "What am I, a goddamn pharaoh?"

"I think the word you want is pariah," I said. "There's nothing going on between Cynthia and me, and you must know it. Why do you talk like that?"

"Talk like what?"

"Try to stir things up. All you do is make a fool of yourself. You're about as funny as a burning orphanage."

"Oh Christ, don't you start. I thought you liked me." After checking his Timex, Lightning added, "What's the holdup? Are you still on duty?"

I locked the door, closed the blinds, brought out the office bottle and two Tim Hortons mugs, poured an inch of Teachers into each and shoved one across the desk. Lightning drank his in one gulp. I poured him another and said, "Okay, start talking. You have a lot of explaining to do."

"I thought you were finished for the day."

"I won't squeal if you don't."

"I guess you've learned to roll with the punches, Silas," he snapped. "I never have."

He'd lost me. "What are you talking about?"

Lightning had become defiantly angry—maybe it was the Teachers. "I'm talking about guys jerking your chains just because you're an Indian or making fun of me just because I'm a fifty-year-old constable," he snarled. "Seems like I joined just yesterday, but it's nearly thirty years since I started pounding the pavement. Bootlickers with twenty years' less seniority than me are wearing sergeant's stripes. Oatmeal Savage kissed ass and polished brass right up the food chain to chief inspector. Where the hell did I go wrong?"

I could have told him.

We sat in the room's semi-darkness, occupied with our different thoughts. I was wondering how to broach the topic of Maggie's grisly death when Lightning said, "When I get this mess sorted out' I'm retiring. Take my pension. Move to Arizona and live in one of them trailer parks."

"You can't. You're talking about a career, not a merry-go-round. People don't just . . ."

Lightning interrupted. "Why not? Think anybody'll miss me? I've been planning this on the quiet. When I go, there won't be no tears shed for Lightning Bradley. The whole department will be glad to see the back of me. I used to go fishing with Bernie Tapp. Now, he won't even give me the time of day. As for Oatmeal Savage and Superintendent Mallory, they hate me too."

He was suffering, but what he said was true. Lightning had few if any friends, and no close ones that I was aware of. "Oatmeal" Savage, who ran the uniform branch, hated Lightning with a burning passion. I wondered why Lightning had chosen to let his hair down with me.

"Don't be a jackass," I said.

"I mean well, but sometimes I rub people the wrong way. Like just now with Cynthia. It was just a lousy joke, Silas. I screw up all the time, and not only on the job."

His smile was a stiff grimace, because a genuine smile is hard to fake.

This time when Bradley reached absently for a cigarette, I didn't stop him. He lit the cigarette, blew smoke out the side of his mouth, and said quietly, "Something happened. I should have told you and Bernie Tapp about it when you and him showed up at Collins Lane. But Bernie treated me like I was dirt underneath his boots. Made me look stupid in front of

Mrs. Milton. I was so pissed off I kept my trap shut. That's days ago, and if I tell Bernie what I know now, after all this time, he'll go ballistic. I just don't need it, Silas. I've got all the problems that I can handle right now."

"Talking to me is the same as talking to Bernie. If you tell me something that I think he should know . . ."

"Screw that! This is off the record, strictly between you and me. Maybe it'll help to break the Cho case. I know you're working on it. But it's strictly private, and maybe I'm making a mountain out of a molehill. Maybe what I saw isn't important after all."

"Let me be the judge of that."

"I want your word, Silas. If I tell you, I want your word that you'll keep it under wraps while you do some snooping on your own. If what I tell you helps to crack the Cho murder case, all well and good. Nobody needs to know you got the tip from me. If it doesn't help the case, no harm has been done."

"Are you serious about quitting your job?"

"Dead serious," he said, tapping a bulge on his inside breast pocket. "The papers are all filled out, and when I leave here I'm gonna stuff 'em in the mail. This time next month, I'll be on a plane heading south with the snowbirds."

I thought, *No you won't*, but what I said was, "What about Maggie?"

"She's dead and gone, there's nothing I can do about it. It's a relief in a way."

"Do you know how she died?"

"I only know what I read in the paper," he said incuriously. "I haven't been home for days."

Lightning exhibited an eerie calm. He seemed totally uninterested in the reality of Maggie's death. It was as if some important aspect of his normal psychological makeup was missing, or had been amputated. God only knows what strange beasts roamed his psyche.

I was silently brooding when Lightning said, "Look at it this way. This visit to your office is the same as an anonymous call."

"You're not anonymous, I know who you are. You want me to lie for you? I'd be in the soup too."

"It wouldn't be the first time, would it Silas?"

I shrugged. Telling convincing lies, dealing with liars and interpreting the truth behind other peoples' lies is a big part of my job, that's just the way it is. Some of my scruples go missing occasionally too along the policeman's highway.

"Here goes. I'm relying on you to do the right thing, Silas," Lightning said in a rush of words. "Last Sunday I'm in a patrol car with that punk, Ricketts. We've been told to keep a lookout for a couple of Native girls. I spotted 'em on Echo Bay Road, and Ricketts stopped the car. The girls start running. Ricketts is younger'n me, so he took off after 'em. I followed, but I'm too out of shape for chasing people through the boonies, so I went back to the car. Then I get a call from Ricketts. He says there's been a murder at the waterfront house. I'm heading over there. With the trees and all, there's dark shade along Collins Lane. I came around a bend and collided with another car. The other guy was speeding, and he went off the road into the trees. It's a miracle he didn't get killed. I stopped my car, and then I backed up to make sure he was okay. He was alive, but he was out cold. I didn't see no blood, I just figured he was shook up. I figured he'd come to, snap out of it. Instead of staying with him and reporting the incident, I panicked. I drove away, I left him to it. I guess it worked out okay, because I know that the guy did come to, and he managed to drive himself off."

"How do you know that?"

"Okay, I don't know for certain. But it's a fair assumption, because when Wondertits Leach drove me home later on, the car was already gone."

"What kind of a car was it?"

Lightning was a thousand miles away. He pulled himself back and said, "What?"

"The car you ran into. What make was it?"

"Oh yeah," Lightning sighed. "It was either a Lexus or it was a Mercedes. Late model, black."

"Okay, you had an accident en route to the murder house, but there are still bits missing from your story."

"What bits? What are you talking about?"

I remained silent. I thought it better to conceal police knowledge that cocaine had been found in Lightning's blue-and-white, and in his house. That Lightning's latent prints had been lifted from the inside of Cho's BMW.

I said, "Let's talk about Maggie."

"I'm sorry she's dead, but it's been over between me and Maggie for years. We weren't even friends anymore. We didn't even talk politely to each other," Lightning said sombrely. "That's it, it's all I've got to say. Thanks for the drink, Silas. You're a White man inside."

"There's more. You can't go yet."

"I've said all I'm going to say."

"In that case, I have to take you in."

Lightning shrugged, shook his head, and reached inside his jacket. I thought he'd bring out his cigarettes again. But Lightning was wearing a shoulder holster, and he brought out a 9mm Glock instead.

He winked with an effort that tilted his mouth and said, "Don't think I won't use it, Silas. My back is against the wall. If you try anything, I'll shoot." He conjured up a thin smile. "But I know you won't shoot *me*. We've known each other too long. No way you'll shoot me, so there's no sense pushing it." Lightning stood up. "In case it's bothering you, I'm not running away. I'll be back. Next time though, I'll bring my lawyer."

Lightning went out. I didn't try to stop him. Moments later, I heard footsteps in the corridor outside. Lightning was already back. With one hand holding the doorknob, he poked his head inside. A ribald grin on his face, he said, "You and Cynthia have got something going, Silas, right? Now there's a nice piece of ass."

I should have wrestled Lightning to the ground, stomped his lights out just on general principles, and then dragged him across to headquarters in handcuffs, but he still had the Glock in his hand, and besides, my brain felt tired.

I reached for the bottle to pour myself another drink but it was only a procrastinating reflex. I didn't need another drink. I needed to drive out to Collins Lane and do some snooping, except it was pouring down outside and I'd left my raincoat in the car.

Rain clouds covered the entire sky. People hurried past with their heads down, water streamed off their umbrellas. My head and shoulders were soaked by the time I got into the MG.

About halfway along Collins Lane, I reached a point on the road where a sharp bend coincided with a sudden incline. For a moment, my view of approaching traffic was partially obscured, and I took my foot off the accelerator. I kept going for another hundred yards. Then I parked in a pullout beneath the dripping trees. The bush in that location was dense and nearly impenetrable to everything except small animals and birds. I put my raincoat on, and hiked back to the bend in the road. Within five minutes, I found small pieces of shattered white plastic and white-enamelled metal lying scattered along the soft shoulder. This, it seemed likely, was the place where Lightning Bradley's Crown Royal had collided with a supposedly black Mercedes. After putting a few items in an evidence bag and storing them in the MG, I grabbed a shovel and poked along the road until I reached a footpath that led into the bush.

Indian kids learn early in life that what's important lies off the trail. Things such as berries, edible roots, a bird's nest, poison plants, dye plants. You have to get off the trail if you're a vision quester on a religious journey. Plenty of rain had fallen by then, and moisture was penetrating the overhead canopy. The damp ground was littered with fallen rotting trees covered with moss and freshly sprouted mushrooms, some but not all of which were safe to eat. It was very dark in places. Maria Alfred could have remained safely hidden in these woods for weeks, except for Nicky Nattrass and his tracker dogs.

It took me many minutes to reach the petroglyph site. The skeletal figure and the wolf were already obscured by more leaves, dirt and other debris, but this time I didn't brush them clean because I was more interested in finding out whether there was a cave nearby. Using the shovel, I dug around until I found a narrow cavelike opening. I crawled into an ancient, irregularly shaped sandstone tunnel, perhaps fifteen feet long and about a metre in diameter at its widest. The walls were daubed in red and black pictographs—human and animal figures made long ago by an artist who had used red ochre and carbon pigments instead of store-bought paints. A mummified male corpse lay on the dry earth. I knew he'd been buried alive, because if he'd been buried after death, he would have been interred in a box with his knees pulled up tight beneath his chin.

I'd seen enough, and crawled back out.

Back in my car, I phoned Bernie Tapp. I said, "Now we know how that Crown Royal ended up with a twisted frame."

"Oh yeah?"

"Remember when Constable Ricketts found Mrs. Milton hysterical on the beach, Lightning was sitting in his Crown Royal on Echo Bay Road?"

"Of course I remember."

"This is what appears to have happened. Ricketts called Lightning and told him about the dead man. When Bradley was driving to join Ricketts at the house, he was involved in an accident on Collins Drive. The other car was a late-model convertible, possibly a Lexus or a Mercedes. Lightning didn't report the accident because he panicked. It was a hit and run."

"How do you know all this?"

"Lightning told me all about it a few hours ago."

"He phoned?" Bernie asked me incredulously.

"No, he dropped by my office. Right now I'm on Collins Lane. I found a bunch of white plastic and metal lying beside the road. Smashed automobile parts, the remains of an accident. It shouldn't take us long to confirm what kind of a vehicle they came from."

"Okay. Now I want to talk to Lightning. Put him on the blower."

"I can't; Lightning is not here. I don't know where he is."

Bernie sighed. I could imagine him, tearing his hair. He said angrily, "Let me get this straight. Lightning comes into your office for a little conversation. Then you shook hands and turned him loose?"

"No. Lightning pulled his Glock on me. He threatened to put a hole in me if I tried to arrest him."

"Apart from that, you've had a quiet day?" Bernie hung up.

I drove across town to Ted's garage. Ted was out, but his foreman wasn't. I dumped the bits of white plastic and metal on a workbench and asked him if he could tell me what kind of a car the parts belonged to.

The foreman picked up one of the pieces. He pointed to symbols embossed on one of the larger parts. "I know exactly what kind of a car they came off, because we've had one in the shop a few times. It's a 2008 Nissan Infiniti 350Z Roadster. There's not too many of 'em around in Victoria yet."

"Is your customer's a black convertible?"

"No, it's blue."

CHAPTER EIGHTEEN

I was frying eggs for breakfast. The sun was shining, and I was thinking about a certain vehicle that I'd noticed recently. It had been parked under tarpaulins in Tomas Gonzales' yard. Who knows what make and colour it might have been? The phone rang. It was Bernie Tapp. He said, "What are you doing right now?"

"Having breakfast and taking care of a sick bird."

"Felicity's ill?"

"No. The bird is a pine siskin. It has a damaged wing, but it's getting better every day."

I held the phone away from my ear while Bernie enjoyed a coughing fit. When he finished, I said, "By the way. The car that Lightning ran into was a 350Z Nissan Infiniti Roadster."

"Better put out a BOLO."

"I've done that already."

"Good lad. Now stay put, I'm on my way over, we're going for a drive."

BERNIE SHOWED UP in an elderly Toyota Land Cruiser. A noisy, broken-down diesel that he had borrowed from the carpool. Its rear seats were separated from the front seats by an impermeable plastic security screen. With Bernie sweating and coughing beside me, we chugged out of Victoria and up into the mountains in low gears. Scorched air rising above the blacktop made the horizon shimmer. We turned off Highway 1 before we reached the Malahat summit and drove past Shawnigan Lake. An abundance of waterfowl, mainly Canada geese, flapped in the air and used the lake's unruffled surface as a landing pad. Summer cottages, a motel, a general store and a restaurant with a *Closed* sign in its window lay along the green forested road like splashes of white paint.

A few miles beyond Shawnigan Lake School, we ran out of blacktop. We bumped slowly west along narrow washboarded logging roads into the boonies. The whole area was rugged and remote, peppered with small lakes and dense forest interconnected by twisting narrow roads, and seldom visited except by hikers or off-roaders driving all-terrain vehicles.

I told Bernie about my visit to the house on Jinglepot Road, adding, "I sent Maria Alfred's stuff across to HQ. Maybe Forensics will find something useful."

Bernie's grunt changed into another cough. As we travelled farther west, the heavens opened up. Rain fell unceasingly. Bernie locked the hubs, put the Land Cruiser into four-wheel-drive and drove on with sweat dripping down his face. He was holding the steering wheel like a running back holds a football and driving too fast, as usual. I bounced around on the Land Cruiser's deflated shotgun seat, hanging onto the overhead grab bars during the wild, bucking ride.

Creeks overflowed. Water, loose earth and small rocks cascaded down from deforested slopes, creating minor avalanches and transforming the road into a ribbon of liquid mud. It took us over an hour to traverse one five-mile stretch. The vehicle's noisy diesel, its busted muffler and the groaning springs made conversation impossible till Bernie stopped at a fork in the road. One fork led to an abandoned logging camp. After consulting an ordnance survey map and getting our bearings, we opted for a fork that ran alongside Sumatch Creek. On we went, with one or all of our wheels spinning without traction half the time, until we were forced to a stop by a red alder that had fallen across the road. Bernie locked the brakes and said, "Silas, I feel wrecked, a bit dizzy. Goddamn summer cold, so I'd better take it easy for a minute."

I reached for the emergency axe and got out. Sweating, ankle-deep in liquid gumbo, I chopped the alder's bushy branches off, dumped them over a bank, and then wrapped a choker around the trunk of the tree and dragged it out of the way with the Land Cruiser's bumper-mounted winch. Soaked, my boots full of warm liquid mud, I got back in the car and we resumed our journey.

A couple of miles before it reached the sea, the creek widened into a small lake spanned by a single-lane bridge. Soon afterwards, a constable wearing yellow rain gear waved us down. We skidded to a halt. "If you go on for another couple of hundred yards, you'll see parked emergency vehicles," the constable told us. "I suggest you leave your vehicle there and take the footpath down to the creek. Careful, gentlemen, the footpath is very slippery."

The next thing we saw was an ambulance and other emergency vehicles blocking the road. Bernie and I got out of the Land Cruiser and slithered down steep muddy slopes to the creek's gravel-strewn bank. About fifty feet wide at that point, the creek flowed around a narrow canoe-shaped islet upon which a few spindly birches and cottonwoods had gained tenuous toeholds. The crime scene was farther downstream.

Sergeant Mollard, a uniform branch veteran, was waiting for us beneath a white plastic tent that had been erected on a stretch of matted grass.

Mollard pointed. "Yesterday, a sports fisherman noticed a floating object snagged up against the rocks over there. At first, the fisherman thought it was a chunk of driftwood. As he drew closer, he realized that he had found a dead man. The fisherman waited till this morning before calling us."

Bernie raised his eyebrows.

"This creek is salmon-bearing, it's off limits year-round. There's a $5000 penalty for poaching," Mollard explained. "This morning the fisherman's conscience got the better of him so he gave us a ring. Lucky the body's still here, it's a miracle it didn't wash out to sea in all this rain."

"Where's the fisherman now?"

"Dunno, Bernie. He was cagey enough to call us from a public phone."

The surging creek was heavy with suspended silt and organic debris. Underfoot, the creek's pebbly bottom was loose and shifting. Bernie stayed under the shelter, drinking coffee and popping Tylenol, while I waded through a tangle of bulrushes and reeds into deeper water.

The floater was wearing a Hawaiian shirt and cargo pants. One shoe was missing. His face was submerged; his thick shock of long black hair undulated in the current. A constable raised the floater's head for me to have a look at him. The corpse's face might have been a handsome object once, but immersion in that tumbling river had rendered it ghastly. He was about thirty and he looked familiar. It took four sturdy constables to lift the body from the water, put him on a gurney and wheel him into the tent.

"What do you think?" Bernie asked me, after looking at the corpse.

"I wouldn't swear to it, but it might be Larry Cooley. If it is Cooley, I saw him in Nanaimo's, with P.G. Mainwaring, shortly before it went up in flames."

"Whoever he is, Hollywood can stop calling him now," Mollard interjected unkindly.

I emptied my boots, took my pants and socks off, wrung them dry, and then put them back on again. We waited under the tent, drinking coffee, till Dr. Tarleton arrived. Instead of driving in, the medical examiner had been delivered to the mouth of the creek in a police boat, after which he had been obliged to wade and scramble more than a mile upstream—a journey that had taken overall two hours longer than our trip in the Land Cruiser. Doc Tarleton was soaked, bedraggled and exhausted, but in his usual jovial mood when he examined the corpse.

"I think he drowned," Dr. Tarleton said. "Some of those facial cuts and contusions appear to have been inflicted before death."

I asked Dr. Tarleton how long Cooley had been dead.

"Heavens, I don't know," he answered good-humouredly, "It's all highly hypothetical till I open him up. At a guess, I'd say the poor man has been feeding the fishes for twenty-four hours, maybe more."

Mollard had an irreverent sense of humour. He chimed in with, "One thing's for sure. It's the last time anybody gets a free meal outta the guy."

Bernie turned to me. "Come on," he said, shrugging his shoulders and bending his arms at the elbow in a supplicative gesture. "If it is murder, who do you suspect?"

"I dunno."

"I know you don't know. But you're a detective, and I want you to use your imagination here."

Reluctant to venture an opinion, I said grudgingly, "Maybe it's a natural death. It's too early to start making guesses."

"For crying out loud!" Bernie chided me. "Until proven otherwise, I'm assuming this is murder. You heard what the doc said. This guy was beaten up before he drowned."

"Hang on," Dr. Tarleton said. "That's not what I said. What I said was—"

Bernie interrupted him. "Maybe it's not what you said, Doc, but that's what it boils down to. For the time being I'm working on the assumption that this guy was brought to the bridge back there, beaten up, and then thrown into the creek, where he drowned. If I'm right, that means there's too many coincidences going on. We've had several violent deaths in the last few days. That being so, nobody can tell me they're not related."

Bernie looked at me expectantly.

I shrugged my shoulders. "If this is murder, the field is wide open. Maybe the Big Circle Boys are involved. Tubby Gonzales, Twinner Scudd, the Red Scorpions. Take your pick."

Bernie was exhausted and ready to leave. I said to Sergeant Mollard, "How did you guys get in here without four-wheel drive?"

Mollard shook his head. "It wasn't too bad earlier this morning. We'll have a helluva time getting out."

By the time Bernie and I departed, Nice Manners, Nicky Nattrass and the crime squad had arrived and were combing the scene for clues. If such a thing is possible, it was by then raining harder than ever. Bernie looked like death warmed over, and I wanted to do the driving, but Bernie wouldn't hear of it. Shortly before the Land Cruiser's tires touched blacktop again, we passed an A Channel satellite van uselessly spinning its wheels in a ditch. I suggested we stop and give them a hand.

Bernie floored it and said, "Screw 'em, let 'em rot. Let the Judas who keeps feeding 'em news tow 'em out."

CHAPTER NINETEEN

We got back to Victoria after a 70-mile round trip that had lasted five hours. Bernie's cough sounded worse to me but he said that a good meal was all he needed. Instead of dropping me, at my office, he drove us to the Victoria seaplane terminal down at the Inner Harbour. The terminal's coffee shop heaved with showbiz characters dressed in expensive west-coast casual. Gucci, Dolce and Gabbana, Armani, designer jeans. Everybody was either darling or dahling. The terminal's self-service counter was jammed. We found an empty wall to lean against and eaves-dropped. Another TV movie of the month had just wrapped on northern Vancouver Island. The principal character was either a baby orca, a baby grizzly or an orphaned forest wolf. I could find out by keeping tabs on Hallmark's Fantasy of the Month, except I don't have TV.

Some of Victoria's low-rent paparazzi were besieging an unflappable Canadian actress—the one with famous breasts. Her tiny, haggard face was in real life far more interesting and revealing than the airbrushed facsimile usually pictured on a screen. Most of the travellers were en route to Los Angeles via Seattle. When the next flight was announced, a few people trooped outside. Bernie and I picked up coffees and sandwiches, and grabbed an empty table. Out in the downpour, people were boarding a DHC-3 Otter. Visibility was terrible. We watched the plane take off and disappear into the murk like a ghostly giant bird.

Bernie drank a little coffee, his eyes closed. He was out on his feet. Shaking himself awake he said thoughtfully, "Larry Cooley was a police informant. He gave the squad a few useful phone calls, but the slippery bastard thought he had us in his pockets."

I nodded. "Yeah, I know."

Bernie seemed surprised; he gave me a long look. "You knew that Cooley was a squealer."

"Everybody knew. The question is whether Cooley was an arsonist as well."

Pent-up air escaped from Bernie's lips in a long sigh. "Cooley was stupid. Instead of keeping his head down, he acted like he had immunity."

"It sounds as if he did have immunity, for a while at least."

"Yeah, well, we used to cut him a little slack. If you ask me, Twinner Scudd's boys got him."

I said, "Remember when we went to see Tubby Gonzales at the recycling depot? A car was parked underneath tarps in the back lot. It was about the size of an import convertible."

Bernie smiled. "That's worth looking into," he said.

When we left the terminal, passengers were being turned away. All further flights had been cancelled due to bad weather. Lit by the terminal's halogen lights, Bernie's wet face was all sharp angles—a study of exhaustion in black and white.

"We'd better check that car out now," Bernie said reluctantly.

"Forget it, Bernie. You ought to be in bed. Go home, for Christ's sake."

He offered to drive me home, but I needed a walk while I thought a few things over. Bernie drove off into the night. I pulled up my coat collar and headed uptown on foot.

CHAPTER TWENTY

It was still monsoon weather that night. Along Government Street, sheets of rain streamed from rooftops, creating mini-lakes along the roads where floating garbage had plugged the gutters. Apart from a few passing cars and buses, the street was deserted, except for a pierced hooker twirling an umbrella, wearing a blonde wig and spikes, her shorts hanging off her skinny ass. She stepped out of a doorway and gave me the business as I slowed the MG to make a left turn at Bay Street. After a few more twists and turns, I ended up at the Titus Silverman Memorial Recycling Depot.

It was quite dark by then. The low rectangular building was a pale blur lit by my headlights as I drove into the muddy junkyard around the back. I pulled to a stop next to the tarpaulin-draped car. I left the MG with its engine running and its headlights on. Dragging the tarpaulins off, I got my feet wet and my hands dirty for the dozenth time that day.

The car illuminated by the MG's headlights was a white 350Z Nissan Infiniti convertible that had sustained major front-end damage. Documents in the glove compartment showed that the vehicle was registered to Tomas Gonzales. Lightning Bradley had told me that the car he'd run into was probably a *black* Mercedes.

Things are starting to add up, I said to myself.

Wet as a water rat's nose, I tramped through the junk-clotted mudfield to the depot's back door. In the murky darkness, I kicked the door till it rattled the TRASPASSARS KILLED sign that hung above the doorframe. Nobody answered; the building was unoccupied. Everybody, even the poker players, had given up for the night.

I DON'T LIKE Humboldt Street, and I especially dislike Humboldt Street after dark. Humboldt lies at the heart of Victoria's most ghost-haunted region, and it gives me bad vibes. I sometimes get the same feeling when I visit parts of James Bay. The stretch of Humboldt that runs alongside St. Ann's Academy is supposed to be haunted by one of Victoria's gold-rush era hanging judges. Many people have reported strange goings-on over the years. I was feeling those bad vibes quite strongly when I parked the MG in a five-minute zone outside the Clarion Tower's front entrance. I didn't know it then, but within five minutes, my bad vibes were destined to become much worse.

Built by someone with more money than taste, its exterior facade had Tudor, Grecian, Gothic, Italianate, Moorish and New Brutalist touches, and for good measure it was plastered with precast concrete gargoyles. It has been widely mocked and how it ever snuck past Victoria's municipal planning committee is anybody's guess.

A tall muscular man appeared from inside the Clarion Towers' ornate lobby. Waving his arms, defying the weather in a T-shirt, shorts and leather sandals, he tapped a knuckle against the MG's side window and suggested I find a proper parking space. I dismounted from the car and showed him my police badge. His name was Josefsen, and he was the Clarion Towers' building manager.

I asked Josefsen if he knew Tomas Gonzales.

"Sorry, officer, I'm not at liberty to say," he said respectfully. "We have two hundred people living here. I can't give out personal information about our tenants to anybody who just asks."

"I'm not anybody, I'm a police sergeant. Just answer my question."

Josefsen swallowed. "Well, yes, I do know Mr. Gonzales, as it happens. I had to fix a faulty radiator for him once. His suite in on the twenty-third floor."

Quiet as an undertaker's mute, Josefsen followed as I walked under the cantilevered concrete slab that protects the building's front entrance and pressed the buzzer to Gonzales' apartment. Nobody answered.

Josefsen didn't demur when I told him to take me up there. He used a master key to access the lobby. The two of us got into the elevator and rose in silence to the top floor. The building was soundproofed. Instead of yesterday's dinner, the carpeted corridors smelled of lilacs. When I remarked upon this, Josefsen said, "The air in the public areas is slightly pressurized. When somebody opens an apartment door, scented air flows in from the corridor instead of out of the apartment."

Gonzales' apartment was at the end of the corridor. I pressed a buzzer set in the doorframe. The sound it made inside was inaudible to me. I kept pressing for a full minute, after which I gave Josefsen the go-ahead. He inserted a plastic card into a slot in the door and pushed. Josefsen stuck his head into the opening and murmured politely, "Excuse me! A visitor for you, Mr. Gonzales."

Nobody replied. I put a hand on Josefsen's arm to prevent him going any farther inside. "Wait a minute," I said. "You'll wait out here for me here, please."

I went in and closed the door in Josefsen's handsome face.

Thirty seconds later, I was in the corridor again. Leaving Gonzales' door slightly ajar, I asked Josefsen for his pager number and told him that he could resume his normal duties: I would call him if necessary. I watched Josefsen retreat down the corridor and get into the elevator. After bracing myself, I re-entered Gonzales' apartment.

It was a large seven-room corner suite. In daylight, there must have been marvellous views of the Olympic Mountains, and the Salish Sea. As it was, vast tentacles of electric light stretched away into the surrounding blackness. Gonzales' suite smelled of death. Even after I had opened every window, the stink of death was almost overwhelming.

A man was collapsed in a large wooden chair to which he was secured by yards of silver-coloured duct tape. His face was an unrecognizable gory mess of misshapen, featureless bone. His clothes, the chair he sat in, and the carpet surrounding his chair were drenched in blood. In death, his sphincters had let go. The contents of his bladder and bowels had discharged. Flies buzzed around the mutilated corpse. God only knows how those flies knew that there was a tasty new cadaver waiting for them to lay their eggs in a Humboldt Street apartment.

As in the case of Maggie Bradley, this man had been flogged repeatedly with a heavy blunt instrument. The visible parts of his sallow corpse had bloated in the apartment's stultifying heat. Every one of his fingernails had been ripped out.

Clearly, this was a premeditated crime. Somebody who had planned to pull those fingernails out must have brought a pair of pliers with him for that express purpose.

In death, the only visible sign of Tomas Gonzales physical vanity was the comb-over, which was now pathetic as well as ridiculous. His shirt had been slit open down the front with a very sharp knife. The same knife had then slashed his belly open like a gutted fish. Entrails had spilled from their cavity and they glistened obscenely, like slimy rubber tubes. As in Maggie's case, the scene was so ghastly that for a few seconds I believe that my heart stopped beating.

For a brief period, Gonzales had had it all. Flashy young women to adorn his arm, the big Rolex, the gold necklaces. Now he was a brutalized corpse. Gonzales' skin was cool to the touch. Rigor had set in, fluid had pooled in his ankles. Based on that, I guessed that Gonzales had been dead for more than twelve hours. As Maggie's had been, Gonzales' rooms had been thoroughly trashed. Papers, feathers and furniture stuffing was strewn everywhere, and fine suspended particles filled the air. Drawers had been pulled out and their contents dumped on the floor. Cushions, pillows and mattresses had been slashed. Carpets had been drawn back to reveal bare floors. Cabinets had been dragged away from walls. Hollow metal curtain rods had been taken down and searched. The toilet's tank lid had been removed, photographs had been torn from their frames—all of this by someone looking for something small and very, very valuable.

A minute after entering the apartment, I was once more outside in the corridor, calling headquarters.

When the dispatcher came on, I said, "This is Silas Seaweed. I'm in the Clarion Towers on Humboldt Street. At the moment I am standing in the corridor outside Tomas Gonzales' apartment on the twenty-third floor. Tomas Gonzales is inside. He has been murdered. Better get Serious Crimes over here right away. Don't bother to call CDI Tapp, because he's ill, sick in bed."

Maybe the dispatcher was a poor listener, and maybe he was just following protocol, because Bernie Tapp showed up before the Serious Crimes mob did. Bernie had probably self-medicated with something powerful, because apart from a slight lethargy, he was his normal self. He found me outside the building downstairs, pacing back and forth under the eyes of those precast concrete gargoyles, while I reoxygenated with clean, unscented, unfiltered fresh air.

"Jesus Christ," Bernie said, after looking at what was left of Tomas Gonzales. "There's a serial killer out there somewhere."

"Unless it's a copycat crime. Here's another thing. Gonzales might have been offed by more than one assailant. He was a big powerful man. Tough. No easy pushover for somebody working on his own."

"Unless Gonzales was sucker-punched. Taken suddenly unawares. That way a girl could have done it. A kid, even. Clobbered Gonzales with a bottle, say, and then taped him to that chair."

"A woman didn't do this, a kid didn't do this. It's impossible."

"Impossible?" Bernie said. "Nothing is impossible."

I shook my head. "A man did this, Bernie, and you know it."

"Jesus Christ," Bernie said. "Let me tell you something. Women can stand the sight of blood better than any man. Women get pissed with people the same way men do. They bear grudges, get depressed. Grievances build like steam pressure builds in a kettle. The next thing you know, the lid blows off. Something snaps, and she grabs a rolling pin or a bottle. She looks at the back of his head, and smack! He's a goner, just like Gonzales here."

"Not like Gonzales. I agree that in a fit of rage a woman might knock somebody out with a bottle. But she doesn't then drag him into a chair, tie him down with duct tape and then torture him for hours."

"Silas," Bernie said impatiently. "You're talking about a normal woman. I'm talking about a nutcase. The Beast of Belsen was a woman."

"What? You're pissed at the killer and now you're pissed at me too?"

Bernie summoned a weary grin. He rubbed a hand across his forehead and was about to say something when a voice said, "Excuse me, Chief. No offence, but shouldn't you be wearing booties?"

It was a crime-scene tech, one of the bunnysuiters. He was standing in the doorway, and he was right. Bernie and I ought to have been wearing booties instead of contaminating the scene of the crime with our dirty size twelves. Bernie and I left the apartment and waited in the corridor until Nice Manners arrived.

Visibly annoyed, giving me the icy stare, Manners asked, "What are you doing here?"

"He found the body, Nice," Bernie growled. "Keep your shirt on, for chrissake."

After that, I kept quiet and tried to stay under Manners' radar while Bernie brought him up to speed. A constable handing out blue booties, white paper suits and rubber gloves to whoever needed them offered them to us. Bernie and I declined. We had seen all we wanted of Tomas Gonzales and his apartment for the time being.

Manners, pulling a bulky white paper suit over his day clothes, said, "Raymond Cho: dead. Maggie Bradley: dead. Larry Cooley: ditto. In addition, three people are dead due to that arson at Twinner Scudd's club. And now Tomas Gonzales is dead."

"If it is Tomas Gonzales," Bernie demurred. "It probably is, but you can't be certain by looking at what's left of his face. I've never seen the likes of it."

Manners zipped his white suit up. Stooped down to put his blue booties, on he grunted breathlessly, "Seven murders in less than a week. Are these cases all connected in some way?"

Bernie shrugged. I didn't say anything.

But Manners' question had been rhetorical. He straightened up and went on, "I'm wondering if these murders are all tied to that first killing, the one on Collins Lane? Raymond Cho was involved with drugs, and he was murdered with brutal violence. Ditto Larry Cooley. Ditto Tomas Gonzales. Ditto Maggie Bradley."

Bernie shrugged. "Maggie wasn't a drug trafficker."

"Not directly, perhaps," Manners said. "But who's to say that her husband wasn't? After all, we found traces of cocaine in Bradley's house, and in his Crown Royal."

"Lightning Bradley is a dumb asshole. He's a drunk, which means he's an addictive personality, so he probably fooled around with cocaine once or twice," Bernie responded. "I don't think he was a trafficker. Besides, cocaine is ubiquitous. Nowadays there's traces of it in a majority of used 20 dollar bills."

"Ah yes, well, it's not quite that simple," Manners said. "Forensics now tells us that the cocaine traces we found in Cho's BMW had been cut by the same ingredients and in the identical proportions to the traces found in Bradley's Crown Royal. They were all from the same batch."

Bernie nodded.

Looking at me, but without meeting my gaze, Manners added, "Chief Tapp tells me that you interviewed Twinner Scudd, Larry Cooley and Gonzales recently. So who do you like for this, Sergeant?"

I said without hesitation, "I didn't interview Cooley, but my guess is Twinner Scudd, although I think that the Big Circle Boys and the Red Scorpions should be added to your list of suspects."

Manners responded by pulling the paper suit's hoodie over his head, and going into Gonzales' apartment.

"Twinner Scudd?" Bernie said doubtfully. "Don't tell me you're coming around to my way of thinking?"

"It makes no difference what I think, Bernie. Manners doesn't put any weight in my opinions."

Bernie let that one go. He said "So long," and went home. It had been a very long day; I probably should have done the same.

The sky was full of thin whirling clouds when I drove back to my office, thinking and trying not to think about Tomas Gonzales' unlovely corpse, and his grisly encounter with the finality of death. The smell of death was in my nostrils; the taste of death was in my mouth. Rather than gargling with mouthwash, I brought out the office bottle and poured myself a stiff one.

Then I logged on and spent a few minutes investigating Larry Cooley. That was something I ought to have done much earlier. Cooley's real name was Millray.

Larry Millray was a self-made character who had made several unsuccessful attempts to reconstruct himself with the faulty psychological building materials that nature had given him to work with. He was booted out of Queen's, then Dalhousie, when they found out he'd registered with forged transcripts. After that he lowered his sights, and took a welding course at a community college in Red Deer, Alberta. Millray passed bottom of his class and then worked on a northern pipeline project until inspectors took a closer look at his work and he was let go. He had two convictions for assault, the second of which had earned him six months in minimum security. When he came out, he got into the condo time-share racket. A few scandals later, and another minimum-security jolt, he changed his name to Cooley (his

mother's maiden name) and then somehow slithered his way into
P.G. Mainwaring's enchanted circle.

There were no voice mail messages; no snail mail lay on the floor
underneath my letter slot. There was just me, and that miserable night.
I keep a portable radio in my desk, and I switched it on to lighten my
mood. It was tuned to KPLU, a National Public Radio jazz and blues
station broadcasting out of Tacoma. B.B. King was singing about the
bro in Korea—the war that nobody remembers any more. The Obama/
McCain election was in its death throes, and a newsbreak came on. Palin
and her cohorts were accusing Obama of being a closet terrorist, an actual
socialist and a secret Muslim. I was already sick of America's election
slanders and phantom campaign issues, so I turned it off in disgust. I
had the whole silent building to myself, or thought that I had, until I
heard water running along pipes. I padded soft-footed along the corridor
to my private washroom and used a key to let myself in. The room was
empty, although water swirled in the bowl of my toilet. Evidently, I
wasn't the building's only occupant. That ghost was back. I stayed in the
corridor, thinking and waiting. After a while, footsteps clattered down
the wooden stairs from the second floor. A pair of gorgeous female legs
came into view, then the rest of her.

It was P.G. Mainwaring. She looked tired, not as vivacious as I remembered. Dark circles ringed her eyes, but she was still exceptionally lovely.

"Miss Mainwaring," I said. "What are you doing here at this hour?"

"I've been working," she said obscurely, coming to a stop at the foot of
the stairs. "I should ask you the same question?"

"I've finished work for the day. Now I'm drinking whisky. Would you
like a cup?"

"It may be time to enlarge your social repertoire. All you do is offer
me alcohol."

"If I could get you to drink some alcohol, I'd extend my range."

She was holding herself stiffly. "A drink might be fun, although I
don't normally drink distilled beverages from cups. There's always a first
time, I suppose," she said, relaxing her rigid stance. "Let me have a look at
your office, first."

She moved towards me with easy graceful strides, wearing an
unbuttoned green raincoat that showed off a curvaceous figure beneath

a black blazer, a cream turtleneck sweater and a tartan skirt with a lot of the same green in it. I couldn't read her eyes. The hem of her coat brushed against me as she went past into my office. She had on a perfume, something unusual, but I'd smelled it before, and I wasn't sure that I liked it.

"By the way," I said. "Thanks for inviting me to your memorial dinner. I'm sorry I didn't make it, but I was tied up."

"You can't be too sorry because you didn't RSVP me either."

"As I say, I was tied up, but I'd have enjoyed the dinner."

"Really?"

"Really."

Perhaps unconsciously, she leaned against my desk with one hip out, like a hooker. I studied her and noticed for the first time that age was bringing faint wrinkles to her cheeks and tugging down the flesh under her chin.

PC was out on the prowl. The only things for P.G. Mainwaring to admire were my crummy desk, crummier visitors' chairs, pathetic metal filing cabinets, a drab fireplace, those pictures of British queens and some missing-kid notices.

"How long since this room has been painted?" she said, as regal in her disdain as their Britannic majesties glaring down at us from their frames. "And you should start using room freshener, because I smell cat."

"It smells of cat because a cat is the principal resident, I'm just her designated victualler. As for the paint, the landlord's a cheapskate. This office hasn't been painted in years."

I pointed at the swiveller behind my desk. "Somebody shot me in 2005. I was sitting in that very chair. The gunman was across the street, hiding on the roof of Swans pub. Most of the bullets went into the walls instead of me. Even then, the landlord wouldn't spring for a complete paint job. All he did was spackle the holes and do a bit of touch-up."

"How dreadful for you," she said. "Were you badly injured?"

"Not terribly. The doctors had me on morphine for a while, which was actually quite pleasant."

"And I suppose pretty girls thronged to your bedside, signing their names on your plaster casts, bearing grapes, flowers?"

"Well, yes, a few of them did. One of the pretty girls was called Sarah

Williams. She's a friend of mine. I think you must know her, because she's mentioned your name to me at least once, although not recently."

P.G.'s eyes widened.

I went on, "When I got out of hospital after being shot, I was on paid disability for a few months, which was another plus. I went down to Nevada to recuperate and play a little poker. I even won a few bucks. All in all, being shot turned out to be a positive experience."

"Did you find the man who shot you, and send him to prison?"

"Yes and no. I broke his nose, put him on a boat and sent him to South America."

"How extraordinary," she said, adding in an offhand manner, "You mentioned Sarah Williams. Is she a friend of yours?"

"I run into her occasionally."

"Accidentally, or on purpose?"

"Never you mind," I said jokily. "And by the way; that perfume you're using. Is it patchouli?"

"How clever of you to notice. It's an old-fashioned perfume, but then, I'm an old-fashioned girl."

I showed her my pearly whites. "Why don't you sit down? Make yourself comfortable, and I'll pour you that drink."

She wrinkled her nose. "I don't think so, because I have a better idea. Follow me."

This is getting better and better, I thought, trotting dutifully behind her, admiring those lovely legs and swaying hips as P.G. Mainwaring preceded me up the stairs to the second floor.

CHAPTER TWENTY-ONE

I seldom visit the second floor. Occasionally, when I tramp up the stairs to visit Nobby Sumner's roof garden, for example, I glance in passing along narrow corridors and see frosted glass doors leading to anonymous offices. For the most part, the building's tenants are obscure underachievers like me. Dicey manufacturers' agents, bitter ambulance chasers, a woman who deals in paper ephemera, a podiatrist, jaded astrologers and the like, along with dot.com startups that hang on for a year or two and either go broke or make good and then move on to more ostentatious addresses.

P.G. Mainwaring led me to an inconspicuous door under the stairs. The world is full of surprises. Instead of an office, we went into a large windowless private library with fat leather armchairs, cherry furnishings and sumptuous rugs. When she flicked a switch, sconced wall fixtures lit a banker's desk with a soft golden glow. Ship paintings and oil portraits shared the walls with shelved books. The dark red carpet was luxuriously deep. A door led off to a washroom. Hidden behind a folding screen was a tiny kitchen with a minute sink, a kettle and a two-burner hotplate of ancient design. The ceiling was decorated with elaborate plasterwork urns and swags. After I had helped her off with her raincoat and hung it on an antique brass whatnot, P.G. Mainwaring went to a corner and swung a hinged panel aside to reveal a small wet bar.

"I've no refrigerator, so there's no ice, sorry," she said. "And no rye either. If you like whisky, there's plenty of scotch."

"Scotch is fine."

"How do you like it?"

"Neat, if that bottle I'm looking at is actually the Grand Macnish."

She poured the whisky into two-cut glass beakers and added a little water to her own drink. She delivered mine along with an Irish linen napkin.

"Here's looking up your old address," I said. "It's quite a hidey-hole you've got here, I never knew this room existed."

"That is the general idea." Smiling faintly, she sat down in one of the armchairs, with her knees together. I sat down, crossed my legs, and wondered, not for the first, time how nice it was to inhabit—even if temporarily—worlds where people drank $70 whiskies and used Irish linen napkins instead of paper towels.

"Sorry about the dust. I ran a vacuum cleaner around the room for a few minutes last week, but it really needs wiping down with a damp cloth, except I can't be bothered," she said in an unapologetic tone. "In case you don't already know, and I suspect that you do, I'm the landlord that you were slandering downstairs. This room is exactly the way it was when my grandfather had it fixed up as a hidey-hole eighty years ago. It hardly ever gets used now."

I licked my lips. "You've been using the room a lot, lately."

She seemed mildly alarmed. "How on earth did you know that?"

"Because your washroom is directly above my washroom, and something's wrong with your plumbing. Every time your toilet flushes, it disturbs the water in my toilet downstairs. Until I figured it out, I was beginning to think that my bathroom was haunted."

"My goodness, your glass is empty already. Would you like another?"

"I certainly would, thanks."

"Are you afraid of ghosts?" she asked, crossing to the bar with my empty glass.

"Not particularly. In the popular imagination, ghosts are the disembodied spirits of the dead," I added pedantically. "People who think they're seeing ghosts are probably seeing bog apparitions or wakeful-sleep hallucinations."

"Wakeful-sleep hallucinations? My, you must be cleverer than I gave you credit for," she said facetiously. "Do you Salish people go to heaven when you die?"

"Coast Salish," I chided her. "When we die, we go to another world. We call it the Unknown World, which is a misnomer, because we actually know quite a lot about it. The Unknown World is a bit worse than the world we're living in now. In the Unknown World, for instance, we live the traditional life of our ancestors . . ."

She handed me my refill. "No soap, no metal pots and no plastic raincoats?"

"Nope. We eat most food raw. Everything else is cooked on open fires. We live in unhygienic pit houses or in longhouses, as we did in olden times. Screwing like crazy, shitting in the woods, itching and scratching. We have slaves to do our bidding, which is a plus, but otherwise the afterlife is very like this one, except everything is backwards. The sun rises in the west and sets in the east. When it's summer here, it is winter there, and so on, until we're reborn into the Vancouver Island that we're living in today. Some of us get reborn as killer whales and thunderbirds. I keep coming back as a male human being."

"Let's hope you keep coming back till you get it right," she drawled. "Now. Tell me more about Sarah Williams."

"I met her five years ago. Sarah's cousin had gone missing, and I helped to find her. Sarah called at my office with a man called Charles Service once. She happened to mention that this was one of your buildings." I grinned. "What Sarah actually said was, as I recall: 'This is one of Piggy's buildings.'"

P.G. Mainwaring smiled—the ice queen was thawing. "You're right about Sarah and me. We were at boarding school together. She used to call me Piggywig."

"That would be the Crofton House School in Vancouver. And don't tell me. Let me guess. You and Sarah were best friends and you hated each other?"

"We might have been best friends once, but there's no love lost between us now, I can assure you. If you'd had the disadvantage of a private school education, as I have, you'd know exactly what I mean."

"I went to St. Michael's. It's a private school, but your comment is still too obscure for my tiny brain. By the way, 'Piggy' is rather casual. Your full name is Penelope Grace Mainwaring, so what would you like me to call you?"

She had been softening, but my question made her eyes widen and that snooty look reappeared. "Have you been checking up on me?"

"I'm a policeman; you are a person of interest."

The thin cleft between her eyebrows deepened. "A person of interest to the police? I'm not sure that I like that very much. In answer to your question, my close friends call me Nibsy. You may call me Miss Mainwaring."

I let that one slide right by.

She looked at her hands and said coquettishly, "Tell me, Silas. Sarah Williams is very pretty, of course. Are you sure she isn't something more than just a casual friend?"

"Tell me, Miss Mainwaring. Is it true that you own a thousand apartment buildings?"

"Don't be silly," she laughed, another thaw setting in. "Of course not."

"Close friends address you as Nibsy, and you think *I'm* silly, Miss Mainwaring?"

"Oh all right. Call me what you like. But do tell me why am I person of interest to the police?"

"Because, Nibsy, you own a building recently destroyed by fire. To wit: Nanaimo's. Twinner Scudd's place of business. Three people died, and many others were injured. If that fire was an arson blaze, then those deaths will be classed as multiple homicides. You were seen inside the building just minutes before the fire started. I'm surprised police haven't questioned you already."

"A dreadful business. My lawyer is taking care of it. If you are planning to nag me about it, I'd better call her now."

"Oh, let's keep it informal. Besides, when you're talking to a policeman, you're not entitled to call for a lawyer unless you've been charged with something." I grinned at her. "Cast your mind back to the night we first met. We were in Nanaimo's. When you left the outdoor deck after a few minutes of delightful badinage avec moi, you went upstairs with Larry Cooley and talked to Twinner Scudd in his office. Several minutes later, I saw you leave Scudd's office. In fact, you walked right past me. You looked just as attractive then as you do now, but you were angry. I don't think you noticed me."

"I didn't notice you," she said, adding thoughtfully. "I hate that man."

"Twinner doesn't like you very much either, Nibsy, although I can't think why. I think you're very nice. Very nice indeed. Not to say lovely and accomplished."

"Sarah will be jealous. Aren't you coming on a bit strong?"

"I don't know. Am I? I meant every word that I said."

Maybe I'm getting to her, I thought, because the edges of her mouth turned up slightly and her eyes lost focus as her thoughts went inward.

She had been sitting in a matching leather chair, directly opposite mine. We were facing each other from about six feet apart. Her empty glass was upright on the carpet beside her feet. She picked it up and went slowly across to the bar. My glass was empty again, too, but perhaps she was too preoccupied to notice that.

Instead of refilling her glass, as she had mine, P.G. Mainwaring took a clean glass down from a shelf and spent more time than was necessary to pour the scotch and add water. She had her back towards me, but I could see her face, reflected from the bar's mirrored back. Those circles beneath her eyes had grown darker. She was thinking and playing for time. She pulled herself together finally and returned to her chair.

I gave her another minute, during which time we exchanged timid glances and tentative smiles.

I remarked casually, "Twinner Scudd is a nasty piece of work."

"True. He seems to think I'm a pushover, and we exchanged strong words. Scudd is behind on his lease payments, he owes me a lot of money. My agent hasn't had any luck getting him to pay up, and Scudd keeps ignoring notices to quit. I decided to talk to him as a last resort before we changed the locks and called the sheriffs."

"Did you make any progress?"

"Scudd is a boor," she said crossly. "He was rude and difficult, but he did promise to pay his arrears. He's made similar promises to my agent, so I wasn't optimistic. As you say, he's a nasty piece of work."

"Is Larry Cooley just your agent, or something more than that?"

My sudden change of topic caught her unawares. Her eyes widened. "Larry is an employee. What's to know?"

"When I saw you two together in Nanaimo's, he acted as if he were more than that."

"So what?" she snapped. "Is that any business of yours?"

"It might be," I replied in a soft voice. "You can't always know in advance about such things."

"If you must know, Larry has been acting like an idiot lately. I'm fed up. He's too forward, doesn't know his place," she said, standing abruptly. The glass in her hand spilled most of its contents on the carpet, but she didn't appear to notice. When I stood up and faced her, she extended an arm towards me, her hand vertical and flattened as if to ward off a blow.

Without speaking or taking my eyes off her, I took the glass from her other hand and placed it on a side table.

"I'm frightened, Silas," she said. "Scudd said that if I didn't stop bothering him, he'd kill me. He threatened Larry too. I'm just so terribly worried and afraid. And Larry's gone missing. I have an irrational fear that he might be dead or injured. If they find me, they might kill me too. Why else do you think I'd be hiding in this pokey bloody room instead of living in my house?"

Shivering and crying, she lowered her hand, moved closer and laid her head against my chest. I put my arms around her and made the sort of noises you use to calm weeping infants. Her sobs faded, and she stopped shivering. She pulled her head back and looked deeply into my eyes. In those depths I saw something that had been staring me in the face all night.

Her face moved closer, her eyes were bright with desire. When I kissed her, she put her tongue in my mouth. P.G. wanted to get laid. The next thing I knew, she had unbuckled my belt, unzipped my trousers and was bent over the desk with a pair of lovely frilly silks around her ankles.

"Well hello, sailor," she grunted, hanging onto her grandfather's onyx desk set for dear life as I shoved myself in.

CHAPTER TWENTY-TWO

P.G. Mainwaring had gone. She didn't tell me where she was going. I didn't ask her. I went downstairs to my office instead. To divert my thoughts I switched the computer on, poured myself a hefty dose of rotgut and exchanged glances with PC. Another complicated unpredictable female with a keen understanding of the male psyche. She leapt onto my notepad. After stroking her for a while, my blood pressure probably dropped ten points. "PC," I said, "I've really fucked up this time."

No kidding. I poured the rotgut back in the bottle instead of drinking it and went walking in the rain.

Apart from a couple of security lamps on poles casting moving circles of light as they swayed in the wind-driven rain, the small commercial marina at the foot of Pandora Street was dark. The Johnson Street Bridge loomed blackly overhead. The *Polar Girl*, Twinner Scudd's hundred-foot yacht, moved in the harbour's modest swell. Too big to manoeuvre into any of the marina's inside berths, the vessel was tied up to the marina's outermost float. It was white, an Italian-built liveaboard palace all ready for sea. Twin radars rotated; twin diesel engines thudded. The pilothouse and the main saloons were well lit. Eddie Cliffs, Twinner Scudd's tattooed bodyguard, was moving around on the yacht's boarding deck. I watched him come ashore. Wearing yellow wet-weather gear, he unhitched the yacht's spring line from a dock bollard, then went back aboard and pulled the line in by hand. After coiling the line neatly, Cliffs went into the main saloon. Before he disappeared down a circular staircase, I noticed the shiny metallic splint taped across Cliffy's ruined nose.

Seagulls, dozing atop pilings, opened their beady eyes and watched me move nearer to the boat and find a patch of shadow where I could see the yacht without being seen. Across the harbour, British Columbia's legislative building was lit up like a Christmas tree. Occasionally, cars and taxis rumbled across the bridge. Rain trickled down my neck and inside my shirt. More rain fell before Twinner Scudd appeared in the *Polar Girl's* pilothouse and busied himself at the steering console. Eddie Cliffs reappeared on deck. Scudd's head showed at an open window. They exchanged words, whereupon Cliffs unhitched the yacht's bow line and brought it aboard. White water splashed against the dock when Scudd activated the yacht's bowthruster. The *Polar Girl's* elegant bows inched away from the dock. By then, Cliffs was pulling the stern line aboard. I stopped watching him when a woman who had been lying on a sofa in the main saloon suddenly stood up. She reminded me of someone. She reminded me of Maria Alfred.

Water churned at the yacht's stern as twin propellers bit into the water. The *Polar Girl* was outward bound.

A police siren bleep-bleeped towards the marina from uptown and then abruptly faded.

If I had been drunk, by then I was sober. It was still pouring. I was soaked and a little bad-tempered. The *Polar Girl* had steamed from sight behind Ocean Point. Walking up Pandora Street to where I'd left the MG, I saw an RCMP patrol car parked outside my office. At that moment, a VPD blue-and-white barrelled around a corner. Its screaming siren sank to a purr as it came down the street towards me. I was still walking, fretting about guilt and the way I'd betrayed Felicity, when the blue-and-white skittered to a halt. Two constables leapt out. One was Harry Biedel, a constable I'd known for years.

Biedel was about my height. Six-foot four or so, and built like a bull. But Biedal, nearly as old as Lightning Bradley, was slowing down and running to fat. Breathing heavily, he said, "Great weather for ducks, Silas. How's tricks?"

"Okay, Harry. What's up?"

"Lightning Manners is hot to trot. How come you're not answering your cellphone?"

"I've been walking. Sometimes I turn my cellphone off, but who cares? I'm not on parade twenty-four seven, Harry."

Harry's voice was jovial, but he looked uneasy. He faked a smile. "Yeah, right. We're not all married to the job."

"Is Manners at headquarters?"

"He's on his way. He wants to meet you here."

Biedel walked alongside me, and his partner trailed behind as we went inside my building. I was in the corridor reaching into my pockets for a key before I noticed that two uniformed RCMP constables were guarding the door to my office. When I went to put my key into the lock, one of the Mounties raised his hands. He said, "Sorry, sir. All due respect, but you can't go in just yet. No offence. Our instructions are to restrict you to this corridor until Inspector Manners arrives."

According to the name tag pinned to his chest, the speaker's name was Madison. I didn't know him. I said, "Do you have a warrant for my arrest, Madison?"

"No, sir."

"Step aside. If there's no warrant you have no authority, and I'm going in."

Madison flushed, but he didn't budge till Biedel said, "You heard the sergeant, Madison. Let him by."

The Mountie held his ground for a moment, and then reluctantly moved aside.

I keyed my way into the office, trailed by the others. The four of us stood calmly, avoiding each others' eyes and not speaking, our wet clothes dripping onto the linoleum for a couple of minutes before Manners' car pulled up outside.

I was behind my desk when he strode in dramatically, his face like thunder, wearing a rat catcher's hat, a blue Burberry raincoat, a taupe-coloured suit, and, unless I'm very much mistaken, Ferragamo shoes. I briefly wondered how he could afford such a wardrobe on an inspector's salary. I didn't greet him or speak.

Red in the face, shaking with indignation, Manners pointed a finger at Madison and shouted, "I gave you clear instructions to keep Seaweed out of this office until I arrived."

PC—who doesn't like loud noises and has the gift of being the centre of attention wherever she goes—chose that moment to leave the scrap of carpet behind a filing cabinet where she had been napping. Tail erect, she meandered towards the cat flap.

"What's that animal doing here? Is this a bloody menagerie?" Manners yelled, taking a step towards the cat. With the toe of his right Ferragamo, he booted PC across the room. She flew through the air, hit a wall and was still sliding down it when, wild-eyed with rage, veins bulging in my neck, I went for Manners. He was backing away and I was halfway around the desk when Biedel grabbed me. He had played rugby for the Crimson Tide, and tackling skills were entrenched in his long-term memory. By then, Manners had taken refuge behind the Mounties.

Biedel's powerful arms held me, and he was quivering. I thought he was reacting to the effort of holding me, but he was actually shaking with suppressed amusement. Nobody else had moved.

PC was tough—cats bend instead of breaking; she was all right. She slid to the floor in one piece, squeezed meowing through the door's cat flap and went out. My reptile-brain fight-or-flight response faded; I stopped struggling.

"It's not worth it, Silas," Biedel murmured into my ear. "Hit him after you've got your pension."

I nodded. He let me go. I sat in the swiveller behind my desk, leaned back, folded my arms and waited for Manners to make the next move.

He was dabbing his face with a handkerchief that matched his shirt. Nobody spoke, the silence was deafening. After a while, Manners crooked a finger at Biedel, who went across to see what he wanted.

Manners whispered something in Biedel's ear and offered him a pair of latex gloves.

Biedel took his uniform jacket off, rolled up his shirtsleeves, put the latex gloves on, and then he got stiffly down on his knees in front of the fireplace. He reached up into the chimney flue and brought out a small cardboard box that had been lying out of sight on the fireplace damper. His face grave, Biedel followed Manner's instructions and put the box on my desk.

Looking at me directly for the first time, Manners said, "Open it."

After pondering that order for a moment, I opened a drawer and rummaged among the tea bags, packages of coffee whitener, old socks and paper clips until I found one latex glove. I was still looking for another when Manners snarled, "I am ordering you to open that box. Just do it."

"No chance, Nice. No way. Not without gloves. I'm not gonna put my prints on it."

"I've told you a thousand times! I'm Inspector Manners, I'm not Nice!"

"You said it, Inspector."

"Seaweed. You are under arrest!"

Manners ordered Biedel to put me in handcuffs.

CHAPTER TWENTY-THREE

I arrived at headquarters in leg irons, with both hands cuffed behind my back. It must have been about two in the morning by then. The only witness to my indignity was Sergeant Darcy Clough, on duty at the desk. A woman cleaner, mopping the floor, didn't even glance up from her work.

They shoved me in one of the first-floor interview rooms. Manners ordered Biedel to stay with me in case I tried to commit suicide or defaced the walls with nasty felt-pen drawings. The minute Manners left, Biedel took my cuffs and leg irons off.

A few minutes later, Darcy came in with coffee and doughnuts. "Nice is upstairs with the Mounties," he said. "He's helping them to compose their statements."

"'The statements ought to be good, then," Biedel said. "Nice has been taking creative writing courses at night. Pretentious poetry for mature students."

By then I was too weary to care. I closed my eyes and tried to sleep. Biedel drank both of the coffees, ate my doughnut and tried to keep himself awake playing iPhone games. We were both asleep when Darcy came back at 8:30.

"CDI Tapp got here ten minutes ago," Darcy told me. "He went ape shit when he found out you'd been locked up. He's as hot as a two-dollar pistol. Reaming Nice's ass for not calling him last night. He's upstairs in his office waiting for you."

Bernie was alone, looking at Victoria from his window with his back towards me.

"Sit down," he said, without turning.

I sat down in a chair, leaned back, put my hands in my pockets and stretched my legs.

Bernie sat behind his desk, put his hands behind his head and gave me a penetrating look from beneath his heavy dark brows. "Have you had any breakfast?"

"Not yet."

Bernie picked up the phone and spoke to Mrs. Nairn.

Bernie put the phone down and rubbed a thumb across his forehead. He said sombrely, "Superintendent Mallory will be talking to you in a little while. Me and Manners will be there as well. Would you like me to call the union rep?"

"Do I need a union rep?"

"Only if you want to keep your job."

"In that case I won't be needing her."

"Pissed off, are you?" Bernie asked, grinning like a hungry hound. "A little emotional because Nice Manners slapped you around last night."

"Is that what he said?"

"He said something like that. He told me that he treated you like a common hoodlum because in his opinion that's what you are. Manners is saying that you tried to attack him."

"Manners is right," I said. "I would have attacked him, but for Harry Biedel. I'd have put him in hospital."

"So you agree that Manners was acting rationally when he ordered you placed in restraints and held in custody overnight? It wasn't just pure unreasoning vindictiveness against a pain-in-the-ass junior officer?"

For a fraction of a nanosecond I thought about bringing Manners' Ferragamo shoe and PC's involuntary flight across my office into the conversation, till I thought better of it and kept my big mouth shut.

Bernie said, "That box they dragged out of your chimney last night. Is it connected in some way with the Raymond Cho case?"

"I don't know. I don't know what was in the box."

"You don't know what was in the box?" Bernie's eyebrows climbed his forehead. "Would you care to make a guess what was in the box?"

"No thanks. My brain is tired."

Bernie raised his hands in a kind of acquiescent apathy. "Well, just so you know, I do have a better opinion of you than Manners, only my brain is tired too. It's been working overtime since I came to work this morning and found my old buddy up to his ass in alligators again. *Again*, pal. I think we should call Guinness. A French Foreign Legionnaire holds the current world record for insubordination, but I think you might have him beat."

A couple of pigeons flapped in and perched on the windowsill. When Bernie turned in his chair to look at them, his face softened.

"Tell me, Bernie. Do you know what's in the box?"

"Yeah, I know. Superintendent Mallory knows too. Manners knows. For a while, Manners wondered if it might contain an explosive, so he very wisely took it down to Forensics. Forensics was even wiser. They called the bomb squad. Instead of destroying it, the bomb squad took the box outdoors into the police yard, put it in a cage, and opened it with a remote control device. It wasn't a bomb."

"What was it?"

"Ah, that would be telling, Silas."

"You mentioned the Raymond Cho case?"

"That's right, I did. Raymond Cho, alias Ronnie Chew. Big Circle Boy, cocaine addict, womanizer, amateur pornographer. Cho came to a bad end in a case that's all part of a big humungous mess. A case with more tentacles than an octopus."

Mrs. Nairn came in with a tray, put it on Bernie's desk and went out.

Bernie helped himself to a cup of coffee. I helped myself to an Egg McMuffin.

I was chowing down when Bernie went on, "An octopus, Silas, a humongous great big octopus. Raymond Cho dies. Maggie Bradley dies. Then there's an arson fire at Nanaimo's, and Larry Cooley dies."

"You're certain that it was Cooley we dragged out of Sumatch Creek?"

Bernie nodded. "Larry has a brother, we took DNA samples and got a match. It was Larry, no question."

Bernie paused for another sip of coffee. "Then Tubby Gonzales dies. What these murders have in common is an open question, but recent evidence would suggest that cocaine trafficking might be a factor."

I finished the first McMuffin. There was one left. I said, "Do you want that, Bernie?"

Bernie was talked out and shook his head. I picked it up and ate in silence.

Bernie's desk phone rang. Bernie pushed a button. Mrs. Nairn said, "Superintendent Mallory will be ready for you and Sergeant Seaweed in fifteen minutes, sir."

"Let's get you cleaned up," Bernie said.

We went downstairs to the duty change room, where I washed and shaved, took a sergeant's uniform from my locker, put it on and checked myself in a mirror.

"All finished admiring yourself?" Bernie asked, as I adjusted my necktie. "We'd better not keep the old man waiting."

THEY KEPT ME waiting in the corridor outside Superintendent Mallory's office for half an hour, pacing back and forth with a uniform cap tucked beneath my arm. Eventually the police chief's door opened. Nice Manners emerged and ordered me to go in.

Manners stamped with impatience while I put my cap on, adjusted it to a rakish tilt, and then strode past him. I came to a stop in front of Superintendent Mallory's desk and gave him a smart salute. Manners came in and stood beside me. Bernie Tapp, who was standing to one side, gave me a surreptitious wink.

The chief of police was seated. Holding himself with the full gravitas of his office, ramrod straight, Superintendent Mallory was a big white-haired man kitted in full-dress regalia with medals pinned to his chest.

After a stern warning and the usual procedural palaver, Mallory made a noise in his throat, examined me thoroughly with his glittering blue eyes and asked me if I had anything to say for myself.

"A little," I said unwisely. "Frankly, sir, I'm disappointed. I thought people had a better estimation of my abilities. I thought my colleagues would know that if I had a box to hide, I wouldn't put it where any half-smart jerk with a mission could find it. Sir."

"Half-smart jerk with a mission?" Mallory repeated with asperity. "Watch your tongue. I won't tolerate such language. Who do you think you are?"

"Sir?"

"If you are under the impression that there's a witch hunt in progress, you are very much mistaken," Mallory said. "This is serious business just the same. You are charged with threatening Inspector

Manners, a senior officer. You are also charged with the possession of one kilogram of cocaine. Do the charges have merit?"

"It's true that I threatened Inspector Manners. It is also true that Inspector Manners found a cardboard box that was hidden in my office. As to what was inside the box, or who put it there, I have no idea. If the box contained cocaine, so be it. To repeat, sir: I don't know how the box came to be there. I wish I did know. I would be interested to hear how Inspector Manners came to find out about it."

Superintendent Mallory looked at Manners.

"From information received," Manners said, his voice stony with dislike. "We had an anonymous tip. Somebody told us that Seaweed has been trafficking cocaine."

"Trafficking! And you took this tip seriously, Inspector? Before you say any more, be mindful that Sergeant Seaweed has served this police force with distinction for many years."

"If I didn't take the tip seriously then, I do now. As you are aware, sir, we get much of our information from informants," Manners replied. "Here's the deal as I see it: The present street value of a kilogram of cocaine is a quarter of a million dollars. If this is a setup, as Seaweed implies, there would be much cheaper ways of arranging it."

"A valid point," Manners said. "How do you respond to that, Seaweed?"

"I've already responded to it, sir. I didn't know anything about the box until Inspector Manners and his team showed up."

"If you are right, can you suggest who might have put the box there?"

"No, although several people have keys to my office. Others have ready access."

"Are you are speaking of other policemen, Seaweed?"

"Cops and crooks are sometimes brothers under the skin, sir. Somebody set me up, that's for goddamn sure, and it might have been a cop."

"Rein in your tongue, Seaweed. I won't tell you again," Mallory snapped, with unusual severity. Lowering his voice, he went on, "You are entitled to the benefit of any doubt. Perhaps you are right, Seaweed. Some person as yet unknown may have planted the cocaine. Chief Detective Inspector Tapp will look into that possibility, and we'll get to the bottom of things soon enough. Meanwhile, Seaweed you can help things along and possibly even improve your position if you'll prepare a list of likely candidates."

Superintendent Mallory looked at Manners. "You realize, Inspector, that pushing these charges is a serious matter for Sergeant Seaweed. It could result in the termination of his career. Have you given that any thought?"

"Indeed I have, sir. Ordinarily I might have turned a blind eye. Under the circumstances, I can't. Witnesses were present when Seaweed tried to attack me. He might have succeeded but for Constable Biedel, who intervened. If Seaweed isn't severely disciplined, it will send the wrong signal to the rest of the force," Manners said, his voice hard with resentment.

"Sure that's the reason you want to see Seaweed fired, Inspector?" Bernie asked Manners sarcastically. "Sure you're not trying to change the tires on a car that's still rolling?"

Manners smiled thinly. "Excuse me, Chief Inspector, but I'm not done yet. If Seaweed has been trafficking in drugs, another question arises, namely, how did he acquire these drugs? There's evidence of Native involvement in Cho's killing."

"Go on, Inspector Manners," Mallory said.

"Well, sir, I should have thought it was obvious. Seaweed might have acquired them from Raymond Cho, and then killed him."

"You are accusing Sergeant Seaweed of murder?"

"I'm just raising it as a possibility, sir."

"This is becoming farcical," Bernie said.

"Inspector Manners' reasoning may have some slight merit, Chief Inspector," Mallory snapped. To me he said, with less emotion, "Are you ready to accept my punishment as regards the alleged attack on Inspector Manners, Sergeant?"

"Yes, sir."

"Are you quite sure, Seaweed? Don't take this matter lightly."

"I'm ready for whatever you decide to hand out, Chief."

Mallory stood up. "Very well, you leave me with no other choice," he said without enthusiasm. "Sergeant Seaweed. You are stripped of all rank and suspended from duty as of this instant. I will defer a final decision on your status, and you will continue to be paid until the cocaine matter is resolved.

Turn in your badge and your weapons immediately. That's all, you may go."

I saluted smartly and marched out of Mallory's office with Bernie Tapp right at my heels. Bernie shut Mallory's door. Standing in the corridor, Bernie said, "What the hell's wrong with you? You stood there like a trussed turkey and let Manners accuse you of murder. Why didn't you speak up for yourself?"

I shrugged, because I didn't care. A little voice told me that I ought to tell Bernie that I'd seen a woman who in my estimation was probably Ruth Claypole, hiding aboard Twinner Scudd's yacht. I decided to keep that opinion to myself.

Some things needed my personal attention.

BACK AT HOME, I telephoned Charlie Charley. He lives on Cortes Island and has chronic obstructive pulmonary disease from smoking too many cigarettes. Charlie came on and said in a phlegmy gargle, "Who's this?"

"It's your long-lost friend. The one you could have gone to school with if you'd stayed out of juvie hall."

"Jesus, it's the old ratcatcher. I ain't robbed nobody since last month, so what do you want this time?"

"Has anybody seen Twinner Scudd lately?"

"Somebody told me he came through Campbell River last night and filled his tanks at the Esso dock. He'll be smoking weed on Quanterelle by now, I expect."

"I'm coming up tomorrow if I can catch the 10:30 mail plane. I'll be needing a boat for a couple of days."

"I don't blame you. The sun's shining up here, not a cloud in the sky. And the fishing's fantastic," Charlie said, gurgling laughter rumbling up his clogged windpipes. "What do you need, a day boat?"

"An overnighter with radar. Something I can take into Desolation Sound and run onto a beach if I have to."

"Yeah? I guess I can rumble something up for you, Silas," he said throatily. "If it's Twinner's grow-ops you're interested in, I'll keep you company. We'll rip him off and go halfers?"

"No, this is personal. When I'm done with Twinner, his grow-ops are all yours."

I hung up and phoned Lucas Air.

IT WAS LATE August, but it can get very wet and cold up around Desolation Sound way, even in summer. I put on wool pants, a wool shirt and waterproof Nikes. Then I packed a Gore-Tex jacket, a toque, a thick wool sweater, spare socks, toiletries, fifty feet of nylon rope, string, a butane cigarette lighter, matches in a waterproof box, two pounds of Thrifty's trail mix, five bars of dark chocolate and a water bottle. I put my own personal non-police-issue Glock in the backpack as well, along with a large folding knife with one saw blade and one cutting blade.

Outside my cabin, the pine siskin was trilling plaintively—letting me know that he was out of groceries. I shoved a few bits of meat into the escallonia before I left the reserve and drove downtown. It was exactly 9:15 AM by my watch when I passed the Warrior longhouse.

I left the MG in the Fisgard Street parkade. Lou's Cafe, two blocks away, reminded me that I hadn't eaten since yesterday. I went in and slid into a booth near a window. The breakfast rush was over. Apart from a large, soft-looking woman puzzling over a Sudoku book at another table, the cafe was empty. Lou was wearing a yellow ten-gallon hat, and I had his undivided attention.

"Moran heard you got fired and he left a message for you," Lou said, swishing a damp cloth over my table. "If you're looking for work where nobody won't bother you, there's a janitor's job going in his gym. Five bucks an hour, plus free room and board."

"That's very tempting, I'll give it some thought later. Right now I'm busy."

"Doing what?"

"Ordering breakfast. Got any beef sausage?"

"Is Elvis Presley alive and well and shaking his crotch in Las Vegas?"

"In the flesh at the MGM Grand, all ten of him. Gimme four crispy beef sausages, two eggs fried over medium and two slices of wholewheat toast. Marmalade. A large glass of OJ."

"I know you want your eggs over medium. I know you want crispy sausages. I know you'll help yourself to coffee if you want some. What I don't know is, what I am supposed to tell the boys?"

"Tell them I'm catching the 10:30 flight to Cortes Island."

Lou looked at his wall clock; it was 9:45. "You'll never make it." He scuttered away.

I got out of the booth and helped myself to coffee. There's a wicker basket on a shelf beside the door where people drop their used newspapers. I picked up the local rag and took it to my table.

The item I was looking for was a scant few lines buried on page C3. I was reading it when Lou delivered my breakfast. Written under Dorothy Fredricks' byline, it read:

Police Officer Suspended
Victoria's senior police brass remain tight-lipped as to why controversial Native street cop Sergeant Silas Seaweed has been suspended from duty. Nobody will speak on the record. Insiders speculate that the suspension is connected to a recent surge in local drug-related criminal activity. If the allegations being whispered about this officer's activities are confirmed, severe disciplinary action is expected to follow.

"How'd you feel about getting your name in the paper again, Silas?" Lou asked, reading over my shoulders. "Ain't you learned how to keep your nose clean by now? A man of your experience? Them cops will throw the book at you."

"For what?"

"For what you've done. Dealing in drugs. That's a big no-no, pal."

"It's crap, idle gossip," I said, picking up a knife and fork. "A storm in a teacup, it'll blow over in no time."

"That's not what Fred Halloran told us this morning," Lou said, setting my breakfast down on the table.

"Told who?"

"Everybody. Me. Moran. The usual gym bunch. Fred said they'll bust your balls. He says you'll get five years."

"Fred's pulling your leg."

"It's the worst thing can happen to a cop, going to jail. You'll have to stay in protective custody, or them cons will be all over you with Vaseline and baseball bats."

I cut a piece of sausage and put it into my mouth.

"Fred says in these cases what they generally do, when a cop gets found with his hands in the cookie jar, he gets reassigned to desk duties,"

Lou said. "You haven't been reassigned, you've been sent packing. They've got the goods on you, Fred said."

I finished breakfast in a hurry, dropped money on the table and walked two hundred yards to the floatplane terminal.

Victoria is an island city. Victoria's Swartz Bay ferry terminal is about thirty miles from the Tsawwassen terminal, on the BC mainland. The Salish Sea is too cold for swimming. If you want to get here from there, you either have to come by boat or by air. Most people arrive on one of the BC Ferries. Government-owned, it is the world's largest fleet. Many visitors fly in to CYYJ—Victoria International Airport. Others get here on private boats, or floatplanes.

Regularly scheduled floatplane flights have been servicing Victoria's Inner Harbour since the '30s. The rent-a-cop manning Lucas Air's metal detector was half-asleep, and I had no trouble bullshitting my knives and my gun onto the plane.

That morning, I was the seven-passenger deHavilland Beaver's only customer and I sat in the co-pilot's seat. The plane had one bag of mail aboard. We left the dock right on time. The harbour was busy as usual. The pilot waited uncomplainingly in the takeoff lane while a canoeist who thought he had the right-of-way crossed the harbour ahead of us. The pilot then gave his 450 horsepower Pratt and Whitney engine full throttle. The noise in the cabin was over a hundred decibels when our floats cleared the water. As the plane gained altitude and banked left, the pilot adjusted his controls. The noise diminished, but the sound in the cabin was still too loud for ordinary conversation.

Snowy peaks gleamed like an armada of sails across the entire horizon. Over on the mainland, the Fraser River's wide blue mouth nibbled its way to the sea. Vancouver's highrise towers were easily visible thirty miles north of Tsawwassen. Gazing down from my window, I watched the plane chase its shadow north.

Dozen of fishboats were working the Strait of Georgia between Texada Island and Qualicum Beach. A cruise ship came into view. Immense, white as an iceberg, it was carrying three thousand tourists up the Inside Passage to Alaska. Ayhus, Hernando, and then Marina Island passed beneath our wings.

We were travelling over Sliammon tribal lands now. Approaching the Coast Salish Nation's northernmost limits. Seen from the air, Ayhus—otherwise known as Savary Island—looks like a giant two-headed serpent. According to the Sliammon people, Ayhus was a living snake until it incurred the Transformer's wrath and was turned to stone.

Then the southernmost peninsulas of Quadra Island and Cortes Island rose up, and we began our descent into Desolation Sound. Whaletown appeared as a series of white dots in the pristine blue and green wilderness. The dots grew larger and became a dozen or so houses, a steepled church, a post office, a general store and a government dock.

The tide was running strongly enough to create whitecaps when the Beaver's floats touched water again. Two rocks mark the entrance to Whaletown's bay. It was a choppy ride until we gained the lee of a promontory and smoother water. Fifty feet from the government dock, the pilot cut his engine, opened his door and stepped onto the port-side float. Momentum carried the Beaver forward. A man standing on the dock threw a rope, which the pilot caught and fastened to a cleat. The dockman pulled us in. We tied up behind a large all-weather Zodiac inflatable with a pilothouse and twin 250 Evinrude outboards. My ears were still ringing from the Beaver's engine noise when I clambered ashore with my backpack across my shoulders. The pilot hoisted Her Majesty's mail from the plane and delivered it to Whaletown's tiny floating post office. Small waves broke on the beach and lapped against the pilings underneath the general store.

The Gulf and Dawson Whaling Company created Whaletown in 1867. By 1870, nearly every whale in Desolation Sound and the Strait of Georgia had been killed, flensed and rendered into oil. Gulf and Dawson moved on, leaving nothing behind except a name and a few unemployed diehards. Now the whales are coming back. Whaletown is still a sleepy laid-back place, although things were livelier than usual that day. Children and adults were coming and going. The general store, located at the head of the dock, was having a going-out-of-business sale. A seagoing dentist was making her biannual visit. I counted twenty people, children and adults, before I spotted Charlie Charley.

He was at the wheel of a demolition-derby Ford, parked near the Columbia Coast Mission Church. Charlie, a bloated white-haired giant, was wearing the kind of dark glasses favoured by blind people. He can probably see a barn at a hundred feet. When I came within range of his limited vision, he stuck his arm out the window and waved a white cane. I went over, shook Charlie's hand and threw my backpack onto the back seat.

The car stank of cigarettes, rotten fish and something worse.

"Jesus," Charlie said in his phlegm-laden voice. "You look great, you haven't changed a bit."

"What happened? They gave you an eye transplant, you can see people's faces now?"

"I wish. You're a bit blurry, Silas, but you sound good anyway."

Charlie lit a cigarette, pointed vaguely and said, "Like I told you on the phone, the fishing's fantastic, boats are scarce this month. The best I could do is the *Belle Girl*. It belongs to a widow who's trying to sell it. She's asking seven and a half thousand. Otherwise it'll cost you three hundred a day with a three-day minimum. I checked it out, she's good to go."

Charlie handed me an ignition key. "The *Belle*'s not fancy, but she's reliable, I use it myself sometimes. It's got radar and a good diesel. It's flat-bottomed. You can get it on and off the beach single-handed, so it should do you okay. I threw some groceries aboard and the fuel tank is full. If you take it easy on the throttle, it'll take you a hundred miles on a single tank. Fill her tanks if you get back."

"If?"

"Will you be going ashore on Quanterelle Island?"

"That is the whole idea."

"Be careful, then. Twinner's got pit bull dogs and he turns 'em loose at night. Them dogs will chew your legs off if they catch you."

"Thanks for the advice. Who do I make the cheque out to?"

Charlie's laugh was a strangled, snot-laden gargle. "Cheque? Are you kidding me? I need nine hundred cash up front. There's an ATM in the general store."

It had started to rain by the time I got back from the store. Charlie pocketed the money, and I climbed into the Ford. Its floor had mostly rusted through and was patched with bits of loose plywood.

Charlie put the Ford in drive and aimed it out of town. We went past Whaletown's tiny library and a straggle of tree-shaded houses, after which it was lonely dirt roads and green jungle all the way. A local driver who saw Charlie coming drove his car into the ditch for safety. After fifteen minutes and several near misses, we turned off the main road and bumped down a single-track lane till we reached a moss-covered cabin. Under the wide porch, fuchsias and bacopa spilled profusely from hanging baskets. A couple of rickety Cape Cod chairs faced the road. Charlie honked his horn. A woman who had been working behind the cabin emerged from the trees and plodded towards us with lethargic steps. She was skin and bone, wearing a Dogpatch frock and gumboots. She must have been beautiful once. Now, marred by hardscrabble living and unhappiness, her face was sullen and prematurely wrinkled.

"I've got that money for you, Lettie," Charlie said.

Without a single word or change of expression, Lettie took the money and left.

Charlie put the Ford in low gear. A hundred yards later we reached a sandy beach.

Charlie opened his door and swung his legs out. Coughing and spluttering, he tried to stand up. He didn't make it on the first go.

Charlie abandoned a feeble attempt to unlock the Ford's dented trunk with a key, and pried it open with a tire iron instead. The mysterious stink that I'd noticed earlier emanated from a five-gallon plastic bucket with a leaky lid. Red juice oozed when Charlie lifted the bucket out and put it down on the beach.

"Take this with you," Charlie said. "It's full of old pig knuckles, deer entrails, sheep brains. Shit like that. Plus some knockout drops. Dogs love it. Just dump it on the beach when you get to Quanterelle and I guarantee you it will send Twinner's pit bulls to dreamland."

"I'll never make it to Quanterelle. That smell will send me to dreamland first."

"Jesus, you city people," Charlie gurgled. "If you're so sensitive, put the bucket in a garbage bag."

"Have you got a garbage bag?"

"Lettie will probably have one."

"I wouldn't ask her. Lettie's bushed."

"No. She ain't bushed yet, but she ought to be. Her husband was that logger. The one who was working alone and got killed when a tree fell on him last year. Then he was ate by grizzlies."

"What the hell's she doing then, still living here on her own?"

"She's not on her own. There's two kids. A lodger has moved in with her already."

The *Belle Girl's* stern was in the water; her squat bow was nose-up on the beach. The boat's mooring system was a clothesline arrangement whereby one end of the rope wound around a tree and the other end of the rope wound through a shackle on a buoy anchored fifty yards out.

The boat was a boxy, no-frills, twenty-six-foot aluminum cabin cruiser with a Volvo inboard/outboard. After stowing my backpack and Charlie's bucket of guts in the cockpit, we both got our feet wet shoving its bow off the beach. Charlie stayed ashore while I climbed over the bows and worked my way around the deckhouse to the cockpit. With the tide running at about two knots, I reeled the stern line in until the whole boat was afloat in deep water.

Instead of taking Charlie's word for it, I checked the fuel tanks. They were full. The engine's oil and water levels were where they were supposed to be. The bilges were dry except for a thin film of black grease. The radar worked properly. There was plenty of drinking water. I lowered the outboard leg. When I pressed the starter button, the Volvo started immediately. Waiting for the engine to warm up, I familiarized myself with the ship's radio, the galley and the hand-pumped potable water system. I found out where the lifebelts, fire extinguishers and emergency flares were stored. The loaf of bread, cheese, cans of Spam and some biscuits that Charlie had promised me were in a cardboard box on the galley table.

By then, the Volvo's cooling water temperature gauge showed 210 degrees. Lashing Charlie's bucket of guts to a cockpit stanchion, I looked up and saw Lettie, watching me from the house.

I reeled the mooring line aboard, nudged the *Belle Girl's* controls until she was moving slow ahead, and set a course along Redonda Island's rocky, vast and remote western sea passage towards Toba Inlet.

CHAPTER TWENTY-FOUR

The view along Lewis Channel from the *Belle Girl's* windows was sterile, austere and superb. Faces of sheer granitic rock rose perpendicularly for hundreds of feet on either side of the boat before levelling into forested mountain scenery of unrivalled magnificence. To my left was Cortes Island, and to my right was Redonda, a perpetually snow-capped island with the largest mass per surface area of any place on earth. Redonda's Mount Addenbroke climbs right out of the water and then rises almost straight up to a height above 5200 feet. Apart from squeaking harlequin ducks, mergansers, squawking crows, great blue herons and the crying gulls that follow every sailor's travels, I had the whole country to myself. British Columbia's Coast Range mountains rose in the distance. Range upon range of tremendous peaks receding to apparent infinity in diminishing shades of blue and cobalt and sapphire. Crowning it all was Mount Denman's white, colossal mitre-shaped peak.

After three hours, I reached an indent in the shoreline that I'd been on the lookout for.

A colony of double-crested cormorants, fluttering their throats to cool off, watched warily as I emerged from Lewis Channel and sailed up a short narrow inlet. The tide was ebbing. A type of greyish algae that only grows in brackish water showed me that there was a small creek nearby. The inlet's muddy bottom was clearly visible about two feet below my keel. I stopped the diesel engine, lowered the anchor and raised the outboard's leg.

Miniature lagoons, tidepools and a narrow strip of marsh lay between me and a white sandy beach. Sunstars sidled across the mud like slow-moving octopuses. An eagle trying to torment an osprey into dropping the fish it had just caught reminded me that I was hungry. I lit the propane stove, put a kettle on for tea, made myself cheese and Spam sandwiches for dinner, and sat in the cockpit to eat them. By then, Charlie's bucket of guts had paralyzed my olfactory organs. The stink was no longer noticeable.

Above the beach a terraced rockery, an old orchard and a tottering house were all that remained of an abandoned homestead. After a little while, harsh metallic grating noises told me that the *Belle Girl's* keel was touching the bottom. Gradually, the boat tilted to starboard. After polishing off all the sandwiches and a second cup of tea, I slung binoculars around my neck and waded ashore. Crows were busy beachcombing amongst the rocks. An almost dry creekbed lay a few yards to the right side of the old house.

The sun was nearly down, and the western sky was rapidly losing colour when I set out to walk an old trail that wound uphill from the beach. Scattered here and there in the bush were signs of human activity: a rusted bucket, lengths of wire rope, an ancient stove, a crosscut saw lying forgotten since somebody had dropped it there many years earlier. Second-growth trees crowded out the light. The ascent was very steep and strewn with loose rock in many places. My shirt was pasted to my back when I reached the top of a cliff, where I had a clear view ahead.

Half a dozen small tree-girt islands dotted the water like a pod of giant green whales. According to the *Belle Girl's* charts, Quanterelle was a triangular-shaped island about two miles north. In the failing light, I put the binoculars to my eyes and had a good look at it. A stone breakwater extended its sheltering arm around a small harbour, where a big Zodiac inflatable boat and Twinner Scudd's *Polar Girl* lay stem to stern alongside a dock. Small outbuildings and a Quonset workshop lay along Quanterelle's rocky shore. Scudd's house wasn't visible, but a thin column of smoke rising vertically above the trees alerted me to its probable location.

After scanning the area thoroughly, I returned to the *Belle Girl*, but I'd left it a little late. It was dark under the trees, and it took me longer to get down the hill than up. Back aboard the *Belle Girl*, I brought the charts out and spent an hour studying Quanterelle's coastline. After noting several possible landing sites, I settled down to wait.

THE *Belle Girl* lifted off the mud at about midnight. With the radar going, and using the boat's powerful searchlight, I managed to stay off the rocks and get out of the inlet safely. Lewis Channel seemed larger and emptier when I switched the *Belle Girl*'s navigation lights off. Stars filled the whole sky, except for a thin sliver of moon. There was a slight swell, and Quanterelle's shape blipped on the radar screen. I set a slow course towards it. Phosphorescent sea creatures glowed in the *Belle Girl*'s bubbling wake. At low speeds the diesel engine wasn't too noisy, although the slightest sound travels a long way across smooth water. If listeners— human or canine—were ashore on Quanterelle, they would know that a vessel was approaching.

At last, a fringe of white surf broke against a beach directly ahead. I went in at dead slow and nosed the *Belle Girl* gently ashore about a mile east from Twinner Scudd's private harbour. Leaving the controls in neutral, I grabbed the bucket of guts and carried it ashore. Dogs were already barking in the distance when I dumped the bucket above the tideline, climbed back aboard, and shoved the control into full reverse. Nothing happened when I revved the engine—I was stuck.

I went over the side, and waded ashore again. Three dark running shapes emerged from the trees. They were closing in fast when I put my shoulders to the bows and pushed. Slowly, the *Belle Girl* shifted. The first dog was only fifty yards away when I leapt aboard the boat, lost my grip on the railing and slid backwards. A dog had the heel of my boot in its mouth when I crawled on deck, reached for a pike pole and stabbed the dog with the sharp end. It fell back into the water with my boot in its mouth, tore it to shreds, and then lent its voice to the other barks echoing all around. I backed my boat clear of the beach and headed out.

The dogs were still within hearing when a fast boat emerged from Twinner Scudd's harbour. It was a large Zodiac, silhouetted on the horizon with three men aboard. At that point, I could see the Zodiac's crewmen, although they probably couldn't see me, because I was against a backdrop of black rocks and trees. I put the engine controls in neutral and let the *Belle Girl* drift in the darkness. As a defensive ploy, that worked beautifully until a magnesium flare lit up the sky.

Capable of doing about thirty knots, the Zodiac changed course and interposed itself between my boat and the island. The game was up.

There was no possibility of outrunning the Zodiac or of getting ashore unhindered. So I pushed the *Belle Girl*'s throttle wide open and set a course for Redonda Island.

Twinner Scudd's pot-growing operations were notorious. A few rash poachers had tried to rip him off over the years, but I was empty-handed and in open water. At worst, I expected threats. Possibly a couple of warning shots across my bows. Instead, the Zodiac's crew tried to blow me out of the water with high-powered automatic rifles. I dropped below the *Belle Girl*'s gunwales, crawled into the forward cabin, grabbed my Glock, and then lay on the floor-plates and waited for the fusillade to stop. It did, briefly, when the gunmen stopped firing to reload. By then the *Belle Girl*'s aluminum hull was already riddled with bullet holes; jets of seawater poured in.

What was worse, bullets had penetrated the *Belle Girl*'s fuel tank; the powerful smell of spilt diesel oil wafted into the forward cabin.

Liquid diesel is hard to ignite at atmospheric pressure—diesel fumes are a different matter. The Volvo engine was still running, which meant that the boat's electrical system was energized. I was worrying about an electrical spark igniting the diesel fumes and blowing me to kingdom come when, still face down in the forward cabin, I turned my head and shouted, "Hold your fire. I'm coming out!"

Nobody answered. I was repeating the same message when the gunmen resumed firing.

By then, loose water sloshed in the bilges and was rising between gaps in the floorplates. The *Belle Girl* was sinking. Above the noise of rifle fire and ricocheting bullets came a muffled roar; the boat's interior lit up with oily yellow light. The *Belle Girl*'s fuel tank had blown up. The cockpit became a blazing inferno.

With liquid flames lapping towards me, I tried to open a cabin window. It jammed halfway. I was trapped. By then, my pant legs were ablaze. The cabin was full of black smoke combined with red and yellow flames. I groped blindly down to the cabin sole, and after struggling for a bit, I yanked a floorboard loose and used it to smash the window. I slid over the side.

Black seawater closed around me like a suit of ice and dulled the searing pain of my burns. Instead of swimming hard and making splashes, I did a slow breaststroke that kept my legs and arms underwater. I couldn't see the Zodiac. That magnesium flare had gone out. The *Belle Girl* was well alight by then, burning and going under about a mile off Quanterelle Island. With the tide in my favour, I figured that I had about a fifty-fifty chance of making it to shore. I wondered if Charlie's bucket of guts had immobilized Twinner Scudd's dogs.

Then another magnesium flare went up. The men in the Zodiac found me in about fifteen minutes. When the Zodiac came abreast, I looked up and saw three gunmen wearing black survival suits. Their faces appeared to float, disembodied, like white balloons. One of the men had a metallic splint taped across his nose. Laughing, he went to his knees on the Zodiac's inflated rubber side. I reached out. He grabbed my wrist. Instead of pulling me aboard, he punched my face and then shoved me down and held me underwater for a while. I could hear my heart pounding in my chest, louder than the Zodiac's outboard motors. When he let me up for air, Eddie Cliffs said, "Welcome to Quanterelle, smart guy."

Grinning, Cliffs picked a fishkiller club out of the bottom of the Zodiac and raised it menacingly. Time seemed to slow down as the fishkiller described a slow arc before it connected above my left ear. My head exploded into a universe of red and yellow pain. Eddie Cliffs was enjoying himself. Only half-conscious, I went under again.

I came to my senses when the Zodiac's hull grounded on Quanterelle Island. I was propped up in a sitting position, with my back against the side of the boat and my legs stretched out on the floorboards. Instead of moving, I kept still, opened my eyes a fraction. One of the boatmen had carried the Zodiac's bowline up the beach and hooked it over an iron mushroom. He then continued on up the beach and went into a small hut. Lights went on inside the hut. Another boatman was fiddling with the Zodiac's engine controls. Eddie Cliffs was leaning over the stern, using a knife to hack away strands of kelp that had wrapped themselves around the Zodiac's propellers.

The second boatman said, "I'm all finished here, Eddie. We'll need to gas her up before we take her out again. What do you want done with the cop?"

"When I'm finished cutting this kelp away, we'll drag him ashore. Twinner will want to talk to him when he wakes up."

"*If* he wakes up, you mean. The poor fucker's probably dead."

"Serves him right if he is dead," Cliffs replied hotly. "The fucker busted my nose and nearly broke my fucking knee."

"Asshole, you had it coming, probably. And there was no need to hit him with the goddamn club. Twinner never said nothing about killing him."

"You worry too much."

"And you don't worry enough, Cliffy," the man said, as he stepped ashore off the bows and walked up the beach to the hut.

The fishkiller club that Cliffs had used on me was less than six feet away. It was lying on the floor near the steering console. Cliffs was still busily cutting kelp at the stern. It was now or never, time for me to make a move. I bent my knees, used my elbows to push myself away from the side of the boat, and tried to stand up. I never made it. Weak as a kitten, I raised my ass off the floorboards six inches, and then I collapsed. Cliffs turned. He was grinning. He grabbed the fishkiller.

CHAPTER TWENTY-FIVE

The nightmare that overtook me took place within the pulsing radiant dome that was my skull. I was on Flea Island, following a woman dressed in a hooded black raincoat and gumboots. Rain sheeted down; my throbbing head seared with agony, but my body was cold, naked, shivering. A ravenous horde of fleas feasted on my face and inside my nostrils and mouth. The woman I was following had a black hole where her face was supposed to be, but I knew who she was all right: She was P.G. Mainwaring. Flea Island was about the size of a football field and forested improbably with aluminum Christmas trees. P.G. was walking too fast. I couldn't keep up and lost sight of her once or twice, until she left the trees and went inside an unfinished house. The house had a shingle roof and planked floors, but its walls were just bare wooden studs. I saw P.G. go down on her knees before a fireplace and try to lodge something up in the chimney. The thing wouldn't stay put, and it kept falling to the hearth. When I looked over her shoulder to see what she was trying to hide, her faceless head swung towards me. I saw something horrible under the black hood and raised both hands to block the sight of it. P.G. grabbed my arm and pulled me to her. Instead of struggling, I curled myself into a ball, and waited for the world to end . . .

A voice I didn't recognize said, "Shhhh, take it easy, you're waking up."

Was I dead? No. I was alive and in the real world. My crack-addict dream receded. My head ached abominably; my mouth felt as if someone had driven a blade into my gums and was scraping the dental nerves. I opened my eyes: I was lying on a wooden floor with a woman leaning over me.

"Hold still and keep your eyes shut for a minute. I've bandaged your head. Now I'm going to put a poultice on your face," she said quietly. "It's wild lily-of-the-valley leaves infused with cascara bark. It's a gooey mess, but it'll cool your skin."

"Aaaaargh, gruuugh."

"Try not to speak, it'll make your gums bleed worse."

I fell into another doze. The next time I woke, I was lying on a low couch with a cushion beneath my head. The woman was absent, but a man sitting in a Coast Salish chief's ceremonial chair was watching me. It was Twinner Scudd. Behind Scudd's chair was a giant sun mask from the centre of which a Raven-Transforming-into-Wolf face gaped out. The mask was old. I was wondering how Twinner had acquired it when he got down from his throne and swaggered over. He said, "Having a shitty day, Seaweed? Eddie Cliffs gave you a good hammering, used your face as a punching bag. But you've been stupid, right? You were asking for it and maybe you deserved it."

I opened my mouth to speak, but the words that emerged from between my swollen lips were garbled and indistinct.

"I've been waiting for you to show up," Twinner said with his usual cocky self-confidence. "Not much goes on around here without me knowing all about it. I knew you were in Whaletown five minutes after the mail plane landed. I didn't know *who* you were, not at first. The Zodiac that was tied up to the government float when you landed belongs to me. It's the same Zodiac that Cliffy picked you up in last night."

I licked my parched lips. It didn't help much, because an invisible sadist was tearing at my gums with red-hot pliers. Twinner went away for a minute and came back with a pitcher of water and a glass. He raised my head from the cushions and let me drink.

"It isn't hard to figure out why you came," Twinner remarked. "It's because of her, right? That stuck-up meddling bitch."

Twinner's words made little sense. What was he talking about?

"Do you have any idea how many people depend on me for jobs?" Twinner Scudd went on rhetorically. "Nearly fifty. Fifty of the greedy bloodsuckers, and I'm only talking about full-time workers. I've got grow-ops all over Desolation Sound, and when we start chopping bud in a couple of weeks, I'll need even more of the bastards. Let me tell you something else. Turnover is heavy in my business, and good help is hard to find. Guys rip me off, or try to. Some of these half-smart fuckers can't even follow simple instructions, and the guy who worked you over last night is one of 'em. He's a sadistic bastard, Cliffy is.

"I wouldn't mind so much except unnecessary violence can bring on a shitload of grief. Believe me, Seaweed, I know what I'm talking about," he said, smiling now like a man who wanted to be liked. "Any time you feel like working for me instead of Whitey, there's an opening for you. Come in with me, Seaweed. I'll pay you more money in the next six months than you've earned in your whole life. With what you know about cops and crime, you and me could clean up. You could move off the reserve, live on a big yacht like I do. You'd have money up to the ying-yang, so think it over."

Twinner Scudd went back to his chair and sat down, motionless and silent, until he took his dark glasses off and rubbed the back of a hand across his dark eyes. He put the glasses back on. "I need immunity from prosecution," he said quite humbly. "I'm ready to make a deal with you. A plea bargain, because my ass is in a sling and I want out. I know what's being going on and I'm gonna turn the killer over to you. In exchange, I get to walk."

Which killer? I wondered.

He said, "Are you listening to what I'm saying?"

In your dreams, I thought. But I nodded my head. If I'd been capable of it, I'd have smiled too because, if Twinner Scudd was involved in murder, I'd see he went down for it.

"I can handle a little slap on the wrist, maybe a suspended sentence, because that's all I deserve," he said, nodding sagely. "Believe me, Seaweed, I didn't conspire to kill nobody. What it was, it was just a big misunderstanding. I can prove it."

He might know what goes on in his own neck of the woods, but evidently he didn't know that I'd been suspended. That my present influence with Victoria's police department was zero.

"I've got something to show you," Twinner said. "You still look bad, though, like something the cat dragged in. Do you think you can walk a few yards?"

I didn't want to walk. I wanted to stay where I was until the pain went away. With a big effort, I got up on my elbows and swung my legs off the couch. When I stood up, the world began to revolve.

With Twinner Scudd's support, I shuffled across the floor to a carved and painted wooden screen, and then through a narrow doorway into a small regalia chamber. It was quite dark and silent inside the chamber. Twinner helped me to sit on a ceremonial chief's throne identical to the one I'd seen in the other room. Twinner Scudd made himself comfortable on the floor. He was a soft fat blob sitting in the lotus position holding his knees.

Half a dozen tall men stood silently here and there. Seconds elapsed before I realized that I wasn't looking at human beings, but at carved wooden totem poles. Masks and dancing blankets draped the regalia chamber's cedar-panelled walls. Then I noticed Eddie Cliffs.

Hardly breathing, as still as the totem poles that surrounded him, Eddie Cliffs was standing perfectly still and upright with both arms behind his back. Several more moments passed before I understood that his wrists were tied and that he was partially suspended from a roof beam. His heels barely touched the floor.

"Feel like kicking Cliffy in the balls or gouging his eyeballs out?" Twinner said to me. "Go ahead. It's payback time for what Cliffy did to you last night."

"Coooey ow," I mumbled.

"Did you say cut him down, Seaweed?" Twinner laughed. "Aren't you generous. This is the guy who used brass knuckles on you, knocked you cold. Now Cliffy's feeling a bit of pain himself."

Pointing a finger at Eddie Cliffs, Twinner said, "How's it feel so far?" Cliffy groaned.

"Hear that?" Twinner said to me. "Fortunately for him, Seaweed, Cliffy is still awake. If he flakes out he ends up with two dislocated shoulders. It's a little trick that Bush's CIA pals picked up from the Syrians. They tell me it hurts like a bastard, but that's not the worst of it. The worst of is you end up permanently crippled with two bum shoulders."

"Fo Gogh sake, 'winner," I muttered.

"God's not listening to you," Twinner laughed. "Cliffy's been appealing to God for hours already, and he ain't had an answer yet either. I'm softening Cliffy up for a grand finale in case he don't do what I want him to do and say what I want him to say."

"Help me, Seaweed. I'm sorry what I done to you," Eddie pleaded. "Somebody help me."

Seated like a fat Buddha, Twinner Scudd said, "Seaweed, I'm gonna tell you how Larry Cooley got killed. It was on account of that Mainwaring bitch. I believe she's a favourite of yours, though. You got a hard-on for her, Seaweed?"

I didn't answer.

"Maybe you got a hard-on for her, but every time I see that woman, all I get is a hard time. Did you know she owned the Nanaimo building?"

I didn't respond. Twinner Scudd took his dark glasses off and rubbed his eyelids with his soft fingers. "With me, Piggy's all business," he said after shielding his eyes with those dark lenses once more. "I owed her a little rent money, nothing serious. It's kind of a landlord-versus-tenant game I was playing with her. I was wondering how far I could push her before the sheriff showed up at Nanaimo's. Dumped my possessions on the street and nailed a writ to the door. She came to my office a couple of times. Laying down the law. Telling me how she was going to pull the rug out from under me. The last time Piggy came in throwing her weight around, I got mad. I threatened to kill her. It was just a bluff, Seaweed. I didn't mean it. I was gonna pay her eventually."

Twinner shook his head in wonderment. "But I guess I shoved her too far. She lost patience with me. So what does Piggy do? She gets Larry Cooley to burn her own fucking building down. Christ, the cunt sure pulled the fucking rug out from under me. The building was insured, she won't be out of pocket one lousy cent. But I am out a bundle. My lovely tax shelter is a heap of rubble, Nanaimo's is finished. If I want another club, I've got to build one up from scratch again. It'll cost me a pisspot full of cash and I hate to lose my hard-earned money."

"Ain't that right, Cliffy?" Twinner asked his former lieutenant. "Larry Cooley burned me out. Tossed a Molotov cocktail, didn't he?"

"Burn oo ow," Eddie uttered, in a series of strangled gasps. "Burn oo ou . . . Lemme dow . . . Jesus . . ."

"I'm not letting you down, Cliffy, because you've been a very bad boy. I'm teaching you a lesson you ain't never gonna forget as long as you live. Which won't be much longer either, probably."

Twinner said to me, "Remember what I was telling you earlier, Seaweed? How good help is hard to find nowadays? Nobody's got a real work ethic anymore. Most of my gang can't even follow simple instructions. Cliffy is a prime example. Take last night for instance. We've got a radar setup on this island. Every time a boat comes in and lands on my beach, we know about it. When your boat came in last night, I told Cliffy to take the Zodiac out, chase you the hell off my property. Instead, Cliffy sinks your boat, beats you to a pulp with a set of brass knucks, and then he tries to drown you. Fortunately, the guys who were in the Zodiac with Cliffy talked him out of it. Otherwise you'd be dead by now. You'd be as dead as Larry Cooley.

"Cliffy's a sick fucker, sick in the head," Twinner continued with growing anger. "We know that Cooley set fire to Nanaimo's because Cooley was careless. One of my waiters actually saw him do it. Well, I can't tolerate that kind of crap. In my line of work, if the word gets out that people can fuck you over and get away with it, you are done, toast, kaput, out-of-goddamn-business! So I sent Cliffy around to give Cooley a few bruises. I told Cliffy to rough Cooley up a little, beat some sense into him. It worked, Cooley sang like a bird. Cooley told Cliffy that burning down my club was Piggy Mainwaring's idea. Only it's like I said, Cliffy's a sick fucker, he's got this thing about hurting people now. He gets a kick out of it. Instead of giving Cooley stern words and a few slaps, Cliffy kills him. Ain't that right, Cliffy?"

Eddie groaned.

Twinner Scudd stood up and loosened the rope behind Eddie Cliff's back until his heels were flat on the floor.

"Tell Seaweed here how you done it," Twinner said. "Go on, tell him, Eddie. Give Seaweed the whole nine yards."

Eddie shook his head.

His anger growing, Twinner grabbed a heavy ceremonial paddle that was leaning against a wall and whacked Eddie's knees with it until Eddie's bones made cracking noises.

I told Twinner to stop, that anything Eddie said under these conditions would be useless as evidence.

"Screw that. For now, all I want is for Cliffy to give you the straight dope. Go on, Cliffy, tell him."

Eddie stared at the ground. Twinner went out, came back with a bucket of water and dumped it over Eddie's head.

"We grabbed Cooley downtown," Eddie muttered indistinctly. "Me and Ross. Cooley lived by himself in a house on Rudlin Street. We staked the place out till he showed up one night. We let him go in the house, waited a minute. Then we knocked on his door. We grabbed Cooley when he answered the door, shoved him back inside. Then we put the boots to him. Me and Ross."

"You and Ross killed him?" I asked.

"Not right away," Cliffy answered. " We shoved Cooley around a little for burning down Nanaimo's is all. We didn't go there to kill him. We just asked him why the fuck he went and did it. Revenge, Cooley told us. Punishment for not paying your rent, Twinner."

Twinner smiled thinly. "Then what?"

"Cooley got lippy. Called me a cunt and an asshole. I guess I lost my temper, but Jesus, Twinner, gimme a break. My shoulders are fucking killing me, I can't even think straight."

Twinner loosened the ropes so that Eddie Cliffs could sit on the floor.

"Go on, Cliffy," Twinner said. "We're listening. Give us the whole story, or I'll give that rope another yank."

"Me and Ross left Cooley's house. Later on, I got to thinking about what Cooley had said. Calling me an asshole and that. It got preying on my mind till I got crazy and went back to teach the asshole a lesson. I shoved Cooley's head down the toilet bowl. I didn't mean to kill him."

"You drowned him?"

"I guess so."

Twinner laughed. "You guess so, Cliffy?"

"I didn't mean it, Twinner. Cooley just died on me. When I dragged him out of the toilet, he was gone, he'd breathed in water."

"Then what?"

"I thought I'd try and make it look like an accident. I took him out of the house and dumped him in a creek."

"Whereabouts?"

"Sumatch Creek. I dumped Cooley's body off a bridge and watched him float away. There was a lot of rain coming down from the mountains, and I figured he would just drift into Juan de Fuca Strait."

"Did I tell you to kill him?"

"No, boss, you told me to rough Cooley up."

Twinner turned to me. "Do you think Eddie's telling the truth?"

I nodded. I had absolutely no doubt that Eddie had told us the truth.

CHAPTER TWENTY-SIX

We were aboard Twinner Scudd's yacht, en route to Victoria down the Homathko Channel. Ruth Claypole was stretched out beside me on a cushioned seat-locker. Her tiny hands and feet contrasted markedly with the rest of her. Enormously fat, she looked in her black elasticized bathing suit like a Willendorf Venus.

Twenty yards to starboard, immense granite walls raced past. I saw a patch of colour, reached for the binoculars lying on a table beside my deck chair, and focussed on a painted man with yellow bars radiating from his head. Before he went out of range, I spotted another painted man standing with his arms akimbo, his skinny stick-legs showing below a triangular skirt.

Awakening from her nap, Ruth yawned and stretched.

"Looks funny, doesn't he?" I said, pointing out the pictograph and speaking as best I could with a poulticed face and a mouth that felt as if it were stuffed with cotton batting.

"If you think them paintings is funny, you should look in a mirror."

"Beauty is only poultice-deep," I bragged. "When this dressing comes off, you'll see what I really look like."

"I already know what you look like without a poultice."

From my chair on the afterdeck, I could see the *Polar Girl*'s pilot-house and the back of Twinner Scudd's head.

Ruth got off the seat-locker and knelt beside me. "Listen," she said, putting a hand on my knee and speaking in a low voice. "Twinner was wrong about you. He thinks you came up here because you were after that woman. What's her name?"

"P.G. Mainwaring."

"They call her Piggy. But it's me that you were really looking for, right?"

"Right. I came up because of you. I want you to tell me what happened at Ronnie Chew's house."

"I know you do, but that's not all I know, Silas. I know for instance that Maria Alfred is having a hard time in Wilkie Road. It don't matter, though, because I just want to get it over and done with. Move on with my shitty little life."

"Your life doesn't have to be shitty . . ."

"What do you know about my life?" she responded heatedly. "What's out there for me? Spend my life cutting Twinner's grass up in Desolation Sound? Or a nine-to-five minimum-wager in Victoria and a nightly commute to a crappy room in a mouldy house? Turning tricks?"

"Easy, Ruth. There are other options."

"Not for girls like me," she said, staring at me with sun-crinkled eyes. "Come to think of it, maybe I'd be better off spending my life in a nice minimum-security prison. I'd get steady meals, free clothing somebody else to make all the decisions for me. And besides, how do I know if you'll give me a decent break?"

"You'll get every possible break, you have my word."

"What do you want from me then?"

"Start by explaining exactly what happened on the night that you and Maria met Ronnie Chew."

"Me and Maria just ran into him by chance, we'd never seen him before," Ruth said, her voice still a little angry. "We were in Twinner Scudd's club in Esquimalt. Nanaimo's. Ronnie was sitting there all by himself, looking lonely. He came over and introduced himself. We hit it off right away. We was having fun when all hell broke loose, guys were fighting, glasses was flying. Maria and me were sharing Ronnie's table by then, having a few drinks. It seemed like he had dough. He didn't argue when it came to paying our tab. When the trouble started, the three of us got the hell out of there and we ended up in Ronnie's house."

"And?"

"Don't rush me, Silas," she declared impatiently, "I'm trying to remember . . ."

I waited, wondering if I'd get the truth or a string of rationalizations.

She said, "It was a beautiful house, we figured Ronnie owned it, but it turned out he was just a gardener."

"Yes, he was. Just a gardener."

"I don't get it. Ronnie was loaded; I know he was. He had all these expensive toys: The fancy Beemer, a ton of cocaine, jewellery. He gave me and Maria jewellery, told us we could help ourselves if we'd fool around with him a little, let him take pictures of us naked. That's what we did. Fooled around in his bedroom. He likes fat girls, I guess. Ronnie was doing coke as well. After a while, he ran out of steam and conked on us. Me and Maria decided it was time to go. We couldn't start Ronnie's car, and so we tried to call a cab, but we couldn't find no phone and ended up walking along Collins Lane. Then this old fart stops us on the road. He asks us what we think we're doing. We tell him it's none of his fucking business, which it wasn't. Then we heard a goddamn police siren and two cops showed up. Me and Maria panicked. I don't know why, we should have stopped where we was, because we hadn't done nothing wrong, right? But we panicked and we ran into the woods and tried to hide. Then me and Maria got separated. You know the rest."

"When we get back to Victoria, police will meet the boat. They'll take you into custody for a short while, and there'll be questions. But you needn't worry. They won't hold you long, you'll be back on the street in no time. It's imperative you tell the police exactly what you've told me. No creative additions or subtractions."

"Okay, I've heard that lecture before."

"You said earlier that you knew what I look like without a poultice on my face."

"That's because this isn't the first time we've met."

"So you do remember me?"

"Sure I do."

"You and Maria were walking on Pandora Street. I noticed you particularly because you were both wearing funny T-shirts."

"Me and Maria was watching ravens. You came over and told us you were a cop."

"Correct. A couple of days later you were on Echo Bay with Ronnie Chew. And there's something else. Hidden in the trees above Ronnie's house there's a sandstone boulder with something peculiar about it."

"I don't know what you're talking about. A boulder? You mean a big chunk of rock?"

"The boulder has a skeleton man petroglyph on it, and a wolf."

"Who cares? If you've seen one petroglyph you've seen 'em all. In my opinion."

A PROMISE MADE is a debt unpaid, but things didn't work out as I had expected they would. It was after midnight when the *Polar Girl* rounded Victoria's Laurel Point and manoeuvred into its usual berth near the Johnson Street Bridge. I was expecting to see Bernie Tapp. Instead, Nice Manners and half of Victoria's Serious Crimes squad were waiting on the dock to greet us. With Twinner Scudd at my side, I posted myself at the head of the yacht's slanting gangway. Manners came aboard all piss and vinegar. The poultice on my face amused him. He gave me the brush-off when I tried to explain matters. Manners wasn't interested in what I might have to say. Obsessed with his personal vendetta, Manners slapped me with a writ that commanded me to stay within Victoria's city limits for the next ten days, and ordered me off the yacht.

I stood on the dock while the entire Quanterelle contingent was arrested, handcuffed and brought ashore. Twinner Scudd gave me a glance hot enough to make my cheeks burn when he and the others were whisked off to VPD headquarters in an armoured van.

Manners ordered Harry Biedel to stay behind and guard the yacht.

Looking down at me from the *Polar Girl*'s pilothouse, Biedel said, "How was Desolation Sound?"

"All right, but things have gone to hell since. I was expecting Bernie Tapp to meet me, not Manners."

"Bernie's in Vancouver with Superintendent Mallory. They're attending a tea, crumpets and gang-related crime conference at the Park Plaza Hotel. It was a last-minute panic deal, I gather."

Biedel wished me goodnight and told me to go home. It was good advice, and I ought to have followed it, but I didn't.

It was a cold night in Victoria. The air smelled like rain, clouds dragged themselves like a veil across the stars. I pulled my collar up and tramped off the dock. A draggle of piss-bums were passing a bottle around in a grassy wasteland beside the E & N Railroad terminus. I needed a drink too, and I might have joined them, except they were probably drinking salt-poisoned Chinese cooking brandy or Scope mouthwash. Swans Pub, a hundred yards away, drew me like a magnet. The streets were empty of pedestrians, although vehicle traffic was heavy along Store Street and down Pandora Street.

I was standing across from Swans, waiting for the light to change, when I heard footsteps behind. I turned and from the corner of an eye saw a masked man turn the gun in his hands and swing it down by the barrel. Shock and surprise slowed my reflexes. My head broke the gun's fall. I dropped away into an abyss of scattered blinding light.

SEVERAL HEAVY BLOWS to the head in quick succession were more than even my thick head could tolerate. I was kept in an induced coma for over a week. I have no memories of the immediate aftermath except for a jumble of vague impressions that may owe more to imagination than memory. I know that Little Sam the medicine man came into my hospital room with Chief Alphonse to burn sweetgrass and throw bones in the air. Felicity Exeter made a single visit, although I remember nothing about it. I've been told since that in a delirious state I came clean about my brief sexual dalliance with P.G. Mainwaring. I had a guilty conscience, I'm a jackass to boot, and the truth was out. Felicity went away and she didn't come back.

My first lucid memory involved Old Mary Cooke. She was sitting at my bedside talking about cedar.

In olden days, cedar bark was highly prized. In late April or early May, when the tree sap was rising, young Coast Salish women would find a good cedar tree, stretch as high as they could reach, cut through the bark to the sapwood with a sharp knife, and then pull the bark down. Cedar bark comes off in long strips that can be rolled up in bundles and carried home. The bark is split, pounded between stones, and immersed in hot water. After days of tedious work the cedar fibres separate and can be woven into cloaks, hats and other garments.

Old Mary Cooke told me that a long, long time ago, the daughter of a chief was looking for cedars in the forested slopes above Echo Bay when she came across a house built of wooden planks. Nearby, four wolf cubs were hiding among the exposed roots of a big old cedar tree where a wolf had made her den.

Now, it is well known amongst the Coast Salish that if a whaler skins a young wolf cub alive and rubs it against his canoe, good hunting will follow. The young woman seized the four cubs and put them into her basket, intending to take them home to her brother.

She started towards home and immediately heard a strange sound, as if a great crowd was singing and drumming. When she stopped walking, the noise ceased. Looking around, she saw an old woman, beckoning her from the doorway of the plank house. As the young woman approached the plank house, she looked ahead and noticed that the floor inside the house was littered with the skeletons of small birds. From within the plank house she heard the sound of many voices. She stepped inside and fell down and went into a dream. While dreaming, the young woman saw a series of Bird Dancers who appeared from behind a screen to dance while the old woman sang. The young woman learned all of the old woman's songs. When the young woman woke from her dream, she saw that the old woman had turned into a mother wolf. The mother wolf released her cubs from the basket, fled with them from the plank house, and gave a ritual howl. The plank house turned into a boulder. The young woman was forever entombed in stone.

I WAS IN the Jubilee Hospital, where an overtaxed doctor was soaking poultice off my face with an evil-smelling chemical solution.

"What is this stuff?" the doctor asked, her nose wrinkling at the smell.

"It's an old Indian remedy," I replied listlessly. "Lily-of-the-valley leaves and cascara bark. A woman that I know keeps putting it on every night."

"Cascara bark? The stuff ancient Egyptians used for unplugging their bowels?"

"The very same."

"Holy God, this is one for the books! Feel that, Mr. Seaweed? Skin is peeling off your face in strips, although I must say that your wounds look clean enough underneath this crap. I don't think there'll be much scarring, if any, but you've been damned lucky. What happened to you?"

"I went up to Desolation Sound and fell into a cement mixer."

"Very careless. Now, open your mouth."

I opened it. She put a spatula on my tongue and looked at my gums.

"This must be rather painful," she said a few moments later. "You'll probably lose a couple of teeth, and maybe their roots. I'll arrange for an oral surgeon to look at you when I'm finished."

Candace wandered into the room. Looking sexy in a miniskirt, she said, "My, my, Silas. Don't you look nice?"

"Goddammit, Hilda!" the doctor said angrily. "This is a sterile area."

Candace bridled. "Nothing to worry about, Doctor. I've just had my monthly checkup."

"I know you have, and I don't want you spreading it around in my emergency room," the doctor replied heatedly.

"I have something to tell Silas."

"Listen, Hilda! Just clear off before I call security."

"Hey, Candace," I said, rousing my head from the pillows. "How did you know I was here?"

"Lightning told me . . ." Candace's hands flew to her mouth. "Oh God! I wasn't supposed to tell you that!"

Candace fled.

"Why do you call her Candace?" the doctor asked.

"That's her name."

"Your thought processes may be affected, post traumatic stress probably," the doctor mused. "Her name is Hilda Mullins, she's a hooker."

"Candace is her boudoir name."

"Really? And as for what Hilda might have for you, Mr. Seaweed, how about a dose of the clap?"

Days passed before I went home.

I DRANK MILK through a straw, slurped up some runny scrambled eggs and went outside to my private garden. Existence was bearable, I decided, lying like a log in my hammock. The pine siskin had flown away; my thoughts kept flying away. There was something important that I needed to remember but, lulled by the pleasant chatter of late-summer birds, I found it hard to concentrate. Words buzzed through my head like bees: mulligatawny, lightning, candy striper, tooth implants. I slept for an hour. A car came downhill past the longhouse and pulled to a stop outside my garden gate. The pine siskin returned and made himself comfortable on my stomach. Bernie Tapp, coming into the garden through the gate, scared the little bird into the escallonia bush.

It was the tenth time Bernie had checked in after bringing me home from hospital. He sat down on one of my garden chairs and brought a bottle from his pocket.

"How come you're not resting up at Felicity Exeter's?" he said gruffly.

"I haven't seen her lately. I believe she's in Seattle, attending a Spirit Bear conference."

"You're banged up in Victoria and she's in Seattle, worrying about bears?"

"She's a free spirit."

"I know, it's one of the things I like about her. It's also one of the things that I dislike about her. Does Felicity know how sick you still are?"

Bernie's innocent question made me feel worse. I said, "Wait a minute."

My sense of balance had improved; getting out of the hammock and going to my outdoor privy was easier now. After relieving my bladder, I went back to the hammock.

"Your cheeks are a bit swollen on the left side of your face. Otherwise, apart from those staples, and the bald spots where your head was shaved, you look pretty good," Bernie remarked. "Is it okay for you to have a drink?"

"I'm weaning myself off sobriety slowly. A wee dram would help the process."

"Where are your drinking glasses?"

"You know where they are, Bernie. Help yourself."

Bernie went into the cabin, returned with two moulded glass tumblers, and filled them with Chivas Regal.

"It's time we talked business. Twinner Scudd has made a long statement," Bernie said. "He's still locked up, but we don't know how much longer we can hold him because his lawyers want him out. According to Twinner's counsel, he made a deal with you. A plea bargain."

"That's right."

"That's bullshit. Twinner spilled his guts. He told us that Larry Cooley set fire to Nanaimo's. In retaliation, Twinner Scudd told Eddie Cliffs to shove Cooley around a little. But Cliffs is nuts and things spun out of control. Cooley ended up in Sumatch Creek the way you ended up in Desolation Sound, except Cooley drowned. That's good in a way, because if Cooley had survived, we would have nailed him instead. He's an arsonist, and people died in the flames. He would have been a burden on the state for the rest of his life. It all adds up. We've charged Eddie Cliffs with first-degree murder. The Crown is sure it'll stick. Twinner Scudd thinks he's in the clear and will walk. But he won't walk. Twinner will get five years and he will serve at least three years behind bars before he gets parole . . ."

"Wait a minute. I didn't promise Twinner anything, but . . ."

"Listen carefully, pal," Bernie said slowly and deliberately. "You are not a cop. Not any more. Your deal-making days ended when you rolled over in Mallory's office . . ."

"Rolled over? I told Mallory the truth . . ."

"Dumb, dumb, dumb and bloody dumber! Instead of sticking up for yourself when you had the chance, you played the big hero. You stuck your chin out and invited Mallory to take a sock at it. You left Mallory with no choice but to suspend you. Now it's too late. You've lost your badge. It's all over, pal. Twinner Scudd has thumbed his nose at the law long enough. Crown is rubbing its hands, because for them it's payback time. Twinner Scudd will go down for five years."

"Is this a joke?"

Bernie shook his head. "This is the joke: you are a walking dead man. When Twinner Scudd finally realizes that his plea bargain is an absolute non-starter, your days will be numbered. You will be dead, buried and forgotten by the time Twinner Scudd comes out of jail." Bernie kept talking, but I'd stopped listening.

I tuned in again when Bernie said, "Your disciplinary hearing is on hold as regards the cocaine rap. Oh, and by the way, Lightning Bradley is still AWOL. He's done a runner, and we still can't find him."

I was still absorbing these priceless nuggets of information when Bernie went on, "Ruth Claypole made a statement. It matches the statement that Maria Alfred made weeks ago. It seems that you were right about those girls all along. They met Ronnie/Raymond when they were out on the town having a little fun. They didn't kill Raymond Cho, we've had to turn 'em loose. We'll be lucky if they don't run to a lawyer and sue us. The problem is, if those girls didn't kill Raymond Cho, who did? Who killed Maggie Bradley? Who killed Tubby Gonzales?"

"Who shoved a brick of coke up my chimney?"

Bernie shrugged. "That's not all. We need to do something about P.G. Mainwaring. Nobody knows what. She doesn't deny that Larry Cooley burned Nanaimo's down, but she insists that he was acting independently. Nobody believes her, but that doesn't bother her because her lawyers have told her we have no case. They've told her that she has nothing to fear from police as long as she keeps her trap shut and lets counsel do all the talking. Her lawyers are right. The VPD is left with egg on its face. What do you think we should do about this mess?"

"Ask a policeman."

"You're a policeman."

Instinctively, I shook my head, which turned out to be a very bad idea. My whole world began to spin. Bernie saw my eyes lose focus; he grabbed me before I fell.

I was trying to remember something. Something important about storms and candy stripers and mulligatawny soup, when Bernie took me into my cabin, lowered my spinning head to the pillows, and tucked me into bed.

"You're not mad at me, are you, pal?" Bernie asked, his eyes troubled.

"Jeez, Bernie," I said, and fell asleep.

CHAPTER TWENTY-SEVEN

Heavy black clouds blew in from the north, skewered themselves atop Victoria's telephone poles and wet us with their weeping. The air turned cold. Winter's ruins were upon us, white horses galloped across the waves and dashed themselves to foam on the beaches. Canada geese flew in and circled above Warrior Bay, where they joined dozens of high-flying mallards. Turning slowly, the birds drifted lower and lower before alighting en masse upon the water, where they disturbed drifting trumpeter swans. I could still hear the birds at night, a dark raft of voices.

Red-breasted nuthatches had been yank-yanking for days. I stocked wire bird feeders with suet. My back garden became full of birds: northern flickers with copper-red underwings; black-capped chickadees; downy woodpeckers. I kept my wood stove alight, listened to KPLU, and read *The New Yorker*. A district health nurse popped in occasionally to change my dressings, pull staples out of my aching head, and warn me against lifting anything heavier than plates of food.

Bernie Tapp phoned. He said, "What size boots do you wear?"

"Blimey, guv," I said in a fake cockney accent. "You've got me banged to rights. Them was me size twelve prints in the vicar's rose garden."

With a hollow laugh, Bernie hung up.

Felicity never called me. As far as I knew Felicity, was still conferencing in Seattle; I was sleepless in the Warrior Indian Reserve. Suddenly, I got crazy from sitting around. It was probably a bad idea, but I put a black toque on my aching head, a black raincoat over my out-of-shape body, and did an old man's stiff-legged shuffle to my MG, parked twenty yards away under my carport. After getting my breath back, I sat behind the steering wheel and started the engine. Somebody banged on the roof. It was Chief Alphonse.

"You're not fit to drive, Silas!" he said, wagging a cautionary finger.

He was right; he's always right. I took my lock-picking kit from the MG's toolbox, and stored it in my several pockets. Chief Alphonse helped me back to the cabin. When he left, I phoned for a taxi. A noiseless yellow Toyota hybrid glided in several minutes later. I was easing myself into the taxi when Bernie drove up in his Interceptor. I had to tell the cabbie that I didn't need him after all, and gave him twenty bucks for his trouble. He took the money, called me a useless cocksucker, swore that that was the last goddamn trip he'd make to a goddamn Indian reserve and raced off. His cab number was 1623.

"Christ, shouldn't you still be in bed? You look like hell," Bernie said, as I dragged my hide back to the cabin.

Bernie had brought me a pair of size twelve Magnum Stealths.

"Eighty bucks a pair when you buy these in volume. Guaranteed waterproof, heatproof, dust-proof. Issued to U.S. troops during Desert Storm," Bernie told me. "Good kick-ass flatfoot gear, any colour you like as long as it's black. Try 'em out and tell me if you like 'em."

I tried them on and did a wobbly walkabout. The boots seemed okay.

"Why the taxi?" Bernie asked.

"I need a change of pace. Thought I'd treat myself to a cup of coffee at Lou's."

"Okay, let's go."

When we got to Lou's, Bernie asked for a rain check.

Umbrellas had blossomed like mushrooms on Victoria's streets. I sheltered in Lou's doorway till Bernie drove away. A bedraggled hooker went by like a zombie; greying blonde hair shielded her face. Instead of going inside Lou's, I went next door to my office. I tried my key in the door, and to my surprise, it still fitted. My bottle of Teachers was still intact in the bottom drawer. I poured an inch into a Tim Hortons mug, and took a sip. *I'm going to miss all this*, I thought. And what about PC? Could I take her home, or did she belong to the VPD now?

As a cop, I'd been out there, dragging helpless victims of life's stormy weather out of back alleys and into homeless shelters. Taking care of PC. Big deal. My epitaph, written on wind and water: he made bad choices.

PC followed her meowing wails through the cat flap, assumed the approved sphinx-like pose, and gave me what is known in the trade as a basilisk stare. Fortunately, I can read PC's mind.

"Hasn't Cynthia been looking after you properly?" I asked the little black cat, taking a can of Thrifty's grade-A tuna from a filing cabinet.

"Of course I've been looking after her," Cynthia said, appearing in the doorway. "The way you mollycoddle that thankless creature! She'll put on too much weight. Is that what you want?"

"I want to know where you came from," I said. "Would you like a cup of scotch, Cynthia?"

"No, I'm on duty. I just came in for a pee. You shouldn't be drinking either, a man in your condition."

Cynthia leaned against the mantelpiece, scowling unsympathetically as I sipped my scotch. After scarfing the last molecule of tuna, PC went behind the filing cabinets to groom her shiny fur.

"You'll be interested to know that that mysterious ghost thingy was just a simple plumbing problem," Cynthia said, taking her uniform cap off and tossing her blonde tresses.

I drank another mouthful.

"I just want you to know, Silas. The whole department thinks you've had a bum rap. Somebody whose name will never cross my lips told me all the ins and outs of it."

"That could be Nice Manners?"

Cynthia rapped the mantelpiece. "All I'm saying is, I was told they found cocaine in here, and that's why you got busted. I've been wracking my brains, wondering who might have done it. I know that you didn't do it. Did you?"

I looked her in the eye.

"That's good enough for me, Silas. Maybe I'm responsible."

"How could you be responsible?"

"Well, you gave me a key to this place months ago, remember?"

I nodded.

"And you know, Silas, people are always in and out. Cops use this place like a comfort station; some of 'em want to use your phone. I usually let them. Did I do wrong?"

"I don't know."

"You were framed. Everybody thinks so and everybody is saying so, although not all of them publicly."

"Pretend you're a police person. If I didn't stash that cocaine, who did?"

"That's what I have been wondering. I can't think of anybody, except Nice Manners. He'd be happy to see you fall, but even Manners probably wouldn't frame you."

"Sure?"

"I'm reasonably sure, not 100 per cent sure though."

"Did you ever let P.G. Mainwaring into this room?"

"Who?" Cynthia replied blankly.

"P.G. Mainwaring. She's the woman who owns this building."

Astonishment is easy to fake, but Cynthia's seemed genuine. "You could have fooled me. I thought it was owned by some corporation over in Vancouver."

"Piggy Mainwaring. Tall, beautiful, keeps a private office on the second floor."

"A private office directly above our washroom?"

I nodded.

"Wonders never cease, I realize who you're talking about now," Cynthia said. "I've seen her once. Every time she flushes her toilet it affects ours, or it used to, till Nobby Sumner fixed things properly."

"Cynthia, you haven't seen me today."

"Seen who?"

Grinning conspiratorially, she put a cap on her lovely head, put a kiss on my unlovely cheek, and went out. I washed the Tim Hortons mug, put it away, closed the office and crept upstairs with my lock-picking outfit. It was dark under the stairs outside Piggy's door. I knocked. Nobody answered. I knocked again. Same result. The lock was a hundred years old. It took me ten minutes to crack my way inside.

Things had changed since my last visit. Blankets, bedsheets and pillows, piled neatly on the couch, told me that Piggy had been sleeping in there. There was an electric kettle on the desk, along with canned food, milk powder and a loaf of fresh bread in a brown paper bag. A leather briefcase stood on the floor. I picked it up and placed it on the desk. Inside the briefcase was a Mac laptop and numerous manila folders containing papers pertaining to her routine business activities. The Mac was password protected. I put the briefcase back the way I'd found it and searched the desk drawers. What was I looking for? Whatever it was, I didn't find it.

I went downstairs, pulled my collar up against the rain and headed west along Pandora.

I was standing on the Johnson Street Bridge, cursing my infirmities while looking down at Twinner Scudd's yacht, still tied up at the marina, when a drowned rat said, "Hello, Silas."

Until then, I had believed that the expression "my heart sank" was just words.

Now I know better, because when I looked at the speaker, my heart hit the soles of my Magnum Stealths. She was Chantal Dupree, and I'd been half in love with her once. Now the sight of her was enough to make me weep. I'd lost track of Chantal for years. She'd been working East Vancouver and now she was back. Trying to turn tricks in the rain at midday wearing a crotch-high miniskirt with a tear in the hem. Ridiculously high heels that made it impossible for her to straighten her knees, an artificial-leather bomber jacket. Her blonde hair was greasy and matted. She'd been smoking crack instead of eating. Few people seeing her then would have guessed how beautiful Chantal had been once. I've lost count of the times I tried to steer her off the streets. She was about 30, looked 60, and had 90 year-old eyes. I wanted to turn her over to Joe McNaught's Christians at the Good Samaritan Mission, but Chantal said she'd rather have lunch with me and go to hell instead.

I took her arm and marched her straight into Lou's.

Lou looked at her twice before he remembered who she was. Troubled, not smiling, Lou addressed Chantal by name, led us to a dark corner table and seated Chantal with her back to the room. I didn't need to be told that Lou didn't want Chantal using his cafe and that he was ashamed of himself because of it. Lou had no gripes to air that day, no wisecracks. We ordered Lou's Tuesday special. It was Irish stew.

Chantal's relationship with Lou's Cafe predated Victoria's restaurant smoking ban. She ate a couple of spoonfuls of stew before giving up and trying to light a cigarette. Instead of telling her what she couldn't do, I reached across the table and took Chantal's skinny hand. Her pallid skin felt dry and feathery beneath my fingers. I had nothing much to say to her. Just for the hell of it, I said, "Do you see anything of Candace these days?"

"Hardly ever. The last I heard she was in Reno with Lightning Bradley."

"Candace is back, I ran into her recently. Why Lightning?"

"Lightning is one of her regulars."

"Next time you see Candace, have her give me a call. She probably knows how to reach me."

I SPENT HOURS on the telephone trying to trace Candace. She was listed in the book as Mullins, Hilda, with an address on Cridge. Eventually I called Potter's Taxi, gave them my phone number and asked them to have driver 1623 give me a call.

The phone rang immediately. I said, "This is the Indian asshole who gave you twenty bucks for showing up at my house the other day. Now I want you to take me over to Cridge. Do you have a problem with that?"

After a long pause, he said, "I'll be right over."

The driver was a turbaned Sikh named Ravi. He drove me to an Edwardian house that had been do-it-yourselfed into a crummy three-unit renter. I told Ravi to wait.

Candace had the basement suite. Her front door was four steps below street level. I pushed the buzzer. Nobody answered. I looked through the keyhole. The suite was quiet, dark, seemingly unoccupied. Ravi was listening to his car radio and pretending not to watch what I was doing. I paid Ravi five bucks more than the meter price, told him I'd be in touch and watched him drive away. We parted friends. Maybe.

Getting into Candace's was a pushover—I slid an old credit card between the edge of her door and the jamb, slid it down to the bolt, heard a satisfying click, and shoved the door open.

Apart from a small red glow, about a foot above the floor, it was dark inside. I found a light switch and turned it on. It was hot indoors. That red glow originated from artificial coals glowing in a gas fireplace. The room had oyster-coloured walls and frilly swagged curtains. Plastic flowers bloomed in plastic pots. Two white leather loveseats faced each other across the room's pink carpet. The tiny white kitchen looked as if it had never been used. The twin odours of old sex and cheap perfume became more pronounced as I entered the room where Candace practised her trade. It contained a king-sized bed with a red headboard and a red dressing table. The floor appeared to have been carpeted by a layer of fluffy white cats. Up on the ceiling, a big mirror gave Candace's johns a reverse image of what they were getting for their money.

I found a black suitcase chockablock with hump-flick CDs, black-leather corsets and masks, chromium and leather restraint devices, handcuffs and gags, but I didn't find address books or anything else that would help me to discover where Lightning Bradley might have gone to ground. I went out of Candace's thinking of elephant graveyards—Candace's was a place where love went to die.

Cars parked beneath Cridge Street's leaf-denuded chestnut trees stretched downhill toward Haultain Street. I started to walk. Three houses down, a tall fine-boned guy with a thatch of wavy red hair was working on a purple Pontiac clunker. As I went past, he said, "Is Candace a friend of yours?"

"She's my kid sister," I lied. "What have you got in that crate?"

"A '68 Firebird Q-jet 3245 pounder."

"In your dreams," I laughed. "It looks like a Chevy Stovebolt about fifteen years since its last rebore."

"So Candace is your sister, eh?" he said, a grin splitting his dirty face as he wiped his hands on a piece of cotton towelling. "You sure don't look alike."

"Same mother, different father. The next time you see Candace, tell her to give Freddie a call," I said casually. "Take it easy, pal."

I could feel his eyes boring holes in my back as I went downhill to Haultain and turned right. When I got to Quadra Street, I sat on a bench inside the first bus shelter. I was still resting to get my breath back when my cellphone rang.

A voice said, "Is this Freddie?"

"Hi, Candace. I've been looking for you."

"I know you have," Candace replied tartly. "That kid down the street told me you've been poking around inside my house. Lucky he didn't tell the police first, instead of me. How did you get in?"

"Your door wasn't locked," I lied fluently. "I must see you, it's urgent. Can we meet?"

"Are you kidding me? My door wasn't locked?"

"It was closed, not locked."

"I don't like the sound of this," Candace said. "Better come over right away."

I called Ravi, and he drove me over there again.

CANDACE HAD STOPPED pretending to be mad at me. Now she was draped across one of her loveseats smoking a Turkish cigarette, wearing an opaque pink negligee and a come-on smile. A gold crucifix dangled from the thin gold chain adorning her slim white throat.

"You've been hard to find," I said.

"That's me. Hard to find, but easy to meet. I've just got back from Vegas. They've got these great deals at the Bellagio now. Airfare and three nights for eight hundred bucks," Candace said, winking a catty green eye. "I charge clients three grand for a package deal. They're lining up in droves, especially them old guys who like to play the slots."

"Don't be filthy. You know what I want."

"I probably do, but there's such a thing as client confidentiality."

"Right. What happens in Vegas, stays in Vegas, including your money. But I'm over a barrel until I find Lightning, and I think that you might know where he is."

"He comes and then he goes," she said, with another knowing wink.

I pointed to the golden figure of Christ, writhing in agony between Candace's augmented breasts. "Be serious, your God is listening."

"We meet in hotels now, I never know in advance which one. Lightning gives me a call, tells me where he's going to be, what time he wants me to be there."

"You don't meet him here?"

"We used to. Things have changed since he landed himself in this bit of trouble."

"That's what he said? A bit of trouble? Let me give it to you straight. Lightning Bradley is the central figure in a murder inquiry. I need to find him, and soon."

"I don't know and I don't want to know where Lightning is, Silas, because my life is complicated enough already," she said, making a dramatic show of covering her ears and sprawling full length on the loveseat. As if accidentally, her negligee had opened. Her enormous breasts and that black triangle of hair below her belly were on full display.

I chewed my knuckles, admiring quite dispassionately Candace's crude attempts at seduction.

"I'm all yours, baby," she whispered, beckoning me with a crooked finger. "I've had the hots for you for years. Come on, give it to me."

I didn't want professional sex. I waved my hand with an impatient gesture. "It's imperative I track Lightning down now, Candace."

"Aw hell, I told you, I don't know where he is," she said, giving up on her Mata Hari act and getting to her feet. "I would if I could, but I can't help you."

Money is always a useful gambit in these situations. I opened my wallet and removed ten twenty-dollar bills, one at a time. Candace eyed them with a carnivorous smile.

I said, "This money is all yours, if you tell me what you know."

She lit a cigarette and then strode back and forth, smoking furiously. She said at last, "There is a little something, maybe you can use it. Lightning's a slippery cat, I don't trust him, but he thinks I do. I run a cash business."

"Or VISA. Your ass isn't the only thing that moves with the times, as I recall."

A thin smile appeared. "One time when we were together, Lightning didn't want to pay. He said his card was maxed out, that he'd run out of cash. It happens a lot in my business, but I don't sleep with guys on credit. They either stuff money between my tits before they leave, or there's a shouting match. The way it turned out, we had a shouting match. Then I made Lightning call a taxi. The two of us went over to this parking lot at the back of Pic A Flic Video. Do you know the place I mean?"

I nodded.

Candace said, "I stayed in the taxi. Lightning told me to wait while he brought me the money he owed. What could I do? I had no choice but to wait. I saw him walk down that narrow lane behind Pic A Flic towards that Starbucks outlet before I lost sight of him. I couldn't say where he went after that. Lightning was gone about ten minutes before he came back. I went home and that was that."

"Just one more thing. Whose taxi was it?"

Candace shrugged, shook her head and said negligently, "I can't remember."

"I give you two hundred bucks, and you give me the runaround? I need to know who drove you to Pic A Flic."

"I think it was a black Cadillac taxi. One of those big old Cadillacs? You're a policeman, ask around, it shouldn't be too hard to find him," she said, taking my money and sauntering towards her bedroom with it. Posed in the bedroom doorway with one knee bent, the other straight, one arm stretched up along the jamb, she said, "Say, big boy. Got anything left in that wallet?"

"Candace, when you walk away from me like that, your behind looks like two fresh honeydew melons."

"Implants, it's the latest thing," she said. "Do you like 'em?"

"I certainly do," I said sincerely.

CHAPTER TWENTY-EIGHT

I wasted a couple of days, wandering the street near the Pic A Flic shop, calling taxi companies and just generally trying to find Lightning Bradley, before Candace phoned me again. It was ten o'clock at night. I'd had a couple of drinks.

She said, "How would you like to give me another present?"

"What for?"

She said coyly, "Just on general principles."

"With you, Candace, principle doesn't enter into it."

"Okay, how about for value given and received?"

"As long as it doesn't involve sweaty tussling on your king-sized bed."

"You should try it sometime. Look up at the ceiling mirrors and admire my educated ass."

"It's not your educated ass that I'm interested in, it's your information."

"Okay, spoilsport. Put another two hundred dollars in your pocket and meet me at Pinky's."

"You want another two hundred, and that's it?" I said sourly. "Give me a hint."

"I've given you a hint, darling. See you at Pinky's in an hour, don't be late," she said sweetly, and hung up.

Unless Candace was stringing me along, it was showtime. While looking at the rain trickling down my windowpanes, I tried to make one and one equal four, gave up, and phoned Ravi. The taxi dispatcher told me that Ravi was out. I called headquarters and asked for Bernie Tapp. Second time lucky—Bernie was working late.

"It's me," I said, when Bernie came on the line. "There's no time to explain but I need a wire, tonight. Right now, in fact."

Bernie's answer was a long drawn-out sigh.

I said, "Time is running out, Bernie."

Another long sigh, then, "Where are you?"

"I'm at home."

"A wire? How about asking me for something simple? A ten-thousand-dollar unsecured personal loan, for example."

"Just a simple wire."

"Meet me in the tool crib, but don't make a fuss coming in because mistrustful eyes may be looking and suspicious ears may be listening. A wire will be ready when you get here. I just hope this doesn't land us both up the creek."

I was wearing jeans, moccasins, and a logger's thick woollen shirt. My hair was growing back nicely. My face looked almost normal, and a lingering dread that the blows to my head might have permanently disabled my brain was fading.

I exchanged my moccasins for Magnum Stealths, put a shoulder holster on under a red Gore-Tex jacket, got my car keys from where they'd been gathering moss in a drawer and strapped a dagger to my right ankle. Loaded for bear, I went out. I'd been running the MG's engine occasionally to keep the battery charged. The MG started immediately. The streets were dark, wet and desolate. It was a good night for dirty tricks and a bad night for motorbikes, so business was slow at Pinky's except for a knee-walking drunk with full-sleeve tattoos on his brawny arms and a slinky woman wearing, in essence, a bikini. Of Candace, however, there was no sign. Doyle was minding the bar as usual. When he deigned to acknowledge my existence, he made an elaborate show of opening a drawer, peering inside it for a long moment, and then he was slow to take my order.

I ordered a double Chivas Regal with water on the side.

"I've just checked your tab, you owe me a hundred bucks," Doyle said, leaning across the bar and giving me a sample of his halitosis. "It's against my principles to advance credit to the unemployed."

I raised my eyebrows.

Doyle pointed at the club's ATM. "Your money is waiting over there, and if it's not, you are barred from here till it is."

I drew money out of the ATM, plunked a hundred on the bar, and added another twenty. When my drink came, there wasn't any change.

I tasted the Chivas, put my glass on the bar and said, "Doyle. I'm waiting for the ten dollars that you owe me."

Doyle scowled.

"I'm his witness. Better give him the money, Doyle," Candace said, sliding onto a stool beside me. "Silas will need it to buy me a drink."

Doyle's scowl deepened.

I said to Candace, "Where did you spring from?"

"We're having a party in the back room. Just me and a few very close and dear friends. Feel like joining us?"

"No thanks."

"Do you have my little present for me, Silas?"

I handed her two hundred while Doyle wasn't looking. When Candace's champagne cocktail arrived, and Doyle withdrew to the end of the bar, she drew a scrap of folded paper from between her augmented breasts and gave it to me. Warmed by her body, the paper had an address written on it. I finished my drink and went out.

I DROVE INTO a street of neat middle-class houses located near Victoria's Craigdarroch Castle and did a U-turn before parking so that I could make a quick getaway if necessary. I reached beneath the dashboard, took my Glock from its clip and put it in my shoulder holster.

The house that interested me was a 1960s colonial with white cedar siding. Four slender octagonal pillars supported its long porch. The doors and window shutters were painted pale blue. Wooden stairs creaked as I walked up to the porch and put my finger to a buzzer. After a couple of minutes, curtains moved in a side window and Lightning Bradley materialized behind the dark glass. His face seemed disembodied, like a ghost summoned up by black magic. When he recognized me, Bradley's eyes widened. A grin spread across his white face like a thin smear of black paint. The face receded into darkness. After a few seconds, the front door opened. I went into an entrance hall, where Lightning was waiting for me with a gun in his hand. I became aware of low voices in the background.

Lightning was wearing a rumpled dark navy suit and he had lost weight. I smelled liquor on his breath. Gazing at me with a mixture of hostility and apprehension, he said, "Sorry, pal, I've got to ask you to unbutton your coat and put your hands behind your back."

Lightning took my gun away and put it in a drawer in the hall table. Patting me down, Lightning was careless. He missed the wire. His hand closed around the wallet in my pocket, but he missed the dagger strapped to my leg.

After checking my wallet for improvized explosive devices, Lightning dropped it on the hall carpet. "Now you can pick it up," he said, with a fraudulent grin. My neck hairs prickled when I stooped for the wallet and exposed my back.

"I've been half-expecting you," he said. "Candace told me that you might show up tonight, but you know what women are. You can't always trust 'em, can you?"

"I ought to have known," I said, giving vent to a spasm of irrational disgust. "Candace is playing both ends against the middle, like everybody else in my goddamn life. She charged me two hundred. How much did you give her?"

"Money and fair words," Lightning said with a widening grin.

He pointed down the hallway. "We've got a little catching up to do, you and me. So let's talk. You first, it's that room on the left."

I preceded him into a dimly lit living room. *Jeopardy* was playing on a widescreen TV. He switched it off. "Game shows are all I watch these days. I used to like *National Geographic*, but what with one thing or another, I don't have the attention span any more. There was a show on last night, about these mist gorillas. African gorillas that live in the mist somewhere. Poachers keep shooting them, it's a shame. Why doesn't somebody do something?"

Lightning sat down in a straight-backed chair. A bottle of Bombay gin and a blue glass tumbler stood on a side table at his elbow. I parked myself on a chesterfield, facing Lightning across the room.

Lightning placed his gun within easy reach on the side table and poured himself another gin. Old acne scars that must have shattered his adolescence and poisoned the rest of his life ravaged his skin. Gravity and late middle age was giving him bulldog jowls and a corrugated neck. Some guys have all the luck. Feeling almost sorry for him, I watched Lightning sip a little gin.

He said flippantly, "So, Silas. What do you know?"

"I know how this whole mess started. I know how it will end."

"Did you figure it all out by yourself, or did somebody have to tell you?" he said with a patronizing sneer.

"I don't put a lot of credence in other peoples' opinions, because most of what I've been listening to lately is lies. Including your lying lies."

"Are you calling me a liar?"

"Of course, I am because you are a dyed-in-the-wool liar," I said in a mild conversational tone. "You are a liar and a fraud. You are an asshole front, back and sideways."

He smiled as if I'd paid him a compliment.

I said, "Let's start with when you and Constable Ricketts answered a suspicious-persons call. You were in a blue-and-white. Constable Ricketts was driving."

"Sure. We were looking for a couple of your Native sisters who'd been spotted walking on Collins Lane."

"When you spotted the two women, Ricketts stopped the blue-and-white, and the pair of you followed them into the bush. You lost them. Instead of just giving up the chase, which is what you did, Ricketts kept looking. You went back to wait in the blue-and-white."

Lightning had a faraway expression. "Go on," he said, "this is better than *Jeopardy*."

"After a while, Ricketts called you on his cellphone. He'd stumbled across a murder. I guess you were in a hurry to join him, because while you were driving over there you ran the blue-and-white into a sports car. It was an unlucky accident, but maybe you were a little careless as well."

Lightning nodded. "Right. I came to your office and I told you about that accident myself. Maybe I shouldn't have."

"I remember that visit well, and you were half-right for once. The car you ran into wasn't a black Mercedes, which is what you said it was. It was a white Nissan. You should have kept the accident business to yourself, though. Still, what you told me that day and what I know now, are two different things. I know that there was more to your story than what you told me."

"Thirsty, Silas? There's a glass on the mantelpiece if you want a drink." I shook my head.

"Well, I'm having another," Lightning said, topping up his glass.

"How long have you known Tubby Gonzales?"

My question caught Lightning like a physical blow. He gave a sudden involuntary start. Gin from the bottle slopped onto the side table instead of into his glass.

I said, "Victoria's cocaine market is growing every day. Tubby Gonzales had been supplying a share of it, but nothing lasts forever. Outsiders have been watching Victoria's skyrocketing drug trade, and they all want a piece of the action. Then Tubby Gonzales did some nosing around and found out that a Big Circle Boy had just moved from Vancouver to Victoria."

"How did Gonzales know that?" Bradley inquired negligently.

"Hell, Bradley, you know the answer to that as well as I do. The VPD is full of blabbermouths. Cops who'll call the press when something juicy happens. Traitorous cops with friends on the street . . ."

Lightning tried to interrupt me, but I kept talking. "The drug scene is wall-to-wall with finks. The ordinary crackster will sell his own mother for a five-dollar rock. Somebody blabbed, Tubby got to hear about it, and he traced Raymond Cho to that house on Echo Bay. Raymond Cho, alias Ronnie Chew. Tubby Gonzales murdered Cho by cutting his throat."

"Cho's isn't the only throat that Gonzales cut."

"I know, Lightning. I know more than you think I know. So just be patient, I'll get around to that in a minute."

A lopsided sneer pulled Lightning's mouth out of shape, but he kept quiet when I said, "Tubby Gonzales just happened to be watching Cho's house on the night that Cho brought two young Native women home. Gonzales bided his time till the women left. Then he went in. Gonzales suspected that Cho had cocaine stashed in the house. Gonzales tortured Cho until he told him where the cocaine was. Then Gonzales killed Cho and drove away. Things spiralled out of control almost immediately."

Lightning was gazing at me with rapt attention. He said, "Keep talking."

"Things went out of control because the car that Tubby was driving ran into your blue-and-white. Gonzales lost control of his car, and it veered off the road. You escaped injury although your car sustained heavy damage. When you stopped and checked, you found Gonzales behind the steering wheel. I assume he was either knocked out or dazed temporarily.

You found Cho's cocaine in Gonzales' car and stole it. Coke worth hundreds of thousands of dollars. You left Gonzales to fend for himself and drove to the murder scene. How am I doing so far?"

"You're doing fine, Silas. I couldn't have described things better myself."

Lightning wasn't looking at me then. He was staring into a deep dark hole. His gun was within easy reach of his right hand. I could see the safety catch, and it was off. He may not have been listening when I went on, "Unfortunately for you, Gonzales probably wasn't totally unconscious when you robbed him. He either knew then or figured out later that you had taken the cocaine. Gonzales wanted it back, so he went to your house. You weren't there. Gonzales found your wife Maggie instead. She was helpless and alone, in a wheelchair. He tortured Maggie to death."

"Yes, he did," Lightning said. "Gonzales tortured my wife. He thought Maggie would know where the cocaine was, but she didn't know."

Lightning's voice sounded normal, but a single tear squeezed from the corner of his left eye and trickled down his cheek. "Maggie didn't know anything about the cocaine. It was one of the few things about me that she didn't know. Maggie knew about my womanizing, she knew a lot of bad stuff about me."

"Yeah, right," I said derisively. "You've done a lot of bad things in your time."

"I came home and found Maggie dead. It was horrible," Lightning said. "I knew that Gonzales must have done it. But what goes around comes around, and then it was my turn. I caught him unawares in his apartment. I treated him the way he'd treated my wife. I enjoyed every minute. I enjoyed watching him bleed and squirm, I kept him alive as long as I could, till his heart stopped."

"I know you did. I can even understand that part of the story, in a way. But I don't understand the rest of it. Maybe you'd like to tell me."

He looked at me without making eye contact, and shrugged.

"Go on, tell me," I said, "try to make me understand."

"It was a dirty trick I played on you, Silas. I'm sorry."

"You're sorry?" I said, revulsed. "What did I do to deserve it?"

"Nothing," Lightning said, pouring himself another drink. "You didn't do a goddamn thing to deserve it. But I was a little crazy back then, Silas. I thought it was my way out. I thought I could get away with it."

Disgust must have shown on my face. I stood up and took a step towards him. Lightning picked up his gun and said, "Make another move towards me and you're dead. You're more use to me dead than alive."

I sat down again.

"You were wrong about some of the details. Cho had four kilos of cocaine in his house," Lightning said. "It was worth a fortune, a million bucks at least, if I'd only known how to market it properly. I had the coke, but it became a curse. I was trapped. I knew that Bernie at least would figure it all out and get me eventually. Then I had an idea. I threw Bernie a patsy."

"Yes, me. I was to be your patsy."

"Yeah, why not?" he grinned lopsidedly. "It was either my ass, or yours."

"You're the one who mugged me from behind when I came ashore off Twinner Scudd's boat. You're the one who put coke up my chimney."

"Correct. After stashing the coke, I called the *Times Colonist*. The TC called Nice Manners. Manners hates your guts, he was only too ready to believe the worst of Silas Seaweed. Manners would love to hang this whole case around your neck, because you're not everybody's best friend, are you?"

"You're crazy."

"Crazy or not, I've made plans. I'm flying out of here tomorrow. Me and Candace."

"Does Candace know about that yet?"

"Not yet. But she knows that I'm worth big money, which is what interests her. She'll do whatever I want her to do."

He was right. I said, "Manners wants to see me fall, but Bernie Tapp doesn't. I cut corners, I tell the odd fib, but I'm not a murderer. Bernie will get you eventually. You might be on top of the world now, but the only way you can go is down. You'll spend the rest of your life running and worrying. Worrying and fretting. Because every time you hear a knock on the door, it might be the police."

"I've given that a lot of thought too," Lightning said.

With the gun in one hand, he reached into his pocket and brought out a wrapped candy. He struggled ineffectually, trying to get the wrapping off with one hand, and then he gave up trying and threw the candy across the room for me to catch. "Here, Silas," he said. "I'm not all bad. Have a breath mint, maybe it'll sweeten you up a little."

I caught it on the fly, threw it back and said, "I'd prefer to have some of that gin now."

Lightning's lopsided grin reappeared. "There's only a few drops left, sorry."

He kept the gun pointed at my chest, but didn't argue when I went across the room, grabbed the gin bottle, and went back to the chesterfield with it.

"Remember what else you said to me in my office one day, Bradley? You told me that I was one of the few people in the force who ever treated you right."

"Yeah. I know, and I'm sorry. It's like I've always said, Silas. You're a White man inside."

Sighing, Bradley picked up the candy and put the gun on the side table while he removed the wrapping. He put the candy in his mouth, said, "Well, here goes. It's been nice knowing you," and chomped down on it.

Lightning's face reddened almost instantaneously; he slumped backwards.

I leapt from my chair and was across the room in a second, trying to open Lightning's jaws and take what was left of the candy out of his mouth, but the tendons of his face and neck were already rigid with seizure.

Lightning was dead.

I opened windows to dissipate the smell of burnt almonds and went outside to the porch.

It had stopped raining, and the stars had come out. Bernie Tapp and other officers appeared from the darkness where they had been staked out.

"Lightning was ready to go. He took cyanide, I couldn't stop him," I told Bernie.

"Good riddance because the wire worked, we got every word," Bernie said. "It's just as well."

CHAPTER TWENTY-NINE

I wanted us to go by road, but Old Mary Cooke and Chief Alphonse were adamantly opposed. So I arranged to borrow Charlie Mangrel's aluminum skiff and we went by boat instead. I got down to the Warrior wharf at ten o'clock, as arranged. Old Mary and Chief Alphonse showed up only a half hour late, but an hour later Little Sam the medicine man was still missing. I went looking for him.

I found Little Sam asleep on a stool in his workshop. Across his knees was a slab of cedar upon which he had used black and white pigments to represent a rudimentary human figure. Approximately three feet long, a foot wide and an inch thick, the figure had a black hat, a white shirt with black chevron stripes, and black trousers. It had an eyeless face and no mouth. The figure had no arms either. Instead of feet, its legs terminated in a single wedge-shaped point. It was an earth-dwarf manikin.

The four of us left the Warrior Bay jetty at about noon and we headed out towards Echo Bay. Buffleheads rode the waves like corks. The tiny ducks had come back again after breeding and spending the summer on northern Vancouver Island. Buffleheads are monogamous and brave. They can live through ten cold winters. Sometimes I recognize the same pairs diving for minnows and crustaceans around Colby Island. It would be nice, I thought, to be like a bufflehead and have a steady reliable girlfriend.

The Salish Sea was calm for a change. When the sun came out, the water shone like mercury, although things were a bit choppier in the tiderips around Trial Island. We reached Echo Bay without getting wet, and I carried Old Mary ashore on my back. She weighed a ton.

Tudor Collins was waiting for us on the beach. He helped Chief

Alphonse and me to half-drag and half-shove Old Mary Cooke up the ravine and over the rimrock to the petroglyph site.

When Old Mary Cooke got her breath back, she sat on the ground with her skirts covering her legs and told us a story about wolves.

In addition to Little Sam's earth-dwarf manikin, we'd brought a shovel, a wooden coffin and the shaman's medicine bag that Ricketts had found months earlier.

Little Sam threw bones in the air. Old Mary Cooke, Chief Alphonse and Tudor Collins watched attentively as I dug a hole with the shovel, crawled underground into the sandstone cave and picked up the mummified corpse. I could feel loose stick-like bones moving under his leathery skin when I carried him out to Old Mary Cooke. She wrapped the corpse with cedar-bark cloths, and then I placed him carefully in the coffin along with his medicine bag.

"He won't get out of that coffin in a hurry," Tudor Collins observed as I nailed the lid down.

I dragged the coffin into the cave, propped the earth-dwarf against it and then, after a last look at the pictographs painted on the cave's sandstone walls, I crawled out and blocked the entrance with tamped-down earth.

"There won't be nobody meddling with that fellow no more," Little Sam announced portentously. "That earth-dwarf will see to that."

Old Mary Cooke gave Chief Alphonse, Little Sam and me small pieces of white bark cloth as a remembrance of the dead. She gave Tudor Collins a ten-dollar gold piece for the inconveniences he'd been subjected to.

"Little Sam is right. That old shaman will rest easy now," Old Mary Cooke told us. "He won't be reaching out to people no more."

I PUT A fresh shirt and tie on, brushed my uniform, spit-polished my Magnum Stealths, adjusted my cap to a rakish angle and glanced out the window. Brisk winds and heavy waves were delivering fresh loads of winter firewood to the Warrior Band's Beach. A long ribbon of black funnel-smoke trailed a freighter inbound from the Pacific along Juan de Fuca Strait. Rays of sunlight slanted through breaks in the clouds above Colby Island. Farther north, storm clouds showed where it was raining hard on the Malahat.

I went out to the MG, drove to police headquarters and failed to find an empty stall in the underground parkade. I had to back out onto the street and pay two bucks for a temporary parking slot outside the Memorial Arena. Two lousy bucks. Money out of my own pocket, because I no longer had an expense account. It seemed like a bad omen. One more thing I'd miss about being a cop.

Bernie was in his office, feeding pigeons. It helps to lower his blood pressure. Bernie acknowledged my arrival with a grunt and tapped the Raymond Cho murder book that was lying on his desk.

"I've got to hand it to you, pal. You're a dope about most things, but you were right all along about Tubby Gonzales and nearly everything else. We couldn't have broken the case without you. Congratulations. Too bad Mallory's gonna boot your ass. You could have rejoined the detective squad full time. Put your abilities to better use."

I sat down and thought about Tubby Gonzales. Bernie opened a leather pouch and filled a corncob pipe with dark shag tobacco.

"Tubby wasn't very clever, but he was too clever for his own good," I remarked sagaciously.

"Yeah, there are a lot of half-smart people in this town."

"Just so I'm sure, Bernie. There's nobody left who thinks that Ruth Claypole or Maria Alfred had anything at all to do with Raymond Cho's death?"

"Hell no, even Nice Manners accepts that now. Tubby Gonzales killed Cho. Ruth and Maria just happened to be in the wrong place at the wrong time. Gonzales planted that slavekiller club to muddy the waters."

Bernie tamped tobacco into the bowl of the pipe with his thumb. "Tell me again how it went, just so I've got it fresh in my mind."

"This is the way it went. The girls had gone when Gonzales entered Cho's house. Gonzales murdered Cho after torturing him to find out if he had any cocaine. Gonzales made off with four bricks, and those bricks ended up with Lightning Bradley."

Somebody knocked on the door. "Come!" Bernie shouted.

Mrs. Nairn came in. "Superintendent Mallory is ready for you now, Chief." To me she added, "We're going to miss you, Silas. Good luck."

"Luck won't enter into it," Bernie said crustily.

Mrs. Nairn went out. Bernie put his corncob pipe on the window-sill. We both put our uniform caps on and went along the corridors to Superintendent Mallory's office.

"Wait here a minute while I have a word with the boss," Bernie said.

He went in. They kept me waiting for a few minutes, and then it was my turn. Victoria's senior policeman was sitting at his desk. Bernie Tapp and Nice Manners were facing Superintendent Mallory from separate corners of the large room. Nobody looked very happy.

Mallory stood up to return my salute, sat down again and told me to stand easy.

I tucked my hat under my left arm and remained standing with my feet together.

"I've received CDI Tapp's final report, Seaweed," Mallory said, his voice slow and grave. "As regards the cocaine possession charge, you are exonerated. These are sad times for the Victoria Police Department. Constable Bradley died in disgrace, and your career is finished. I commend you for your role in solving several recent murders. With one notable exception, you've been a credit to the force and to the uniform. I take no joy in this occasion, believe me."

Mallory stood up, walked to a hat stand by his window, and put his uniform cap on. Scowling at Nice Manners he said, "Did you hear me, Inspector? Sergeant Seaweed's police career is finished. Do you have anything further to contribute?"

"No, sir," Manners replied with a voice and manner that reminded me of TV's bible punchers. "This is a sad day for the Victoria Police Department."

"You don't think, Inspector Manners, that under the circumstances you might consider dropping the attempted assault charge against Sergeant Seaweed?"

"I have considered that possibility, sir. I've thought about it long and hard. However, in all sincerity, I think Seaweed must be dismissed. Otherwise, department morale is bound to be undermined."

Mallory's voice was troubled. "What about you, Silas? Don't you have anything to say in your own defence? Surely there must be something?"

"No, sir."

"That's it then," Mallory was saying, when Bernie spoke up.

"Excuse me, Chief. There is one last small detail we should clear up before Seaweed gets the push. As Inspector Manners has pointed out, department morale will suffer otherwise."

"All right, get on with it!" Mallory said irately. "For the sergeant's sake, let's not drag this farce out any longer than necessary."

The word *farce* brought a bit of colour into Manners' cheeks.

Bernie marched to the door and opened it. Harry Biedel and two RCMP officers were waiting outside in the corridor. Bernie brought them in and paraded them in a line alongside me. Superintendent Mallory looked mystified, but he remained silent.

"These three officers were present when Inspector Manners removed the suspicious parcel from Seaweed's chimney," Bernie announced. "Will you correct me if I'm wrong, Inspector?"

Manners nodded.

"Isn't it also correct that just before that event, you kicked Seaweed's cat?"

"Kicked a cat?" Manners said, startled. "Well, I may have done, although you're making it sound worse than it was . . ."

"Rubbish!" Harry Biedel shouted. "Manners kicked the poor little creature so hard it flew across the room and hit a wall. That's why Silas went for Manners' throat . . ."

"Silence, Biedel!" Mallory bellowed. "Hold your tongue until I give you permission to speak."

"Be damned to that, sir," Biedel shouted angrily. "Silas loves that cat and everybody in Victoria's police department knows that's why Silas went after Manners' ass. Too bad I held him back. Manners deserved a whipping. Too bad we haven't . . ."

"Constable Biedel. Get out of my office! Leave this instant, I'll deal with you later."

Biedel saluted and went out.

Silence reigned until Bernie said soberly, "Chief, we're in a predicament. If Inspector Manners insists on punishing Seaweed, I will have no option but to charge the inspector with cruelty to animals. Animal cruelty is a firing offence."

"Wait a minute," Manners said. "Animal cruelty isn't a firing offence . . ."

"It is if the charge is pressed by a senior officer," Mallory corrected him. "Pity though. It means that I'll lose two valuable officers instead of one."

"Here goes," Bernie said soberly. "Inspector Manners. You are hereby charged with . . ."

"Wait a minute, wait a minute, let's not be too hasty," Manners interrupted. "When I consider all of the ramifications . . ."

"I can hardly believe my bloody ears, Inspector!" Bernie yelled. "A man of your high and mighty moral principles! Don't tell me you're having second thoughts?"

"All right, don't rub it in, Tapp," Superintendent Mallory bellowed. "I've heard enough nonsense and bad language for one day. Sergeant Seaweed, you are reinstated without loss of salary, seniority or privileges. Inspector Manners, you wait here with me. The rest of you get out."

Mallory waited till the door closed before starting his excoriations, but didn't trouble to conceal his anger or lower his voice.

Out in the corridor, Harry Biedel and the two RCMP officers were listening and grinning their heads off.

"Way to go, Harry," Bernie said. "I don't think you have anything to fear from Mallory. He might even give you a medal."

CHAPTER THIRTY

Bernie wanted to close up shop and buy me lunch, but I was feeling a bit peculiar after the day's events, so I declined with thanks and drove to my office instead.

Cynthia Leach was out. PC was out. I left the window blinds shut, took out the office bottle and poured myself a drink. I toasted Queen Elizabeth—whose majestic gaze seemed severe that day—and thought about life.

I was back in harness. Big deal, so what? What did I have to look forward to? Dragging small helpless children from the clutches of drunken abusive parents. Enforcing Victoria's open-container bylaw. Arresting angry high-school dropouts wasted on crack. And Twinner Scudd and his cohorts were going to cause a problem for me down the line, but maybe I had it coming. He had probably saved my life, but I hadn't done much in return. When I tried to intervene with Crown prosecutors, I'd been told that Twinner had undoubtedly conspired in several recent killings. Five years meant he was getting off lightly.

A motorist with giant speakers was parked outside Swans pub, listening to vintage, high-volume rock and roll. When Dire Straits finished singing "Money for Nothing," it was ZZ Top's turn. They were still belting out "Velcro Fly" when my desk phone rang.

It was Piggy Mainwaring. She was wondering if I knew what Mae West used to say about men?

"Mae had a lot to say about men," I replied, "most of it accurate. In *She Done Him Wrong*, Mae said: Is that a gun in your pocket, or are you just happy to see me?"

"In *Diamond Lil*, Mae West said: Why don't you come up and see me sometime."

"Mae's real name was Mary Jane West," I said, just to show off.

I put the phone down, finished my drink slowly, and after some more thinking, I hiked upstairs to the second floor. Piggy's door wasn't locked. I entered her office without knocking and sat in one of those fat leather club chairs, admiring her beauty without speaking.

It was obvious that Piggy was no longer in hiding, because the blankets had gone. The canned food and dehydrated milk had gone. The place was the same as it had been the first time I'd seen it, but Piggy wasn't. Ms. Mainwaring had aged ten years in a few weeks. She was 40 years old and now she looked it. Before, she'd looked 30, but rapid-onset aging is the price you pay for contributing to the deaths of three innocent partygoers.

P.G. Mainwaring was still desirable and very beautiful, though. She was wearing a black suit and black pumps, and the sexual force field that surrounded her was powerful enough to made my balls ache. While she poured me a drink, I tried not to think about her bent across her grandfather's desk with frilly silk pants around her ankles, but I was thinking about it, and it probably showed in my eyes when she gave me a glass of Grand Macnish and kissed me on the lips.

I tried to be indifferent, and wasn't.

She leaned back against the desk and said, "Hi, Silas."

"Hi, Nibsy."

"Well, handsome, where do things go from here?"

"Eddie Cliffs and Twinner Scudd go to jail. Larry Cooley and Lightning Bradley get cremated, and I get my job back. You are just as you were before, except older."

"How's that?"

"You? Okay on the outside, looking after a thousand apartment buildings."

"Why am I on the outside?"

"That, Nibs, is the way these things go."

"Don't be difficult, darling. I want to know about you and me."

I heard myself say, "It's like a wartime romance after the All Clear sounds. We leave the air-raid shelter together, but you go back to your mansion and I go back to my reserve."

"Pretentiousness doesn't suit you, darling," she reproached me. "Do you really think you can walk out of my life like this?"

"It's over, Nibsy, let's not kid ourselves."

Moisture appeared in Piggy's eyes, and her lower lip trembled before she pulled herself together and went into the bathroom. I poured myself another scotch.

She came out of the bathroom looking perfect, just like an ice queen.

Without another word, she locked up her grandfather's office and we went downstairs arm in arm. Out on the street she stood on tiptoes, kissed my cheek and told me that she loved me.

I said goodbye and watched her walk away down Pandora Street.

Then I went back to my office and had another drink and thought about Felicity Exeter until PC came in.

ABOUT THE AUTHOR

STANLEY EVANS' previous novels are *Outlaw Gold*, *Snow-Coming Moon* and the first four books in the Silas Seaweed series: *Seaweed on the Street*, *Seaweed on Ice*, *Seaweed under Water* and *Seaweed on the Rocks*. Stanley and his family live in Victoria, BC.

5, 6, 11, 12, 24, 26, 34
49

ISBN: 978-1-894898-73-7

ISBN: 978-1-894898-34-8

ISBN: 978-1-894898-51-5

ISBN: 978-1-894898-57-7

"Makes great use of the West Coast aboriginal mythology and religion."
—*The Globe and Mail*

"The writing is wonderful native story telling. Characters are richly drawn . . . I enjoyed this so much that I'm looking for the others in the series."
—*Hamilton Spectator*